Newport Wedding Belles

Everyone wants to be on the guest list...
except the reluctant bride and groom.

COLETTE HARRINGTON

ARCHWAY
PUBLISHING

Archway Publishing books may be ordered through booksellers or by contacting:
Archway Publishing
1663 Liberty Drive
Bloomington, IN 47403
www.archwaypublishing.com
1 (888) 242-5904

Because of the dynamic nature of the Internet, any web addresses or links contained in
this book may have changed since publication and may no longer be valid. The views
expressed in this work are solely those of the author and do not necessarily reflect the
views of the publisher, and the publisher hereby disclaims any responsibility for them.

Any people depicted in stock imagery provided by Thinkstock are models,
and such images are being used for illustrative purposes only.
Certain stock imagery © Thinkstock.

ISBN: 978-1-4808-3019-6 (sc)
ISBN: 978-1-4808-3017-2 (hc)
ISBN: 978-1-4808-3018-9 (e)

Library of Congress Control Number: 2016906632

Print information available on the last page.

Archway Publishing rev. date: 05/05/2016

Contents

Chapter 1

Prescott Borden tumbled out of bed like dice itching to be rolled.

"I'm in love and this time I mean it," the devilish bachelor mused to himself on a wicked hot May morning in Boston.

It was the city's second straight week of blistering heat, and across New England, everyone was on fire with spring fever. Particularly Prescott. He could hear chirping birds and smell the blossoming flowers from Bean Town's famous Public Garden beckoning him to the balcony of his Four Seasons penthouse suite. Even though the sliding glass doors were closed, in his mind romance was springing up everywhere.

For Prescott there was no bigger thrill than finding the one true love of his life. The incorrigible single firmly believed in "love at first sight" since it happened to him so often. And last night was no different than many others. Boy sees girl, boy likes girl, and boy decides to spy on girl - from a non-stalking distance, of course. Very few things fell into the stockbroker's hands by accident. There was always a bullish plan of action. But the only inside information he'd gathered about the "head turning" blond checking into the luxurious hotel was her room number, 508. A mere 10 floors down from his penthouse. He might need to "accidentally" get off on the fifth floor and linger around the ice machine. Certainly, his old pal Joe from security, who he needed to speak with anyway, could help facilitate an accidental meeting. With cameras rolling everywhere and a handsome tip, the entire hotel was a player's paradise.

He pressed zero on the hotel phone and got an earful of elevator music. He rolled his eyes and tossed linens around the room searching for his bath robe as if the operator would somehow know that he was in the buff. Not that he was ashamed of his well-toned body, but at that moment, his love-addled mind was switching into business gear.

Today, he was closing on the purchase of the Four Seasons penthouse suite. It was officially "not for sale," but his generous offer to hotel management changed that sign to "sold." The lawyers on the deal couldn't contain their laughter over the outrageous cash offer whose only written stipulation was that the sale be kept private until after the closing. They figured by tomorrow the whole city would be laughing at the poor bastard's overpayment. For two years in a row, he'd shelled out a fortune paying the extravagant monthly rate for Boston's prized penthouse. The payments were exorbitant, and many New England bluebloods found the entire situation "tasteless and low class." Particularly when they wanted to entertain guests there, only to find that the suite was permanently booked.

The notorious tycoon paid no attention to their whispers and complaints. As far he was concerned they could keep on being annoyed, along with the mockers who second guessed the trend-setting businessman's decisions. He planned to lease the penthouse to some

Chinese associates who agreed to a five year term. He'd show the naysayers in Boston's elite circles how to be "tastefully classless." He'd make his cash investment back in three years plus still have the best mailing address in town. In the meantime, he'd hang out at his seaside Newport mansion and at a few girl-friends' apartments in Manhattan. His education at Harvard Business School taught him a thing or two about making deals and living large, but an Ivy League education didn't stop the 35 year old from behaving like a mischievous kid given the keys to Disney World. He loved a witty, one-up prank even if he was the only one who appreciated it. Only those jealous of his lifestyle called him "lucky" and "nouveau riche" - while women called him often.

"Good morning, Mr. Borden," the operator said. She was breathless from running across the lobby. A co-worker had waved her over: Prescott was in the building and on the phone.

"Hello? Hello, hello," she said. The cute college girl, who'd not quite outgrown her baby fat, bore a slight resemblance to Jackie Onassis and shared the same first name. She kept repeating herself, afraid that he might have hung up. She looked forward to their phone chats, all 399 of them and still counting. "Hello!"

He swung his robe around over his shoulder, "Is this my little Jackie O? Darling, it's 7 a.m. What are you doing working so early?"

She giggled. "Just waiting for you to call."

"Is Joe from Security around yet?"

"No, Mr. Borden. He's on vacation for two weeks."

The dark haired blue eyed man thought for a moment, then winked at his own reflection in the mirror like Elvis getting ready for a show. He brushed back his wavy hair with his fingers, the only comb he ever needed.

"Joe's on vacation? Hmm, a vacation. Now there's something we all need." He cleared his throat to lower his voice, something he always did when closing a deal. "What do you say we take a little vacation day at work? Take some time off for a little fun…Just you and me. Are you with me Jackie?"

She froze stiff like a scared cat. Her eyes widened as she held her breath. His hushed voice was tasty like an ice cream cone filled with scoops of temptation and intrigue. Maybe this would be the moment she wished, hoped and prayed for…

He continued, "I have a mission for you, Jackie Double O Seven, if you should choose to accept."

Wait, she'd heard that line before. "Hold on there just a minute. Oh nooooo, I'm not falling for this again. I almost got fired for your last mission impossible. I can't, I just can't."

"I completely understand. I don't want you to do anything you don't want to do. Don't worry about letting me down." He rubbed some Moroccan oil through his hair and counted to himself: 1, 2, 3….

"Well, maybe I can. But I'm not going to get in trouble again, am I? Because I can't give you anyone's cell phone number that's checked in, not after last time. That girl was getting married and her soon-to-be husband practically had a heart attack from all the screaming and yelling. I can't afford to take another chance and lose this job. That wedding was almost called off."

Maybe the bride-in-waiting should have had the courtesy to mention she was getting married and looking at a venue, instead of hanging out at the bar and then sleeping with him. Which explains why she didn't leave her number after slipping out in the dark early morning hours.

"I promise that will never happen again. Scout's honor." He held up three fingers with two crossed. "Besides, I don't want a number, just a name - Room 508."

"No. I am not doing it." Still, she looked up the room number and remembered the attractive woman from Charleston checking in. "I'm doing you a favor. She's not your type."

"Why so suspicious? I might know her from someplace else, you know? And what's my type, by the way?"

"The three T's. Tall, tiny, and twenty. Room 508 is old - maybe even thirty - and short." The operator had assessed her odds of going out with Prescott and determined she wasn't his type either, but it didn't stop her from flirting and trying. "Maybe you should try going out with people like me. Just normal and all."

"I wouldn't let you go out with some old wretch like me, young lady. But when you're older you'll have to get a restraining order."

Speaking of restraining orders, he now remembered the original reason he called and wanted to speak with retired cop Joe, now head of hotel security.

"But your girlfriend Monica's only 21," she protested.

"She's a much different kind of 21 than you'll ever be. Trust me on that. In fact, thanks for reminding me. If you see the lovely Monica Dees, will you tell her that I checked out for a few days?"

There was a loud pounding on the twin mahogany doors to his suite. "Damn it, Prescott. Open up. I know you're in there! I just heard what you said, you effing lowlife. Who breaks up through a text?"

Monica kicked away at the door's brass handles. The five-foot-ten super model with a black belt was supposed to be on a shoot in California. But here she was at his front door and heading in, Boston Strong.

"You're a freaking jerk, and I'll show you exactly what kind of 21 year old woman I am!" Her famous red hair matched the color of her temperament.

He whispered into the phone, "Forgive me, Miss Onassis, for anything you might overhear. I am watching a tasteless movie filled with vulgar language."

"Hah - I'll bet you are. I saw her in the lobby a few minutes ago. Have a good day, Mr. Borden." She was hanging up with a little smile, confident mad Monica represented all the women who ever felt rejected by him, including herself.

"Hold on there. After all we've been through together, you would hang up on me like that? I am going to have to speak with the company's president concerning your ruthless treatment, unless of course, you send a dozen roses with an unmarked card to the sassy blond in room 508."

She took in a deep breath. She'd had enough of being stung by all of his honey bees. "Don't you have enough problems with temperamental women already, *SIR*?"

Her point was proven correct as Monica tried to body slam her way in through the groaning door.

"Who, me? Problems? No problems at all." The door started to show signs of surrendering even if he was not. "Just temporary setbacks. Now, send a dozen roses to room 508. Gotta go." Monica was almost in.

Before he could hang up, he heard an annoyed operator mumble "fine" but not in her usual cheerful way.

"Young lady, I can hear you. Don't sound so down. Trust me, one day, when you're old enough, you'll make some guy like me very miserable." Click.

And he was right, because later that same day, the news stories weren't about his slick penthouse purchase but a Tweet by a wannabe journalist - 4seasonsjackyO - picked up by gossip and business columnists alike.

Financial rock star Prescott Borden had a bear's day at the market as his penthouse suite suffered $12,000 worth of damages. A "no comment' remark came from representatives of the Four Seasons Hotel. Guests say it may have more to do with the temperamental super model Monica Dees who was seen cat walking around the hotel's Bristol Lounge in a hiss over the power couple's break up. Stay tuned.

The bad publicity held up the closing of his prized penthouse and started a gossip-starved media on a dirt-digging frenzy that included chasing him. He wasn't able to come and go without at a camera stuck in face for the rest of day.

Chapter 2

A tipsy Tiffany James twirled around the hotel's revolving door, missing the entrance twice, much to the amusement of the doorman. Room 508 was back after missing a night's sleep in her expensive room. Her long, emerald dress and champagne-induced hiccups caught the attention of the Four Season's 7 a.m. breakfast crowd as well. They were mostly men dressed in power suits who weren't used to witnessing "the walk of shame" at such a high class place. Oh well, she didn't have anything to hide. She rarely drank and never partied all night - except on this one special occasion: the dress rehearsal of her first play. The producers took her out on the town and raved over the performance. They had a serious discussion about "Marble House" having Broadway potential. The night concluded with hugs and wishes of great success, but no one said "Good luck," as it's theater taboo.

"Break a leg," everyone said as they flagged down taxis and headed their separate ways. They all needed to rest up for the big night when critics and theatre goers would determine their future.

An overly excited Tiffany couldn't wait. Instead of going back to her hotel and getting some sleep, the wide-awake playwright showed up on the director's doorstep to share the good news. "Broadway bound" was the buzz word for the night. Or maybe it was the two bottles of wine they drank that had them so buzzed up, much to the annoyance of his boyfriend who kept pounding on the bedroom wall as a hint for the duo to pipe down.

Their only response was to pound back more.

The toasting finally came to a halt when the inexperienced party girl passed out on their living room couch. She was awakened by someone flicking cold water on her face.

"Time for your curtain call," the annoyed boyfriend said, while practically pushing her out the door early the next morning. She didn't even have time to freshen up.

She didn't mind the abruptness of having to leave. Nothing was going to bring her down, not a catty boyfriend or a cab driver who spoke little English giving her shameful glances in his rear view mirror. Like she was Jezebel reincarnated for staying out all night and appearing still under the influence.

"Welcome to America," she wanted to say to Abdul (the name displayed on his taxi permit), but she was rarely snippy to anyone, even people who deserved it.

There was too much to be happy about. She lived in a country where dreams *can* come true. To think she'd almost given up hope of one day having a star on Broadway. There were many nights when setting fire to rejection letters was the only heat in her tiny apartment. Ten years of living off her small reporter's salary, coffee, and little sleep had finally paid off. Nothing could go wrong now, besides the minor annoyance of seeing a busy hotel lobby filled with raised eyebrows at her disheveled evening attire when everyone else was showered and dressed for success.

A redheaded teen boy pointed his finger at her and held his stomach like he was laughing while she waited for the elevator. Under normal circumstances, Tiffany would keep to herself, but today was special, so for giggles she stuck her tongue out at him like a fellow teenager. She unintentionally caught the attention of the boy's father who gave her a stern look and shook his finger at her.

She cast her eyes down and mumbled to herself, "Why do New Englanders have to get up so early and be so damn judgmental? A bunch of finger pointers."

She pressed the elevator button three more times in hopes her getaway chariot would arrive sooner. Much to her relief the brass doors opened, but inside were two Wall Street types having a conversation. They both chuckled at the sight of her.

"Fun night, eh?" the ugly one of the two asked.

"Certainly better than your boring day," she said.

They nudged each other and started laughing as they exited. She wanted to say something more creative but decided it was best to ignore their taunts. What could be so bad about a woman getting in later than expected? She got the shock of her life after seeing her reflection in the elevator mirror. No wonder they were amused. Her blond hair was standing straight up without bobby pins. She gasped at the sight only to see vampire teeth stained from the bottles of red wine she shared with the director and her black bra strap showing under the shoulder of her green evening gown. She tried to readjust while the elevator climbed up through the floors. She was still feeling woozy, even after a few hours of trying to sleep it off.

The elevator doors opened, and Tiffany peeked out to see if anyone was standing nearby. Not that it mattered much, but it's always best to be prepared when doing the "strut of shame." Thankfully, the coast was clear so she let all pretense go and wobbled down the hall on heels too high for comfort. Finally, something was going her way and she'd get some sleep. But for some reason, things looked different than she remembered from yesterday.

"Am I on the wrong floor?" she wondered.

The loud moans of what sounded like a primate in heat caught her attention. Out of curiosity, she followed the odd noises around a corner and down what appeared to be a private residential corridor. Even her vivid imagination and years of reporting experience could not prepare her for what she witnessed next.

A half-naked man was squirming around on the hall floor and fending off blows from a tall, bird-like creature. The thin-looking woman whacked the guy everywhere using her clog shoes as boxing gloves. He groaned and covered his manhood with one hand while fending off attacks with the other. He had been the recipient of a hard blow to his privates, which rendered him defenseless.

"Apologize, apologize!" the attacker said.

"I'm sorry I opened up the door, you crazy witch," was the only thing Prescott wanted to say, but instead he tried to breathe. He had told the front desk to call security if Monica Dees came by again. Whoever was working the morning shift wouldn't be employed there for long as far he was concerned.

Yesterday's big breakup had not agreed with the "no-one-tells-me-what-to-do" super model, and she was out for more revenge on something far more valuable than his penthouse: his organs - and one in particular. Having a black belt in Karate didn't discipline her dyna-mite-loaded mind the way it was intended. *Good investment Prescott!* It was easier fighting off her potty mouth than her karate chops.

The only thing Tiffany's reporter's eyes saw was a hundred-pound girl pounding the heck out of some guy who most likely deserved it. If that sight wasn't absurd enough, noticing his heart covered boxer shorts with the words "I love you" not completely hiding his manhood sent her over the edge of reason.

"Oh my," she said. She definitely was on the wrong floor and maybe even at the wrong hotel.

Monica's attention turned away from Prescott after realizing someone else was present. She jumped up and gritted her teeth while trying to regain her composure. She smiled at the observer as if noth-ing odd was going on. Tiffany immediately recognized the world famous super model.

"You're Monica Dees!" she said in a star struck kind of way.

The red head looked up and down at the blond hot mess. Just great, now she'd have to deal with a drunk fan ready to ask for an autograph. Her smile disappeared as she realized the other woman was actually "hot" and not just a mess.

She growled, "Who's this? The next whore of the week?" Her nostrils flared like a gorilla warning rivals to stay away.

Fear told Tiff to get the hell out of there, but it was too much information for her senses to absorb. Her newspaper reporter's curios-ity left her motionless. She couldn't respond to the voices in her head screaming: "Run for your life."

Prescott, sensing what might happen next, made a quick recovery. He bolted up and wrapped his strong arms around his out of control former girlfriend. She squirmed like a spoiled kid stuck in a car seat but still managed to snap off a kick that landed straight on Tiffany's nose. The model's long legs and aim were both perfect. Down fell the writer in a pool of fast-pouring blood.

Prescott let go and raced to Tiffany's rescue, but Monica dived in first and landed on the victim's back. She started pulling out mounds of honey blond hair and yelling obscenities.

"Busy-body bitch," she said, while smashing the stranger's face into the ground.

He tackled the crazed assailant who kept on kicking and screaming.

"I'll freaking kill you. Both of you," Monica said, while trying to inflict as much injury as possible to each of them.

He needed to put an end to the madness. He didn't care about himself or the damage to his penthouse, but now there was an injured person involved. He straddled the cover girl and without thinking slapped her hard across the face. His remorse was instantaneous and more painful than her initial kick in the groin. He could have ended the assault on him sooner, but he had always vowed to never hit a woman, even one like Monica whose power punches were as strong as a brawler on a hockey team. He reasoned that she'd eventually run out of steam, and he'd walk away the victor for being true to his word. He never thought someone else would end up getting hurt.

There was a strange silence between the two notorious lovers. Both their worlds stopped moving as they realized that their infamous relationship had reached a crescendo. They both wrestled with the idea of what to do next even though she was pinned down.

"How could you do this?" he asked Monica, referring to the knocked out victim.

She didn't shed a tear or even have a look of remorse on her otherwise perfect face. Prescott grabbed the model's arm and pulled her up. He escorted her to the emergency stair exit and opened the door, then pushed the attacker out. It couldn't be reopened from her side without a key. But it didn't matter, she had no plans of kicking her way back in. She knew the sleazy paparazzi would descend upon the place like bats to a cave now that "another woman" was involved and injured. It was time to catwalk her way to the bottom parking level and pay whatever the fare was for a cab ride to New York. Another scandal meant losing millions of dollars in endorsement contracts, so she'd let her lawyers and PR rep handle the mess from there.

Overwhelmed, Prescott dialed the hotel operator from the hall phone. Just his luck it was Jackie O, who picked up. He was deliberate and unfriendly. He knew she was the reason the media picked up yesterday's penthouse trashing.

"Get an ambulance here," he said.

"Absolutely sir. What's your emergency, and are you a guest at the hotel?"

"Jackie, it's Prescott Borden. Someone's been injured on my floor."

"Really? That's terrible. Do you know the name of the person? What should I say is the extent of *her* injuries?"

Her phony concern annoyed him, along with the fact that she said "her." What kind of game was this girl playing? Only Jackie knew about Monica being in his apartment yesterday and then witnessed all the workmen coming up to repair the damage done. He was also convinced that she was the reason Monica was able to get through

the hotel lobby today without security being alerted, which were his
instructions.

"Jackie, do your job for a change and call now!" He hung up,
much to the offended operator's dismay.

"Well, two can play at that," she thought to herself.

Prescott sat down next to the injured Tiffany. He cradled her head
as she started to come to. He took his torn white tee shirt and like a
gentle nurse cleaned up the blood gushing from her broken nose. His
own nose had been broken three times during his semi-pro hockey
days. Hockey taught him all he needed to know about life. How to
fight hard and never take on a battle unless you can walk away the
clear winner. He never lost at anything again. But this time it looked
as if Monica got the better of both of them.

Tiffany's almond-shaped eyes opened. They were a toasted golden
color that lit up even under the darkest of circumstances.

He smiled. "Aw. You're going to be okay," he said. Something tender must have struck his heart because "aw" was not in his vocabulary.

Now he recognized her. Room 508. The same room he sent flowers to in hopes of having a "happy ever after" short-term romance
together. She looked so sweet, even though her evening gown was now
torn to shreds. He didn't know she'd spent half her life's savings on
that dress and planned on wearing it again tonight. The rest of her savings went to the Four Seasons hotel for a three-day stay in a suite. She
planned a party for the cast, and even some critics had agreed to go.
Then they'd all talk about her play, her crown jewel: Marble House.

A strange thought occurred to Prescott as he waited for help to
arrive: "There is no way she'll go out with me now."

She'd surely sue him before sleeping with him. The loss almost choked him up. Or maybe it was the worry that Monica's people might strike a deal with the injured girl before he'd get a chance to at least try. He could come across as the aggressor and bad guy in this affair. That's how these scandals usually go down. No one knows the real story when high profile reputations are at risk and big money taints the truth. Time to cancel all plans, personally deal with the paparazzi, and camp out at her hospital bedside for however long it took to be cleared of any wrong-doing.

* * * * *

An ambulance headed to Mass General with the patient and Prescott inside, now fully clothed in an Armani suit and looking prepared to deal with anyone from the police to the press. He'd be upfront about it all. He was, however, not prepared to show off his own swollen private parts as evidence. He desperately wanted to ask the paramedics for an ice pack but instead held Tiffany's hand and had to make a conscious effort not to squeeze too tight from the throbbing of his own injuries.

As the emergency vehicle disappeared from sight, the hotel staff started congregating in small groups outside of public view, each one sharing what little knowledge they had about what was going on.

Jackie O fired off texts to every media source she could think of with a promise to give an exclusive interview. She'd "tell all the inside happenings between the super model, billionaire and injured guest," while putting herself center stage. She then held court with her colleagues.

"He practically stalked that woman from room 508," she said to the three employees listening wide-eyed with anticipation. She kept lowering her voice so that they each had to inch in closer. The power

of having everyone's attention was going to the 20 year old's head like
a third-world leader with a nuclear bomb.

"He wanted me to personally spy on her in exchange for favors
that I won't mention. Let's just say, I told him I am too young to
even think of such naughty things. Then, when I refused, he told me
I was going to make a lot of men miserable and hung up on me. I'm
worried he'll have me fired for not going out on that twisted date he
kept begging me for," the exaggerator said.

Even the janitor rolled his eyes at the chubby girl's claims.
Everyone at the Four Seasons had witnessed the parade of women,
from socialites to Hollywood elite, chasing Prescott down over the
years - many of which he turned away. Jackie couldn't pick up the signals that the hotel staff was whispering a nursery rhyme joke behind
her back: "Liar, liar, pants on fire."

She kept repeating the same script despite the looks of disbelief
on other's faces she mistook for "jealousy." She'd show them all who
was queen bee. She'd claim the hotel staff allowed her to be sexually
harassed if they dared cross her. Surely, a lawsuit would be forthcom-
ing if anyone tattled on her for breaking the signed confidentiality
agreement concerning hotel guests. As far as she was concerned, the
marriage contract between silence and anonymity was over. She was
now free to be ravished by a swooning media, even if her colleagues
weren't all that impressed. She'd speak the truth as she saw it. She
might go as far as to claim Prescott and she had been lovers for a long
time, since there was no way of proving otherwise. She went from
being a part-time Boston college student majoring in journalism to
thinking she had a Harvard law degree. Unfortunately she would
flunk the bar exam for being wrong on the facts of this particular case.

No one in the media cared about the chunky girl's wishful thinking or potential sexual harassment suit. She'd have to be a lot better looking to be taken seriously as a player in the game of celebrity gossip.

The real inside scoop was leaking from hotel security like strawberry ice cream in a sugar cone on a hot day. A dribble here and dribble there. Security cameras had caught only part of the cat fight: the super model being slapped down by her boyfriend and then her slithering off after he pushed her down the emergency stairs. Some thought of bootlegging the tape and quitting their job for the best offer, an amount equal to 10 year's salary. But it was too late. Hotel management had seized the video and was prepared to hand it over to Boston P.D. if asked.

Seasoned employees just listened in carefully to each new rumor and waited for the national media to arrive. They'd been through the scandal drill before. Hundred dollar tips were about to fall like heavy hail on a new car. And they weren't disappointed: The paparazzi came barreling in with cameras loaded and a $10,000 bounty for the real story, plus a number to be negotiated for the security video.

The Four Seasons executives responded to the paparazzi parade by closing the doors to anyone except registered guests. But the damage was already done, and by mid-afternoon, even mainstream reporters were emailing in stories with headlines like: "Cat fight: The Super Model vs. the Playwright." "Down and Knocked Out at the Four Seasons." And one that would really bother the first-time playwright: "Marble House is a big Kick in the Ass." Named after her play, which had yet to see an opening night or even one critical review. Acknowledgement for Tiffany's work finally arrived, but in the wrong package, at the wrong time, and there was no return address.

Chapter 3

The thing about Sugar Lynn Limehouse is that everyone could hear her long before she entered a room. From her booming voice, turned up a decibel too high, to the pounding sound of her high heels carrying too much weight, everything about the buxom blond filled up space. She appeared much larger than her actual size 10. The hospital staff - even the doctors - inched towards the hall's walls as her curves cleared the way like a hundred mph speed boat on a lake. Everyone was left in her wake.

"Honey, you can tell her Sugar's here - that's the only credentials I need," she said to the security guard standing outside of Tiff's room. He'd been hired by Prescott to keep out unwanted visitors, mainly the press. But her self-assured manner backed the sentry down from his post. Her Jedi powers always managed to open doors. He moved out of the way, against all his instructions. He was not messing with the big-haired Texan. Everything about the blond lady screamed the Lone Star State, even though she was from Charleston, a common Yankee stereotype that all Southern belles are one and the same. Besides, his measly pay grade was not worth the hassle of finding out any more information, and frankly, he was too scared to ask.

The newspaper publisher marched into Tiffany's room. Who in heaven's name sent these world-class bouquets since they both knew all the same broke people at the newspaper? She hated staring at the gorgeous floral arrangements and being empty-handed but there were no time for stops or restroom breaks on the fastest trip ever from Charleston to Boston.

She'd pushed the pedal to the metal after hearing the morning disc jockeys discussing her best friend on her way to the airport. All the media was abuzz with speculation about the throw down between the supermodel and the business tycoon at the Four Seasons Hotel in Boston. The center of all the fuss? Her friend Tiffany. And to think only yesterday the two childhood pals were excited about the play's opening night and celebrating its success. Now their worlds were turned upside down - including Tiff's nose.

The plus-size beauty plopped down in a chair next to the hospital bed. No hellos were expected or exchanged. The friends always talked to each other as if their conversations had no beginning or end. Which for all practical purposes was true. They lived, worked, and grew up together.

Sugar didn't sound so sweet at that moment. "You just wait till I get my hands on that twig Monica. I'll beat her to a skinny pulp. I'll make you look pretty compared to that hellcat."

She took a closer look at the patient. It was far worse than she'd imagined. "Not that you ain't pretty honey, underneath all that raccoon makeup and bandages. Your beauty shines from within."

Tiffany cried, "Some good that does me. Look at me. I can't go anywhere. This was supposed to be the biggest day of my life." She choked on her sighs, but then remembered something. "Wait a minute. Last week you told Helen in editorials that her beauty shined from within. Then you told me that's all a person can say when someone's born with an ugly gene. You're telling me I look homely," she concluded as tears ran down her face.

"Aw, honey, don't believe anything the shallow and narcissistic say. I've changed my evil ways since then." Sugar had a tendency to use humor when feeling helpless. But deep inside she felt sad because Tiffany looked like she was in a lot of pain. She touched her friend's head with tender care. "I know everything seems bad but there is good news. I listened to the radio the whole way here, and you're the biggest star in the country. You're famous."

"You mean infamous and ugly," she sobbed.

"Not true. Most of the reporters stood up for you over Monica. They even said you're gorgeous and don't you forget it. There are photos of you all over the internet. You're the most Googled name in the country. The show is sold out. People can't get enough of you."

"Are you serious?" The playwright started to perk up. As of yesterday there were still 1700 tickets available in a 2000 seat theatre. Sugar nodded and clapped her hands like she was the president of her friend's fan club. "You have the world's attention, and they're lining up out the door to see your show."

Tiffany wanted to go to opening night and see the theatre-going crowds enjoying her work. She grabbed a hand held pocket mirror sitting on a food tray hoping she could do something to fix herself up. A few hours of makeup might make her look presentable.

Sugar snatched the compact, then stomped on it with her six-inch black pumps. Crunch. "There, now you'll have seven years good luck. Besides honey, it's best not to look until you've had a few days to heal up. I'll go to the show and take lots of pictures," she said.

"Darn it, Sugar. That was a family heirloom and belonged to my grandmother." She was more upset about having to accept the reality of not being able to attend the premier. "I'm sorry. I'll get over it."

"No worries - I'll fix it." The big beauty started crawling around the floor trying to put the pieces back together. "I'll glue it all up like brand-new. Now you just close your eyes and pretend like I'm not here," she said, hoping the patient didn't see it was a lost cause. "I won't say another word. You get some rest." She stood up and almost ripped her snug pink outfit. She let out a little "oops" giggle.

She pulled on the shoulders of her bra straps and gave a little wiggle, making sure her ample cleavage fell back in the right spot. She stopped just short of perfection as she felt a chill creeping up the back of her spine. She sensed there was another powerful Jedi-like force in the room, one even grander than hers. She turned around and saw Prescott, armed with a cell phone, sitting in a corner chair.

He stared at the buxom woman like a guest who had overstayed their welcome.

She crossed her arms. "What's wrong with you? Haven't you seen a woman in a pink pants suit before?" She brushed off any dust from her knees. "Well, don't just stand there, come in for a group hug." She put on her best sugar-coated smile, the one most men couldn't resist.

He didn't move but spoke in an Elvis-like voice, the same one women found irresistible. "Darling, you need to slow down there. Doctor's orders: no group hugs. Give the patient a chance to recover - and the rest of us too." He went back to checking stock quotes and ignoring her.

Sugar looked at Tiffany as if to say: Why didn't you tell me anyone was here?

The writer had been asleep for six hours and didn't know for sure herself. She grinned and shrugged her shoulders. She was too giddy to even speak. One of the world's most desirable bachelors was hanging out in her hospital room.

Sugar decided to handle the introduction in her usual tactful way since his negative vibe was getting on her nerves. "Well, if it isn't Prescott Borden. Must be quite a big day for you making headline news. Usually, you're third-page news in the business section. The cheapest place to advertise besides the classifieds."

Tiffany smacked her friend's hand as if to say stop.

Sugar didn't take the hint and kept on going as if he wasn't there. "Why have you been keeping this scoundrel a secret from me? Everyone on the radio says you two have been up to no good. I wake up only to find out my best friend is sleeping with the biggest sinner in the world, hiding it from his super model girlfriend, and me too for that matter. Talk about shock. Now I know why they're called shock jocks," she said.

"Darling, I bet you've shocked a few people yourself back in your day," he said, while scrolling through his messages.

"Honey, you better be talking to that over-used piece of crap," Sugar replied. Then she turned back to her girlfriend. "And you better have used protection on that thing because according to everyone in the know he's been around. He's dated every ho from…"

"Stop it. I just met him. He's the one who saved me. My hero."

Tiff grinned at her knight in shining armor, and he gave a little wave back.

Sugar's eyes widened. All she saw was a devil with two horns, a pitchfork, and a pair of Bruno Magli hooves.

"Evil's a-lurking," she said and made the sign of the cross with her two index fingers.

Tiffany laughed, "You'll have to ignore her colorful commentary. Everyone else does."

Sugar's face turned to glue: white and pasty.

Tiff tried to take back her words with a glowing introduction. "Prescott, this is Sugar Lynn Limehouse. She's the publisher of the Charleston Gazette and our city's most talked about icon."

"We are not doing interviews with anyone. You do not have my permission to quote anything I say," Prescott said.

"I beg your pardon? I am not here to profit on my best friend's pain. I'm here to celebrate her play. God only knows your intentions. I heard on the radio today everything I ever want to know about you and then some. In fact, maybe it's time you left so WE can do a little research and find out exactly what kind of devil we're dealing with."

"Satan herself should know," he said. The disdain growing between the two visitors was like a staph infection at a hospital – literally so, since they were sitting in Mass General.

A stunned Tiffany tried to play referee, but she sat up in bed too quickly and let out a painful screech. They both rushed to her side. She held up her hand as a gesture for them to stop. "You two need to quit making a fuss over me and fussing at each other. Can we just please start over and give each other the benefit of the doubt?"

"Honey, we don't have time to start over with some guy who

watched while you got clobbered. He needs to go now. We have business matters to discuss without this bozo chiming in."

He threw his arms up in the air in dismay. "Of course, a clown like me from Harvard Business School wouldn't know anything about business. Bozo better get back to the circus before he misses the opening act." He usually was in good spirits, but something about her just pissed him off.

Tiffany tried to smooth things over by being even more accommodating than usual.

"Now everyone, let's be nice and start over. Prescott let me introduce you to the most amazing person you'll ever meet. She's the sole investor in my play and **my boss**." *Hint, Hint: back down*!

Then she turned to her best friend. "Allow me to introduce you to a man who saved me from being beaten to death. He's my hero." *Hint, Hint - I like him - shut up!*

Sugar snapped: "Hah."

Prescott took offense to Sugar's "hah" and said, "Don't mind me, little darling, I am just the clown with the big red nose who happened to protect your friend from being beaten down by a black belt," he said.

"Don't you dare 'little darling' me honey bunch. Take a look at what a fine job you did. Your handiwork speaks volumes."

"Stop it, both of you!" the weary patient said. She had more problems than the banter going on between the outsized egos. They were giving her a double-size headache, and someone had to go. She couldn't ask her best friend, investor, and employer to hit the road. Or could she? He was the most handsome man she'd ever met. But as tempting as he looked, art was the love of her life. She'd sacrificed everything for writing success, including years of dating. Besides, she'd never stand a chance with a guy who dated Vogue covers and hot starlets. Reality beat down her giant imagination for the first time ever.

"Prescott, I'm sorry but I have a serious issue with my play opening tonight, and as you can see, I'm in no condition to go. Sugar and I have a lot of decisions to make. Maybe we could talk in a wee little bit?" she said, praying he'd wait in the hall.

"It was nice to meet you. I don't want to be a bother," he said and turned away. He rolled his eyes at Sugar who grinned at him in a "good riddance" kind of way.

Tiffany's heart started to beat faster. To her massive embarrassment, the sounds could be heard on the hospital monitor.

Prescott stopped just shy of the door as the beeping sounds hit a record high, like a 911 bleep – bleep - bleep alert. An emergency code went off. She turned as red as the flashing lights. *Good Lord, could someone please shut that damn thing off?* With all of Tiffany's might, she ripped off the monitoring cord and everything stopped.

Prescott smiled to himself. He did a 180 degree turn and waltzed back into the room relieved he didn't have to wait in the hall - which is what he planned on doing.

"Tiffany, forgive me for being so bold, but you have more than an opening night problem, and I can't leave here without at least offering my assistance."

Sugar rolled her eyes. *Oh no, he's back!*

He sat down in a chair next to Tiffany's hospital bed. "I'm not sure if you're aware of it or not, but Monica has pressed felony assault charges against you. She claims you attacked her first. She's sought medical attention and has been released. The police will be here to question you soon enough."

Dead silence overtook the room. Even Sugar decided to sit down and listen for a change.

"I have my sources tracking the situation, and they've been in touch via text. Trouble is brewing." He waved his phone like a hypnotist.

The playwright's eyes started to fill up with tears. Her life was becoming as ruined as her broken nose.

"Aw, honey, don't worry. We have nothing to hide. The truth is the truth," Sugar said.

Prescott leaned in closer to the bed. "I have a copy of the hotel security tape if you'd like to see it."

Both women nodded. He played the evidence on his I-phone while narrating the scene.

"There is a drunken you riding up to my floor - which is not good, since you had no business being there…Oh look, you're making a weird face in the elevator mirror and showing off your red stained teeth."

Tiffany's face turned as blush as the red wine she'd been drinking earlier.

He continued. "Now you're on the penthouse floor tiptoeing around like you're up to something. You can tell me what you were doing there later, but people will assume you're a celebrity stalker. Saying something to the police like: 'I was drunk and didn't know I was doing' won't fly. You need to come up with a rock-solid excuse."

Even Sugar questioned her friend's motives. "Honey, what were you doing there?"

"I was drunk and didn't know what I was doing. Now be quiet and let him speak."

Prescott heeded her request and continued. "Then the next image we see is Monica smashing your face in, but it does not show why or what happened before. The camera rotates around in a circle and missed the most critical part. You could have easily started the fight," he said.

Sugar piped in. "No one is going to believe Monica. Look at Tiff's face. It's not even a hot mess, it's a horrible mess. A train wreck."

"Is it really that bad?"

Prescott put down his phone and tried to get the conversation back on track.

"Darling, your face will look pretty again, but your reputation could be ruined forever. Ladies, I am certain her people have seen the tape too. They're concocting a story of how you attacked her first. She has millions of dollars in endorsements and people out to protect their skinny cash cow. They're getting ready to let the pit bulls loose and attack your character and your version of the story even if it's the truth. They'll drag you through mud and rip you to shreds," he said.

Tiffany's mind was pounding with too much information. She'd been trying to come across as being mentally together, but in reality she was ready to pass out. Still, a part of her thought to herself: *Did he just say I was pretty?*

Prescott leaned in closer. "I feel terrible about all of this. But here's the good news: There is one thing that saves you and supports your story, and that's me," he said, as he flashed his perfect smile.

What he deliberately failed to mention was that **he** needed Tiffany's testimony. The camera caught Prescott tackling Monica to the floor and then slapping her hard across the face. The eye in the sky caught something else even more damaging. It appeared he was trying to push her down the emergency exit stairs rather than get her away from Tiffany. From a legal standpoint, the video incriminated him in the attack and alleged injuries to Monica.

Sugar scrunched up her face. Something about Prescott Borden's grin just didn't set right with her. "We appreciate your offer of assistance Mr. Bored-Dumb but we can handle things from here. We can dig up as much dirt on her as she can on us. We're the press and know how to work sources."

Tiffany replied, "Sweetie, now let's think before we speak to our gracious guest. We're a Charleston paper with local connections and limited resources. The police are coming to question me, and my opponent has unlimited resources. Prescott's help is invaluable."

"Doubtful," her Sweetie replied.

"Darn it, Sugar! Can't you just be open for once?" she asked and then took in a deep breath to help soften her tone. "I'm just saying that it's good to get as much help as possible."

The two girls rarely disagreed. That's because Tiffany always let Sugar win. They were both only children and next door neighbors growing up. They each had distant fathers, and mothers who died a year apart. Sugar's mom passed first after years of alcoholism. Tiffany felt so sad for her playmate that she'd let her do, whatever she wanted, including stealing her Barbies. Their relationship hadn't changed much even after Tiff's mom died of breast cancer. She needed someone to tell her what to do, and the older girl did just that. Each handled their losses in different ways. Sugar bossed her way through pain, and Tiffany wrote hers out in diaries. "Marble House," tonight's play, was the story of their survival.

Prescott wondered why the sweet girl put up with the demanding diva, but he had his own agenda that needed to be accomplished. He wasn't leaving until Tiffany and the she-devil surrendered to his better judgment.

"How much does this play mean to the both of you? Because I can tell you right now you're going to lose it because of a media horde out for blood and a highly paid PR team working against you. Everything is riding on a decision you'll have to make concerning tonight's performance."

Sugar's blood starting boiling so hot she was about to turn into caramel. She exploded. "What exactly are you proposing? That we close the play? Then what? I'll lose my newspaper if this play does not at least get my investment back in ticket sales. Box office receipts are through the roof now that Tiffany's the most Googled name in the country," she said.

The playwright had her own motives for wanting the show to go on. "Some of the producers think Marble House can go to Broadway. Now that ticket sales are up, maybe there's a chance. I am not losing my baby or best friend's money. What exactly are you saying?"

He unbuttoned the top of his shirt then ran his fingers through his dark curls, something he always did before giving a business presentation. Sugar started feeling a little sweet on him but quickly changed her mind. *Come on, he is just a bad Elvis impersonator.*

"Darling, I'm saying you're going to need to rally harder than you ever have in your life. Even though you have a broken nose and scheduled surgery, you need to go to the play. Let the world see what Monica did to you," he said.

Sugar laughed. "That's it? That's your plan? She can't put her health in any more danger. The press can come here and see for themselves."

Prescott continued. "I'm not finished yet." He crouched down so he was level with the hospital bed. He spoke softly and directly to Tiffany. "Let's walk into that theatre tonight hand in hand. The press will have nothing to report on other than the show's opening night and that you and I attended together. Every newspaper and gossip column will give a synopsis of the reviews. Marble House will be a nationwide hit provided the reviews are in your favor."

"The press will report on Tiffany going whether it's with you or without you," Sugar said. She too had now come to the conclusion it was of the utmost importance the playwright attend.

He couldn't tell if he was getting through to the writer or just pissing off the investor more. He could usually guess which way a person was leaning from the movement of their eyes and the twitching of their face. But the patient was too swollen up to tell anything, and she was fading fast. Barely able to keep her head up. When in doubt, Prescott always switched gears faster than a finely tuned Ferrari. He revved it up another notch.

"You need a man of my stature and influence to bring credibility to your story. Otherwise, you'll be a victim to crazed fans who don't like it when their favorite celebrity is seen in a bad light. It's why I put a security guard out front and bought you all these flowers. I want to make sure you're safe and comfortable. In a few short weeks, once you're shining in your own spotlight, I'll fade. Simply fade away."

Sugar was incredulous. "In a few weeks? Just what kind of publicity stunt are you pulling here? Twenty-four hours should be good enough for someone with such a BIG…stature." She was referring to more than just his celebrity status. But part of her knew he was right. She never wanted anything bad to happen to Tiffany and having him around could help sell tickets.

Every deal has a decision maker, and he finally relented to the real boss. The only thing that made Sugar semi-tolerable, as far as he was concerned, were those smoking-hot green eyes. So he made his final sales pitch while looking at his shoes.

"You'll get your investment back and then some. You'll sell every seat for the entire run with me around generating publicity. I might even pitch in for a Broadway show as a favor for all your troubles. Are you 100 percent positive the play is that good?" he asked.

"Yes, it's that good!" Sugar replied.

He looked the "she-devil" in the eyes. Damn, they really were pretty. Too bad the rest of her was so impossible to be around. "Then we have a deal?"

"We have a deal," she said.

Tiffany appeared knocked out cold. She'd hit the wall.

He snapped his fingers. "Say, Sugar, why don't you go out and buy two of the best dresses in town compliments of me? Get Tiff and you all prettied up." He was hoping to give the patient time to rest without the pink panther prancing around.

She took the bait. "Hand over your credit card."

He looked at her pink pants suit as if seeing it for the first time. *Ghastly.* That uniform wasn't fit for an over-the-hill Hooters girl serving lunch to her five kids on a picnic table in Kentucky.

"Wait. What am I thinking? I'll just get my personal shopper Hubert over here, and he'll get you both fancied up. You have much more important things to do. You need to concentrate on getting your girl rested up for the big night. I hope Marble House is as great as you say," he said, while making a mad dash for the door.

Once a deal is closed, he never hung around for small talk. He'd provide tonight's wardrobe and escort service. In return for these small services, they'd verify his story with the press. Plus, he'd make some money too. He looked for dollar signs in every endeavor, and Marble House had green painted all over it. He wanted in on the action.

The business tycoon had read the play earlier compliments of a PI who gave 50 bucks to a stage hand. Prescott then forwarded it to Stewart Hamilton, an old school chum turned producer. The accompanying message read: "Drop everything. Read this. Here is your next big hit. Then check out the entertainment news. Let's springboard it into something bigger."

The producer texted back: "Marble House makes a better movie than Broadway show. Enjoyed the script and the bad publicity too. Makes it much easier to get investors when a play is making national news. If the critics love it, we're a go. Call you tomorrow."

What Stewart Hamilton didn't know is the media frenzy was just starting, and there'd be more surprises than if Prescott Borden became a priest. The real blockbuster was happening now before their very eyes.

The notorious lady's man had gone from interested lover to Hollywood power broker. Now he had to sprinkle a little poison into Sugar's pot because he could tell she was not going to give him even a quarter teaspoon of love. Especially when it came to him taking

charge of Tiffany's jewels - her written words. Sugar had invested a
fortune in them, but now he wanted control, without the obnoxious
best friend being tagged in every photo. But he was still a man of
honor when it came to business and was willing to write her a big
check to go with her big behind – which he intended to push out the
door.

What he failed to keep in mind was that Sugar Lynn Limehouse
was no man's fool. She didn't dig a dead newspaper out of the grave
and bring it back to life without getting dirty from pulling off a lot of
maggots. Her alcoholic father had buried it, preferring booze to working, but that didn't stop her. She quit college and never went back.
Running a newspaper became her education and was worth more
than any paper degree. She'd let Prescott think she bought into this
whole "investing as a favor" deal. She'd take all his free publicity and
ticket sales and create some more. She thought maybe it could lead
to a Hollywood deal, and they could just skip right over Broadway to
the L.A. big bucks. Scheming minds think alike. She just needed to
find some a cheese. A pretty young thing to rattrap his private parts
and prove to Tiffany what rodent he really is. One big snap and the
pest would be a gone!

Chapter 4

Tiffany fought the good fight, attended the production, and stood by her man. Or rather, her "imaginary lover" who came to life in the form of Prescott Borden. Just like Barbie's Ken. He was just arm candy. All plastic and not real. Although she hoped for more, along with the rest of the country, who was cheering for the new "it" girl.

Gossip columnists and entertainment shows had everyone guessing. Was billionaire Prescott Borden in love with playwright Tiffany James instead of the most watched woman in the world – super model Monica Dees? Did he choose brains over beauty? And who attacked who? Did the skirt-chasing tycoon really beat up the cover girl? Or was he just protecting the real love of his life Tiffany? Did the writer jump on the model's back, provoking the fight, as Monica claimed? And was Justin Bieber somehow behind it all? (Just throw in his name and everyone watches.) "Stay tuned," was the tabloids' only answer.

Tonight's charade further proved that the two had been lovers. They smiled at each other and waved to those in attendance. Theater goers were texting out messages faster than dandelions growing on a suburban lawn. Even the highbrow crowd wanted to improve their social media status, so they took photos before the announcement of "Turn off all cameras and cell phones," which no one did of course. They put their I-phones on silent and snapped a few shots during the performance. "Marble House" turned out to be hottest ticket around. Audience members had made themselves part of the show with tweets like: "They're holdings hands," "She may not be a super model but she's super beat up," and "Wow this play is good."

Poor "Barbie" looked puffy, black and blue, and exhausted but held herself with a grace that would have made Mother Theresa proud - minus all the lying stuff. She clung to "Ken's" hand throughout the night to keep herself grounded in reality. She was on an all-time high, but it wasn't from seeing a packed theater enjoying the play. Or from relishing the performance. Or having the hottest date in the world. She was soaring from a few too many white pills called codeine. Her feet were on the ground, but her mind was in the theater rafters.

As the show came to a climax, so did she. She sat stoic, unable to move, about to fall into a coma, like a woman having the worst sex ever. Nothing was moving besides her fingernails, which kept digging deeper into Prescott's skin, drawing blood. He never complained because he was completely engaged in "Marble House" and didn't feel the pain.

He saw her beauty shining in the performance. He felt he knew something very personal about her. He saw her past come to life before his very eyes. He was sorry she missed the experience of seeing a live audience's reaction. (Clearly she was there but not mentally present.) He couldn't wait to take her to see the show again.

The crowd went wild at the end of the performance and de-manded five additional curtain calls. The actors kept returning to the stage encouraged by the non-stop applause. But enough was enough after two standing ovations for "Barbie" and "Ken." The "fairy tale" lovers had to go before their coach turned into a pumpkin. Tiffany's mind had become like pumpkin mush.

They made their way through the aisles touching the hands of all the people reaching out to them. There was no rush for the exit doors as there was after most shows. It was as if the crowd expected something more to happen, like Monica Dees rushing in with a samurai sword.

The exit was just a step away. A chance to breathe. The couple burst through the doors hand in hand, only to find the great outdoors even more claustrophobic with cameras flashing and some of Monica's fans screaming obscenities. Photographers wanted that million dollar tabloid shot and kept yelling Tiff's name so she'd look their way.

The sights and sounds all blurred into one. Tiffany's mind couldn't fight her body any longer and she passed out. Her handsome prince swooped her up in his arms and carried her to the waiting limo, like he was starring in an epic drama. He put her inside the waiting car but purposely left the door open. He paused an additional few seconds for the cameras to capture him ripping off his bow tie. He tore off a piece of his shirt so he'd have something to pat her sweating head with. He then slammed the door closed as if to tell the press they were not welcome. Even with the cameras off, he continued caressing her head, but this time not just for show. She looked so pretty in pink despite his recent disdain for anything that color - particularly pants suits. But on Tiffany, every shade looked adorable. He let out a long sigh of relief.

He heard clapping from inside the black stretch limo. "Bravo, well done. You should have been an actor in the play," a voice said.

He looked around and there "it" was. Laying across the white leather seat, in a purple sparkly dress, with a glass of champagne in "its" hand. Sugar Lynn Limehouse whose parents should have named her Vinegar, because she made everything sour as far as he was concerned.

He rolled his eyes. "You've been out here all this time? Some best friend and key investor you are. You're just a bad actor."

"Hah!" she said and sat upright. Not worth her time to think up a witty comeback. The champagne was far more intoxicating than dull Prescott Borden. She took a long sip from her glass and finished it in one gulp. She put down the crystal flute and started examining her friend, who appeared unusually quiet.

"Honey, open up your eyes. The show's over. The cameras got it all."

But Tiffany didn't respond. She moved in closer and started lightly patting the patient's face. The injured playwright just shook her head "no" and went on sleeping.

"Oh, my Lord. Look! What have you done to her? She really is passed out!" Sugar jumped up and pounded on the glass window separating the driver from the passengers. "Freaking step on it. Mass General Hospital," she said, while pounding away.

"Darling, you need to calm down. The driver knows where we're going - it's only five minutes away. There's a private room waiting, as well as a doctor and a whole slew of professional caregivers. She's knocked out from being loaded up on too many pain pills. Why'd you give her so many?"

She stopped pounding on the glass, turned around, and crossed her arms. "Because of bad advice I got from a certain doctor. Dr. McDumbknuckle. That'd be you in case you're wondering." She fell back in her seat.

"I didn't say give her a whole bottle," he protested.

"Perhaps you should stick with the only profession you're qualified to speak on. Screwing super models." She poured herself another drink to calm her nerves. She held up the glass as if to say "Cheers," then downed it.

He shook his head. "Darling, what's wrong with you? Why don't you just slow down and enjoy the ride in a fancy car? Stop being a pain in the ass all the time."

She ignored his judgmental stares. She adjusted her bosom in her pushup bra, wondering if he even noticed. Or did he just like dating girls with boys' figures?

He snapped his fingers and pointed at her. "Seriously. I saw the character based on you in that play tonight. Who could miss you? Chubby wannabe princess telling everyone what to think and do. Hell, that actor did a better job of playing you than you do in real life. Because I enjoyed watching her performance. She made me laugh and smile, but every time I see you I just wanna stab my eyes out."

Sugar pleaded with him. "Oh, please don't stab your eyes out. Spare yourself and all your fans too. Give us something to believe in. You. All you." She said in an over-dramatic kind of way.

"There you go again. That's exactly what I am talking about. You're not funny like the character in "Marble House." In fact, you're not even worthy of being called a smart ass because half of what you say doesn't even make sense. You're like a Dolly Pardon-me blow-up doll filled with hot air. You're floating all over looking for a place to land. It must scare the hell out of every man you meet."

She laughed. "I'll tell you what's scary. Your expertise with blow-up dolls. Aren't models with fake balloons satisfying enough? You need to sleep with plastic toys too?" She said, trying to egg him on.

He was unfazed. He figured out her problem. "For someone who hates me so much, you sure are fascinated with my sex life." He leaned in close. "Are you sure you're not a little disappointed because you'd never stand a chance? Maybe that's your problem. Sexual frustration." He smirked and pulled away.

She sat up so her enticing bust was in his direct line of sight. "Oh, that's it. Someone like me can't get sex anywhere. I am begging you to please have sex with me." She fell back in her seat. "Oh, but wait - never mind. I'd have to starve myself into a size A bra to satisfy your taste in anorexic girls and not real women."

He mumbled. "You forgot to mention getting a facelift and li-posuction." He figured that last comment would back her down permanently, even though he felt kind of mean saying it. He took out his cell phone, confident their exchange was over but feeling a little shallow just the same.

Sugar, who had no question about her curvy good looks and pretty face, didn't flinch at his plastic surgery remark. She never second guessed her over estimation of herself. She was a 10 on the good looks scale. OK, maybe more like an eight, but it was still a good number and matched her zaftig figure.

She sweetly inquired, "I am just dying to know what it's like to be you. Oh, please, please, please, tell me all about it." She dropped all pretense of being nice. "Because I'd sure like to know what it feels like to wake up and see God every day." She took another drink and half felt like throwing it at him.

He cleared his throat as if getting ready to say something important but kept on pretending to check messages, when actually his phone was dead.

She chuckled. "You're an easy read. You're not really reading texts. Just posing. I've got your number written on the back of my hand."

"Darling, I sure as hell hope not. I've had that number for 20 years. I don't want to have to change it." He put his phone down wondering how in the hell she knew he wasn't reading anything.

"Now you're wondering how I knew that…I got your number all right and your act too. Whereas my character can be seen in a Broadway bound play, you're performing live in a Memphis honky-tonk. You're nothing but a cheap Elvis knock-off in an Armani suit. May God rest his soul. Wait, don't get confused. I am talking to the real God, not you."

He was now done with feeling guilty for slamming her back. She pissed him off in ways that were almost inexpressible. Still, he'd give it the old college try.

"Maybe you should start praying to yourself. Because the only God you know is you. You walk into a place like you don't even have to stop for a security guard because you're too damn important. You throw the word 'honey' around like it's everyone's first name. Or maybe you don't even bother with names because you think everything is about you."

"Whatever you say, Darling."

A dazed Tiffany sat up. She covered her eyes from the light. She spoke in a voice louder than Sugar's highest pitch.

"That's it! You two have got to take this down a notch. Can't you see that I am barely breathing here?" She fell back down on the limo seat and mumbled, "A bunch of self-indulgent pigs." She took her fingers and stuck them in her ears.

They both looked to be more in shock than the poor patient. They tried to soothe her by touching her hair and back.

"Stop it both of you. Don't touch me. Leave me alone."

He scratched his head and whispered so as not to disturb the injured, "Did she just call us pigs?"

Sugar lowered her voice too. "No, no, no way. She'd never say anything like that. Never. She called us kids. Self-indulgent kids, not pigs. Trust me on this, I might not know much, but I know Tiffany. She'd never say anything like that about anyone."

Prescott was skeptical. "Well, maybe you don't know her that well. Maybe you should have come to the play to find out what's she's all about. Some best friend you turned out to be. You were at the wrong theater production. You're more like the cowardly lion. Big roar but didn't have the courage to see yourself on that stage. Or get to know Tiffany better." He stretched out his long legs and crossed them like he was watching a movie at home.

Sugar's indignation could be felt by the limo driver hidden behind a glass barrier, even though her voice was barely above a whisper.

"Are you kidding me? I lived that show. That's our life. Meaning mine and hers. That play is as a much me as it is her. I'm the one who pushed her to work at the newspaper and hone her talents. That girl would still be talking to herself in diaries if it weren't for me. I am the one who edited every article she's ever written and every story she's told, including "Marble House!" I know her better than anyone. I'm the one who discovered her talent, not you, so bug off." She pushed his legs off her seat. What was he doing putting his dogs next to her anyway?

The limo pulled into the patient drop-off area at Mass General. There was a nurse waiting. They all got out of the car and helped Tiffany get into a wheelchair.

"Hi Tiffany. I've heard a lot about you. I am so glad to meet you. I'm your personal nurse, Betty Raney. I'll be taking care of you for the rest of the night."

Tiffany nodded. The codeine was wearing off, and the pain from her injuries was kicking into high gear. She felt wide awake now. The kids (or was it pigs) followed behind.

Tiffany yelled, "Everyone stop. **We** are not going forward."

The nurse leaned down to speak with the non-compliant patient. "You're in bad shape. You need medical help," she said.

Tiffany looked straight into her caretaker's eyes. "That's right, but I don't want these two coming along. Get them out of my sight and ban them from seeing me for two days. I need to get some rest."

Did she just say two days? Both Prescott and Sugar looked at each other in panic. They needed her, but for different reasons, all of which were self-centered. She needed Tiffany promoting the play with the press. This was a chance for her to make money and save her newspaper from going bankrupt. He needed to be cleared of assault charges, turn "Marble House" into a money-making movie, and who knows what else? Maybe a short term romance was still possible.

The two schemers ran in front of the wheel chair to stop it from moving, and both got down on their knees.

Sugar spoke first, "We need to do interviews and sell tickets. I've invested everything in you, including the newspaper."

Tiffany held up her hand up like a stop sign. "Sugar, quit making me feel guilty for your own investment choices. You've made a lot of money on me throughout the years. I'm sorry times have changed. Newspapers aren't what they used to be, but you can't keep holding that over my head. You've clearly come out a winner today. We never expected the show to sell out opening night."

For the first time ever, the writer stood up to her boss and best friend, and it felt good, despite the raging headache.

Prescott took his turn. "Tiff, darling, I know you're hurt, but we talked about this today. Remember fighting for your play to be number one? Using the media momentum to skyrocket you to Broadway or maybe even Hollywood? I might be holding a card or two up my sleeve. Hollywood baby. Come on and work with me." He winked.

Tiffany looked at him in dumbfounded amazement. Here was the world's most eligible bachelor down on his knees, in front of her wheel chair, and the only thing she wanted was for him to get the hell out of the way.

She took in a deep breath while trying to be civil. "The play will be a success on its own. I don't need you. I saw its potential on the night of the dress rehearsal, and the reaction of tonight's audience confirmed my suspicions. It's a hit. Now move along, Buster."

His ego couldn't believe his ears. He tried once more to reason with her. "Of course it's a hit. But remember we have a press conference to do about Monica tomorrow. And then there's that little tiny issue with the police and felony charges against us. Both of us, not just me."

Sugar agreed, but for ulterior motives. "He's making sense. The time is now... not two days from now. Let's all make "Marble House" a hit and punch out the crazy woman who did this to you. Let's do it for the good of humanity," she said in a cheerleader kind of way.

Prescott scrunched up his face and looked at Sugar in an annoyed way. He spoke as if they were the only two present. "For the good of humanity? Now that's some sales job. What kind of ridiculous comment..."

While they started up with their carping, Tiffany held her hands to her head. They'd worn her out as much as the beating from Monica. Nothing was getting through to either of them, so once again she'd have to sacrifice her better judgement for some peace of mind. Whatever they wanted, she'd give them, provided she could just get to her hospital bed and sleep.

She shook her head. "Look – I've had enough. Do whatever you want to do. You two cook up whatever you want me to say. Sugar, no one knows my voice, so you can do phone interviews pretending to me. Sell tickets. Prescott, take Sugar to the press conference and tell the truth about what happened at the Four Seasons. She's my official spokesperson now. I exempt you both from any liability. Besides, you can't screw up my life any more than it already is. Now please, leave me alone!"

The nurse felt Tiff's pain. She pushed the wheelchair forward like she was mowing down weeds. The tagalongs both moved out of the way just in time for the elevator doors to open.

"Wait," Sugar said, while watching her friend being loaded in. "What about the hotel key? I need a place to sleep other than my car. My credit cards are maxed out."

Tiffany hit the wall of being reasonable. "Are you kidding me? Do you think I have any idea where that key is after all this? Go to the box office and take out some of that cash you're dying to get your hands on. Or better yet - here's an idea: You can sleep over at my pretend boyfriend's place - and in his bed for all I care. Maybe Monica will break down the door and join in. Invite the press. Make it a paparazzi party and you can all promote whatever it is you're trying to sell. I am not playing. I am done - I quit. You're a bunch of self-centered…"

The elevator door closed taking the patient out of sight.

Prescott nudged Sugar. "I bet she just said pigs and not kids."

She rolled her eyes and smacked his hand for nudging her. "Shut up and never touch me again. She's obviously been hanging out with you too long. I never heard her talk like that before."

They walked together down the hospital corridor in silence. They each independently realized it was time to put their plotting minds together. They both had agendas that could only be accomplished through working as a team. But instead of having an adult conversation, they got inside the limo and sat like pouting kids pretending the other didn't exist.

Prescott found himself turned on by Tiffany's toughness under pressure. "She's a little frisky," he thought to himself. At least he hoped that was the reason for his sexy mood. He glanced over at Sugar and the feeling ended immediately. Thank God. Now he could get a good night's sleep before the two competitors had to partner up. He'd buy her a hotel room on the first floor at the Four Seasons, far away from his penthouse suite.

Chapter 5

"What do you mean the hotel is sold out?" Prescott questioned the girl at the desk. He saw a night manager standing by the elevators and ran over to him.

"Dave, how are you buddy?" he said as the two shook hands.

The manager smiled. He looked more like the owner of the four-star hotel, dressed in a gray pin stripe suit with a perfectly pressed red tie and matching pocket square. He was even better dressed than Prescott but wasn't nearly as handsome and was a little balding. Both men were around the same age and had enjoyed cigars, discussions about women, and tipping drinks occasionally.

"Hey guy, it's so good to see you. I've been hoping you'd stop by. I'm so sorry about the penthouse sale falling through. We're going to miss you," he said with sincerity.

Prescott looked confused. "What are you talking about?"

"You haven't heard? I'm so sorry." He lowered his voice. "After all the bad media coverage and damage done to the suite and then the injured guest...well, the deal was taken off the table. I thought you knew."

The entrepreneur held his hand to his head and bent over, looking like he'd just been hit in the gut. He straightened up and tried to get a hold of himself. His beloved penthouse that he spent countless dollars rehabbing, in the belief that he'd be closing soon, was now gone. His attorney had warned him not to move so fast and stop all renovations or at least wait until the ink was dry on the deal, but he could not foresee anything going wrong.

Dave put his hand on his friend's shoulder, "I didn't mean to be the bearer of bad news. I worked hard to let you stay until the end of the month, but they're only giving you a two-week notice. I am really sorry about all of this," he said with compassion. His tone changed after seeing a hot looking number who seemed to be observing their conversation.

He nudged his friend. "But at least it looks like you'll be in good company tonight. Sweet!"

Prescott was confused. "What are you talking about?" He looked around. Then he saw Sugar swinging her pink suitcase back and forth while her blond head was bobbing all over the place, checking everything out.

"You're kidding me, right? You think I'd take that thing home?"

"Oh, you're not with her? I think I'll go over and introduce myself." He winked.

"No, no, no. Don't do that."

"Why not?

Prescott searched for an answer. "I mean, not that I care or anything. You can do whatever you want. I wouldn't take her home with me because...because she's my cousin. Yeah, my cousin from North Carolina."

"Is she single?"

He started laughing. "I am quite certain she is."

"Can you introduce me?

Prescott remained silent.

"Hey guy, is there something wrong with her?"

Prescott stayed quiet for a few more beats and said, "I'm sorry. I'm just trying to figure out an answer to that question." He snapped his fingers. "Hey! I have an idea. I'll give you an introduction if you can get me a room for her to stay in."

"The hotel is booked and so is everything else in town. What exactly is going on here? You've got plenty of room in your suite."

Sugar made her way over to the two gentlemen.

Small beads of sweat started breaking out on Prescott's forehead. He nervously said, "Dave, I'd like you to meet my cousin Sugar from North Carolina. Dave's the general manager here. My cousin is in town for a few days. Right *cousin*?"

She didn't miss a beat and put on her best sugary southern accent, one that would have raised Scarlett O'Hara from the dead. "Well, I am just so pleased to meet you, kind sir. This is such a fine hotel. You look like the perfect host for such a lovely upscale establishment." She held out her hand to him.

He reached out and kissed it. "Thank you, pretty lady. I'd be happy to give you a tour."

Prescott squeezed himself between the two. "Hold off there, cousin Sugar. We've got a lot of family business to take care of. Lots of phone calls to make in the morning. Remember? We have to be the voice for that family member who can't speak for herself on account of being injured," he hinted, hoping she understood he was talking about Tiffany.

She made a cute pouty face at the hotel manager. "Aw, he's right. I'll take a rain check if that's OK? Now, don't you go getting too far out of my sight."

He laughed. "Not a chance. I'll check in with you tomorrow. I have your cousin's number on speed dial," he said, while smiling ear to ear.

Prescott grabbed Sugar's arm and pulled her towards the elevator doors. He yelled back, "Great to see you Dave. We gotta go."

As they rode the elevator up, Prescott started imitating Sugar. "Well, don't mind me. I'm just a little old wall flower from Kentucky. So nice to meet you kind sir. I have always relied on the kindness of strangers. La-De-Da," he said.

"North Carolina. Remember? You said I am from North Carolina. See, you're already having trouble keeping your lies straight. Cousins? What exactly was that all about?" she inquired.

"He thought you and I were together. As in a one-night stand. I had to save my reputation."

"Save it from what? He seemed pretty damned impressed."

"Well, I suppose if someone likes it all hanging out for everyone to see it's impressive. Some people prefer a little modesty," he said, referring to her ample cleavage that he kept trying to avoid staring at. He couldn't help himself.

"You mean some people prefer starved scarecrows with straw for brains instead of women with clout and curves."

"There you go again! Is this how it's going to be for the next few days? One dig at me after the next."

"You tell me. You're the one who just started it up all over again. You have some nerve mocking me, all because you're jealous of some other guy who took an interest in me. Admit it. You're just plain old jealous," she said, and then resorted to childish sing-song accusations. "You're just jealous, you're just jealous, you're just jealous."

He made no response.

She, on the other hand, entertained the thought a little longer than expected. Especially for someone who hated him so much. But for some reason, the idea of Prescott Borden taking notice of her flirting seemed intriguing to her. She glanced at him in the elevator mirror, checking to see his response to her taunts. Why did he have to be so damn good looking anyway?

He turned to her. "Don't you even think about starting again with that jealousy crap. Don't humor yourself." He looked straight head. "You're insane, you're insane, you're insane," he said in the same sing-song style.

Actually, maybe a little jealousy had slipped in - or rather a lot. That was the first time he saw her flirting with another man. Why didn't she try to be charming with him?

He glanced at her in the mirror. Her full lips and sparkling green eyes were super inviting. He had to admit that was the real reason he'd rushed her away from Dave. Their connection bothered him on a number of levels. He'd show her who was boss around here. He'd make her life miserable over the next few days if she didn't start being attracted to him or at least flirt it up a bit. Just for the sole purpose of telling her: "Don't bother. I'm not interested – at all."

Silence and sexual tension took over the small space as the elevator climbed. Both the thought of him taking notice of the flirting and the actual jealousy itself rapidly changed the temperature in the room. The car seemed far too tiny for the two big personalities and the intense heat. He pushed the "up" button to his penthouse harder, over and over again.

She slapped his hand. "Stop it."

He in turn grabbed her arm. "Make me."

He pulled her in close. They were looking at each other face to face now but neither made a move. Their sexual energy was too electric. The elevator door opened. He let go of her arm. They stared at each other for an additional second, then put their heads down as if nothing had happened and walked out.

He took out a key card to open up the double mahogany doors. The red light kept flashing.

"Damn it," he said.

"Let me try." She took the card from his hand and slid it through. The green light appeared. Both of them took hold of the door handle but didn't make it inside. He spun her around and kissed her like she'd never been kissed, pinned up against the doors. Sugar let out a deep sigh, as she felt the power of him taking charge. He pulled on the front of her sparkled dress and ripped it wide open. Her face felt flushed, but she didn't try to cover up. She didn't know what to expect next. He backed away and looked her up and down. For the first time since he met her, she looked vulnerable and he liked her that way. Her blond bangs dipped below one side of her green eyes, her black push up bra off one shoulder. She looked like the pinup girls he fantasized about in his youth.

His powerful hands started rubbing her breasts. She let out another sigh. Again, he pulled away. He wanted to see that same look of surrender like after he'd ripped opened her dress. He wasn't disappointed. She was clearly out of her comfort zone but wasn't about to do anything about it. There was something almost innocent about her passiveness, something he hadn't seen in her before. He touched her lips with one finger tracing all around their pouty shape as she remained perfectly still except for her intense breathing.

His hands clasped her face, and he pulled her in closer. He tilted up her head and put his lips on hers. His alpha presence was almost counter to his gentle French kiss. Softly, slowly and seemingly endless. They both were aroused in such a heightened way that the moment took over any sense of time. They were lost in ecstasy and unaware of their surroundings - an open hotel hall. Clothes started flying, hitting the ground just before they did.

The sex lasted maybe five minutes. It was the fastest, most orgasmic, mind-blowing moment that either had ever experienced. They laid on the hall floor holding each other. They both needed a chance to catch their breath. Her head rested on his shoulder and her body was curled on its side. Neither said a word. It was as if in that moment they belonged together – forever.

Chapter 6

Tiffany had a good night's rest and slept most of the day after being in surgery. Her nose was reassembled, and she felt rested and at peace. Everything was going to heal up just fine, the doctor assured her. Finally, she'd get her life back together.

Maybe she'd been too harsh on Prescott and Sugar. They both really wanted what was best for her. Success was an important element in all of this, even if they seemed unconcerned about her medical needs. They were pushing her to be the most she could be, and she had misunderstood their intentions. Plus, he mentioned something about a Hollywood deal. Could he be her knight in shining armor, clearing the path to L.A? Something most playwrights are rarely able to achieve.

Life was starting to feel good again. Her room was filled with flowers (all sent by him), and now newspapers featuring spectacular reviews of *Marble House*. Of course, there were a few hits below the belt. The New York Post had a photo of Tiffany looking quite beat up at the performance. Next to her, a picture of Monica with the bruise shaped like a handprint on her face, left by Prescott's smack. "*Marble House* is a smashing hit," was the headline.

The staff read the reviews to her out loud, since her vision was still a little blurred, but they left off some scathing remarks. One critic wrote, "The only flaw in the performance was watching the writer nodding in and out through the entire show. It was a distraction for many in attendance. *Marble House* is good. Using negative publicity for attention distracted the spotlight from the actors who mastered the script."

Prescott turned out to be right. Having him by her side made people pay attention to the play. The "no comment" trick worked perfectly. The entertainment media had nothing to report about other than the show and the two of them being there together. Even highbrow publications took an interest purely because the reviews of *Marble House* had been so favorable. But the real reason was because everyone wanted to know more about the billionaire, supermodel, and playwright.

The soft-spoken girl from Charleston was relieved she had given Sugar permission to handle all the media inquiries. Her best friend had the magic touch of captivating a room with her outgoing personality and take charge attitude which always impressed even the harshest skeptic. With the exception of Prescott, who seemed to hate the newspaper publisher.

Tiffany was glad her two friends were now forced to work together and trusted they'd figure out a way to move past their personality clashes. They were, after all, business professionals at their core and quite capable of behaving as such. Or they'd at least figure how to get along because of their affection for her. She figured by now they'd stopped being haters and were acting like adults with an agenda of making the play a smashing success. She looked forward to seeing their joint press conference. They were about to make her even more famous and write her ticket to Broadway and Hollywood. Her dreams were coming true! Even though she had always imagined it would be her work that was in the spotlight and not her personally.

But being famous wasn't so bad. She was enjoying all the attention from the hospital staff. Even her plastic surgeon, Dr. DeAngelo, appeared to be a little star-struck and flirty. Which didn't bother her a bit. He wore thick glasses that made his eyes seem oversized, but underneath the lenses she could see his classic Italian good looks. He didn't have a ring on his finger, but she was starting to believe there could be a chance with Prescott. Stranger things had happened, like their accidental meeting that caught the world's attention. Maybe they were meant to be. They'd be spending a lot of time together on her way to Broadway or L.A. Maybe the bachelor just hadn't met that right special someone. Or maybe that special someone was her.

She laughed at the thought and turned on the TV. TMZ was on. That sleazy show had somehow managed to get a copy of the video. There was Prescott fighting off Monica. *Wow, I'm on TV!* She turned up the volume just in time to see a new image flash on the screen: A press conference featuring her two biggest supporters.

A reporter asked. "Are you sure this is the real deal? You've been known to have quite a few girl friends in the past, including multiple partners several times."

Prescott smiled. "That's just press gossip. My commitment to Tiffany couldn't be stronger. I did the best I could trying to defend her from a mentally unbalanced person."

"Do you know how she's doing?" someone asked.

Sugar jumped in, having no idea they meant Monica. "She's been through a terrible ordeal and is doing the best she can. She's been in surgery. I talked to her earlier (not true since she was banned from contact), and she was in good spirits considering the terrible circumstances. Still, there is a lot to be grateful for. Her play *Marble House* is a huge success, and Hollywood is calling. Tickets for *Marble House* can be ordered online."

A reporter shouted, "Prescott, are there wedding plans?"

He laughed. "Well, it's certainly something to think about in the future. Tiffany is something," he said.

"Don't forget to call Ticketmaster," Sugar said, out of the blue.

Tiffany repeated her friend's words: "Tiffany is something, and don't forget to call Ticketmaster? Too funny," she giggled.

Then her mouth dropped open as another video started playing of a blurry Prescott and Sugar appearing to have sex. And on the same hotel hall where Monica had beat her to a pulp.

The words "kissing cousins" flashed across the screen. She almost went into shock. She pressed the nurse's station button on the side of her bed rail. She was feeling faint. The room was spinning, and her heart was racing. A full blown anxiety attack hit her like a swarm of bees protecting the queen. There were no words to describe the depth of her confusion, anger, and disgust. She tried to calm herself by counting to 100 while waiting for a response from the nurse's station.

Seems hotel manager Dave turned out not to be such a good friend after all. He took an early retirement plan compliments of a video camera he personally installed in front of Prescott's door. He figured there had to more drama before the guy checked out permanently. The Monica fight tape went for a huge dollar amount. It was his turn to cash in. He also let the world know that Prescott's new love interest was none other than the playboy's sweet cousin Sugar from North Carolina. Who Dave still hoped to meet under different circumstance provided she didn't find out he'd already screwed her.

Chapter 7

Sugar sat in bed in her furry pink robe, staring at the TV watching the press conference, sipping on a cup of coffee. She spit it out at the unexpected sight of her having sex with Prescott for the whole wide world to see and the words "Kissing Cousins" flashing across the screen. She didn't bother cleaning up the mess. She felt frozen and trapped in disbelief.

He came out of the shower showing off his rock hard abs and drying his hair with a towel. He shook his head so that his dark curls fell into place. All part of his daily routine. But today it happened twice since they'd been up earlier preparing to meet the press after a 6 a.m. wake up call. Sugar was all business, and so was he. He was surprised by her work ethic and how professional she'd been through the process of their brainstorming. She seemed to be able to separate business from pleasure, an attribute he found particularly attractive, since he himself possessed the exact same talent. He seriously doubted that any woman was really capable of being so deliberate - at least not the ones he slept with. Sugar seemed to be an exception. They'd already had sex twice with no discussions about "where is this going" or even worse "do you love me?"

"What just happened in here?" he said, referring to the brownish coffee stains on his white comforter.

Sugar jumped out of bed and started pointing at the TV. "I just saw our press conference and then some. I spit out my coffee out at the sight."

"What's the problem? We did a good job except for you being a little too pushy telling everyone to call Ticketmaster. Naughty girl." He didn't really care about the coffee stain. He was more interested in something else. He walked over to her and started kissing the back of her neck. The thought of the way she could separate business from pleasure was turning him on. "Guess I'll have to take you over my knee and ..."

She pulled away and said, "No. No. No. Everyone knows. The whole world knows. Oh, Lord. I hope Tiffany didn't see it." She wrung her hands while pacing back and forth on the Persian rug. She started talking to herself.

"How am I gonna be able to show my face in Charleston? Are my employees writing copy on me as we speak? Of course, they're laughing their asses off at my expense." She started pulling on her blond hair. "Oh, my word. What's my dad going to say?" She hadn't said something like that since sneaking out in her daddy's pickup truck at age sixteen and getting caught parking illegally with Billy Parker. Another Tiffany crush that had been crushed.

Prescott stared at her, then at the TV. The words "Kissing Cousins" once again flashed on the screen while the TMZ reporters made jokes about the tryst caught on camera, which they had edited down to 30 explosive seconds. The TMZ host made wisecracks about keeping "it" in the family and southern hospitality.

"What the!" Prescott shouted. He fell backward on the bed with his hands holding his forehead. He stared at the arched wood ceiling in total disbelief. He'd just managed to get a meeting with the hotel's owners to plead his case about renewing the deal to buy the penthouse. There was no point of going now. He was cooked, and he knew it. He wouldn't be seeing those gorgeous curves much longer. Meaning the ceiling, not Sugar.

When did hotel security put a camera right in front of his door? There had never been one there in the past. He wanted answers, but was in no position to ask. For the time being, everyone would be snickering behind his back or maybe even to his face. As he would be too after watching the sight of some other guy having sex with his alleged cousin and finishing prematurely.

His cell and the room phone both started ringing. He kicked one off the dresser and ignored the other. He decided he was not getting out of bed for the rest of the day.

"Aren't you going to answer that?" Sugar asked.

Oh why was she still here? Reality TV is such a turn off when you see it in real time. She was a fine looking, voluptuous girl in real life but on the tape looked fat. What would his buddies think? Would they be more offended by her size or the cousin part? Any other warm feelings he had for her were overshadowed by watching his manhood being permanently trashed by a 30 second edited performance.

She continued, "The caller ID says it's the National Enquirer. Maybe we should respond?"

In a smart ass way, he asked, "And, pray tell, what exactly do we say?"

Her mind started racing, and without thinking she said, "That we were drunk and didn't know better. Yeah, that's the line I'm sticking to. Everyone will think it's true. I've been known for public drunkenness on many occasions." Her excited tone convinced him it was probably true.

He rolled his eyes. "Your fame lives on for sure."

"Well, what do you propose? We can't pretend it didn't happened. It's on tape. We need to at least clarify we're not related." She paused and took in a deep breath. "I didn't have sex with my cousin." She stamped her feet like a spoiled kid whose candy was just taken away.

Prescott mimicked her childish tone, "I didn't have sex with my cousin," then mumbled to himself. "But maybe I should have instead of getting into this mess." He rolled over on his side and looked at the bedside clock. What was the appropriate amount of time before he could ask her to leave? An hour? Two? Maybe twelve?

She wanted out just as badly but needed more time to think about her plan of escape. She left the room and sat down at the oversized dining room table where they'd brainstormed earlier. There was a handsome wet bar with a refrigerator but no kitchen. She wondered why anyone needed a table with eight king size chairs when there was nothing to eat. She had no idea room service provided everything from breakfast to fine dining for any size group. She pulled out a bottle of Bailey's and poured some into her coffee cup.

In Prescott's mind, time was up. He came out of the bedroom, took one look at her and grabbed the bottle and her cup.

"No way, you're not starting that here. You need to get your things

together and drive back to Charleston. I need...correction, we both
need, to put our lives back together. Tiffany's play is a success. You
two are bound for greater things. You're nice girls and belong with
nice guys - not me," he said.

Sugar stood up from the dining room table. "I can't show my
face in Charleston. Maybe you don't care about your reputation, but
I need time to rebuild mine before going home," she cried, while tears
rolled down her face.

He breathed in. He held his hands to his head like he was keeping
it from exploding. Tears were not his strong suit. Maybe he'd been too
harsh. She, like all women, can't separate themselves from the heat of
the moment. He'd have to let her down easier.

The one-night stand break-ups were sometimes more complicated
than the two-year types, which usually ended with an "I hate you"
door slam. He'd seen it all through the years, but a crying girl was
always his weak spot.

"Darling, now don't go on doing that. Here, here take a drink.
It's OK," he said, while handing her back the coffee mug filled with
Bailey's and encouraging her to take a sip.

She refused. "You got us into this mess. Now I'm stuck getting
myself out. I wanted to dump you to the curbside at the hospital. I
knew you were bullshit the second I saw you. Oh, and all that talk
about Broadway and Hollywood. You just wanted to clear your name
from the Monica fight and then have your way with Tiffany but got
stuck with me instead." She marched back into the master bedroom
and started gathering up her things.

He followed and tried to reason with her. "Now stop moving a second. I am glad it was you. Really, really, really glad." He put his hand on her shoulder in hopes she'd stand still and listen to reason.

She turned to face him. His touch still aroused every part of her body.

He lowered his voice. "Darling, we just made a mistake. You said so yourself when I started to kiss you earlier. You pulled away from me because of the reality of watching the sex tape. I did the same thing once I realized what was going on and saw the words 'Kissing Cousins.' Be realistic. Last night and this morning were spectacular. Awesome. But we both have to put our lives back together now. You saw the tape, and so did the whole world." He looked her in the eyes with a tender expression. Still, the message was loud and clear: It's time for you to go.

If she stood there any longer, she was going to kiss him. Like he had tried to kiss her before seeing the shocking evidence. She had a change of heart and wanted to figure out a way of working things out. Why wasn't he feeling the same? She could see from the look on his face her advances would be rejected. She pushed his hand from her shoulder and marched over to her pink suitcase. She tried to unzip it, but it wouldn't open. She kicked it out of frustration. She wanted him to stop her from leaving but knew he wouldn't. She came to the conclusion that he'd used her for something beyond her comprehension.

She pointed her finger at him. "You had to know there was a camera there and recording. Is this how you get your kicks? Watching 50 shades of crap? I don't know what game this is, and I don't care. Mail me the rest of my things." She started cussing to herself and walked out of the bedroom, then through the living room. He followed behind her then jumped in front of the exit door.

"Wait, wait, wait. Hold on there. Listen to me. You need to calm down. Calm down. Just stay one more day. You don't want to go out of here like this," he said.

She breathed in a sigh of relief hoping he'd seen the light, but she needed more information. "You tell me why. Why should I stay here one more day with you?"

He couldn't believe she was being so dense, and he had enough of this drama. "Because as you pointed out, there is a damn security camera right outside my door and the paparazzi are waiting outside the hotel. Let's not make bigger fools out of ourselves than we already have. You stay, and I'll leave! Get your head together, and go out in the early morning when you won't be seen."

The room got quiet. She nodded her head as if what he said made sense. But actually she was acknowledging the hurt she felt down to her very soul.

He cast his eyes down but still stood guarding the door.

A cell phone started ringing. It was hers. She'd almost left it on the dining room table. She walked over and looked at the caller ID. She turned her back on Prescott.

"Hi, Daddy," she said and cleared her throat and paused.

"No, I am fine. What makes you think I'm crying?"

She listened and twirled a strand of her hair. Something she always did when he seemed upset with her.

"Yeah, we need to talk about it. Please don't be mad…Well what can I say? I fell madly in love, and I'm still standing here with him now. That's right, a billionaire tycoon in his penthouse. You should see this place. This one's for real, Daddy." Tears started to fall down her face.

She listened and then started to laugh.

"You're proud of me? For what? Well, I don't think I ever heard you say that before, especially given the video tape." More tears fell down. "You know he's asked me to marry him? But I told him I needed a little time to think it over. So I am coming home for now."

She turned and looked at Prescott. Their eyes locked. He understood that she needed to leave with her head held high and forgave her white lies.

"No, he's gonna stay here for now. He's going to take care of our Tiffany. Give me a chance to think things over." She turned away and walked over to a window. The views of Boston's Public Garden were breathtaking even on a cloudy day. Heavy rain drops started to cover the glass faster and faster. She felt like she was drowning in their wake.

Her dad spoke. She smiled. For the first time, she felt like he was actually listening to her. "Now, Dad, stop that. Don't worry. I'm not going to lose him. He's more likely going to lose me." She waited for a response. None came from Prescott. She almost choked on her words. "I'll drive safely. See you soon. Bye-bye."

Once again, he found himself oddly drawn in by her. She seemed like a teenage girl talking on the phone and making up stories about a boy she dreamed to life, very innocent and sweet. When she was vulnerable, he wanted to be strong.

He walked over and took the cell phone from her hand and stuck it his pocket. He put his arms around her and whispered, "Just stay."

That same sexy feeling overwhelmed his mind and body. He never desired someone more, even though he had plenty of practice with women far more stunning, but never one so sexy as when Sugar let her guard down. He wiped away one tear then kissed another.

She clasped her hands around his face. She needed to look at him. Could this really be happening again? She searched his eyes looking for answers as to what the hell they were both doing. Are they starting up again or just having a final goodbye?

He caressed her gently.

"Are you for real?" she whispered.

"This is real," he said and pressed himself up against her. He picked her up and carried her back into the master suite. He laid her down across his big brass bed.

"I need a Kleenex. I must look terrible."

"You never looked more beautiful to me." What was it about this girl and this moment that captivated him so? He'd been with some of the most beautiful women in the world, and for far longer than a day. Something about her was familiar, but he couldn't place it. He could see the sweetness and complexity of her spirit. Like looking through a kaleidoscope, she kept revealing more.

She closed her eyes.

"No, I want you to look at me." He held her arms above her head and fell on top of her. They were looking at each other eye-to-eye with his body weight resting on hers.

"We've had sex twice. This time, let's make love. I don't want you to close your eyes. Just be with me." Words he'd never said to anyone before.

She nodded in complete surrender. They didn't speak for the rest of the afternoon. They made love in silence but never once stopped staring at each other, as if they communicated through their eye contact and nothing more.

Chapter 8

Monica Dees sat in her manager's office in New York City. Usually she was rushed right in, but this time she was stuck waiting in the small reception area with the general public population of models. Not the super girl category.

A few tried to start up a conversation with her, particularly a 16-year-old gawky teen with mom in tow. The newbie girl happened to be an exact duplicate of Monica at her age.

"I'm your biggest fan. I have your posters and print ads with you all over my wall," the young girl said.

"How old are you – 10?" Monica said without looking at the teen. She'd heard those same compliments a million times and was usually gracious, but this one was from her direct competition.

"Don't listen to her. She's just jealous," her mother said.

This tit-for-tat was observed by the receptionist, who also happened to be Sam Goldstein's mother. A little fact the power broker and mom kept to themselves.

"Monica, Sam will see you now," she said and walked her back through a creaky wooden hall. No one would guess this was the office

of a genius in the industry. It looked more crack den. The receptionist stuck her head in his door before presenting Monica Dees.

"It's working," she said to Sam, referring to the 16 year old they
had deliberately planted at the same time the super star would be ar-
riving. Models were washed up in New York at age 21 unless they had
a name. The constant competition from younger look-a-likes ruined
most careers. Monica had a huge name, but it was turning to mud
faster than a roller coaster ride at Coney Island.

Monica gushed. "Samuel, darling, how could you? Now why
would my favorite guy in the world makes his favorite girl in the world
wait? Don't you love me anymore?" she said with a coy smile.

He turned his swivel chair away from her and looked out the window behind him. He chose enjoying the site of a trashed-filled alley
rather than have to look at his personal discovery, Monica. He sucked
on a stogie that was never lit but always hanging from his mouth.
There were bets within the industry that the cigar was the same one
he chewed when he opened the doors in 1962.

She pleaded, "Don't be like that. It's not my fault. Turn around.
Look at my face. He did this to me." She pointed to the black and
blue slap print left by Prescott. "They attacked me first."

He'd already seen the evidence. It was splashed on every tabloid
from here to Tokyo. He swung his chair around to address his client.
The quick movement caused his dyed brown comb over to stick up.
He was pudgy and red-faced, and looked straight out of central cast-
ing as an over-the-hill agent. Behind his back, people called him the
Penguin. But Sam's days of being the main attraction at the zoo were
far from being over. The Penguin was the go-to guy when it came to
problem models.

He squawked, "The trouble is, my dear, no one is buying your story."

"Not true - I am the most watched woman in the world according to most men's magazines." She showed off her dazzling smile.

He was one of the few men able to look past her beauty and the fact that she'd been featured on the cover of every fashion magazine in the world. "Being watched isn't the same thing as being believable. Models with your name recognition make $40 million a year. You make $1 million. What do you think is the difference?"

She sat down. She had to think about that question. She pondered for a few moments.

"The problem is, I am just too good looking for mainstream deals." She sincerely believed that was the answer to his question.

He raised his thick unibrow. He heard it a million times, but it still amazed him. The giraffe walking down a high school hall goes from the class geek to runway chic. But deep inside she still carries the pain of not fitting in for 17 years. She goes from being the ugly duckling to being crowned national homecoming queen. Then come the men, gifts, trips overseas, and parties. Life is good. But then the drinking and drugs bring back the pain of sitting on the sidelines for the majority of their life. Later, it turns to rage, because deep down inside there's a 5' 10" girl who never made peace with the two worlds she exists in. Most models couldn't figure out they were partly freaky and partly magnificent. They'd prefer to believe they were too pretty rather than an oddity. Monica's acting out and fights with the world were really about the battles within herself.

At least that's how Sam Goldstein saw it. To hell with victims like

Tiffany, provided it didn't affect a cover girl's revenue. He had a job to do, and he did it well.

He got up and waddled over to her. "You are by far the most beautiful woman in the world. Everyone knows it. I can see it. I've represented the best, and you're better. Only no one knows it because no one knows the real you," he said and then held her hand. "You're misunderstood, my love."

She started to tear up. He handed her a fresh Kleenex tucked under his sleeve. He had to put a new tissue in there every time a special needs case walked through his door. Everyone had a story. If he didn't see tears, the meeting was a failure. Besides, it was best to get them crying before dropping the really bad news.

She dabbed her eyes. "I don't know why people take mean jabs at me. It's just really hard to deal with sometimes," she said, managing to shed only a few tears. She was soft on the outside but tough as a black belt on the inside.

Sam jumped up on his desk and sat down so she'd have to look up at him from her chair. A power move he'd practiced many times when dealing with clients much taller than him. "It's jealousy, plain and simple. That's why it pains me to tell you this. Your deal with the lipstick company just fell through. I think it's another case of you being too pretty for your own good. Even people who see you in magazines put judgments on you."

"What? I'm not the Double Trouble lip gloss girl anymore?" A few more tears started to fall.

"You'll always be double trouble to me." The comment went over her head.

There is a point in a troubled model's career when it wasn't worth salvaging. Time to put her out to pasture and let the commercial print people take over. He could see Monica was headed there. That's why he found her replacement a month ago, even before her most recent blow up at the Four Seasons. He couldn't wait to tell the 16 year old sitting in his lobby she was the new lip gloss girl.

But Sam didn't want to give up on Monica, not just yet. Too much tabloid money was out there. There had to be some way to cash in. The mastermind had brokered a deal she couldn't pass up.

He pounded his little flipper hands on the desktop, loud enough to startle her. "So how are we going to get regular people to know you better? So they'll come to love you as is. For the sweet, aah, caring person you are?" He didn't give her a chance to respond.

"You're not going to believe this. But you're going to get that opportunity. You're going to be the star of a TV show called 'Hanging with Miss D.' It's all about you and your fine attributes." He clapped his hands in praise of his genius deal making.

She wasn't feeling his enthusiasm. "Not a chance. I am not doing reality TV."

"Now, don't make a rash judgment. You haven't even heard the premise. Look at Heidi and Tara. They're working the TV circuit. They're pulling in hundreds of millions. That could be you in a few years if you work it," he smiled. In his mind, he was headed to the bank with 25 percent. A larger percentage than he'd normally be owed, but he was going to squeeze it out of her - because this girl was unmarketable. It was all thanks to him and his marketing savvy that she'd have a longer than usual crash-and-burn career.

"What's the offer?" she demanded.

"Five million, three years, but you've got to be you. No holding anything back. So what if you lose your temper? That's how people will come to understand your anger and your side of things."

Monica crossed her arms. "So, you're saying you want me to act like an idiot and cause trouble. Is that what you're saying, Sam? Look, this meeting is over. There are still plenty of..."

He jumped down from the desk and got eye-to-eye with the beauty. They were the same height when she was sitting down and he was standing up. It looked like a scene from "Beauty and the Beast," only there was no magic rose. He moved in one inch over the personal line of comfort, deliberately trying to push her to the edge.

"I'm saying your career as a model is over. No one wants you. That sweet 16 year old sitting out there is interviewing for every one of your jobs, and the answer from all the clients is an overwhelming 'yes.' You're washed up. She's in - you're out. After this last incident, you're done, finished. People can't drop you fast enough. You might as well marry a Prescott Borden and five guys just like him because you're officially broke, bankrupt, a big zero in the modeling world. You either say yes to this contract now, or don't let the door hit you in the ass on the way out. Which, by the way, is getting too big. No one wants you but the tabloids."

He waited for more tears to fall. Or an "Oh, thank you Sam. What would I do without you? You're the only person I trust to tell me the truth." Surprisingly, he heard it many times after giving the straight skinny to over-pampered cover girls.

Monica stood up but didn't leave. She slammed her hands on the desk, just as he had.

"You want drama, I'll give you drama. When can we get my attorney here to sign paper work?"

Chapter 9

Tiffany sat in her hospital room talking on the phone.

"Thanks so much for calling. No, I don't know what to say. As you can imagine, I'm stunned. I guess I'll need to call and say congratulations. Thanks for letting me know. I'll talk to you soon. Bye." She hung up.

No sooner had she put the phone down than it started to ring again. The calls were nonstop. Sugar had not given a single phone interview pretending to be Tiffany like she had begged to do. "Sell tickets, sell tickets, sell tickets." Instead, she had sex with Prescott on a hotel floor. Tiffany cringed at the thought.

There was a knock at the door. She put the phone on silent as her doctor and team of interns walked in. Her mind was still on the phone call. What did it mean? She wished the physicians would leave so she could think about how to handle the situation, which she figured would turn into headlines news soon.

They all circled around her with big grins on their faces and excitement in their eyes. She thought: *Is this what it's like to be famous?* Everyone looking at you with goofball expressions? She wanted to be a respected writer, not tabloid fodder. She wanted to run in literary circles and see plays and live the bohemian life. No more being a reporter by day and wannabe playwright by night. She was always running late for everything and making Lucille Ball entrances, primarily from a lack of sleep. Time to start over and be taken seriously. Maybe a move to New York where her work would finally be appreciated.

For the first time, she had clarity of vision even if her sight had not returned to 20/20 just yet. Everything was crystal clear. The doctor's examination of her eyes hadn't started yet, but the ridiculous questions about the catfight had. She was not in the mood to tell the whole story again.

The security guard who'd been keeping watch over her entered. Clarence never came in when anyone else was present. He was a tall, black kid of only 22 working night shifts and odd jobs while attending school. He had brought in many reviews of *Marble House* and read them out loud to her. Tiffany liked him but couldn't imagine why he was standing there.

"I'm sorry for interrupting, but someone out there that says he want to see you. It's rather urgent," he said. He normally wouldn't do such a thing, but he'd been offered a cash tip and his shift was over. He felt terrible for bothering her, but his rent was behind and he needed to buy some books. The cash offer was like manna from heaven.

She didn't bother to ask who it was. She didn't want to deal with the doctors any longer. Plus, the phone call was embedded in her head. A real game changer.

Tiffany looked at the doctors. "I am sorry everyone, but you'll have to excuse me. Can we do this again in the morning? She knew the plastic surgeon Dr. DeAngelo would say yes because she could tell he had a little crush on her.

"Not a problem. But you're not completely getting rid of me. I'll be back before my shift is over to check in on you," he grinned. The rest of his posse looked solemn and shuffled their way out. Surprisingly, Harvard Medical School residents were not just interested in higher education and the pursuit of excellence. Enquiring minds wanted to know all the juicy details of who did what to whom.

She spoke after they all left. "Clarence, what's going on? Who is it?"

"First I have to tell you something. I am only doing this on account of being offered $1,000 if I get you to do an interview. A reporter wants to talk to you and said it couldn't wait."

Tiffany was disappointed in the lack of integrity of many in the media. "Well, first of all, they're not supposed to do that. But I highly suspect you wouldn't be telling me this if you didn't need the money." She was right.

"I'm late on rent and a few other things. I'm sorry. This job is only temporary and ends tonight. I'm not paid by the hospital but that guy Mr. Borden. He hasn't returned my phone calls. I have been working for free all day."

Tiffany mumbled to herself, "I'm not surprised." She shook her head and then turned to the sweet kid. "Don't be sorry for anything. I'll do it. For you."

He started to laugh. "You're a really sick lady."

"Not true – I'm getting better." She knew sick was the new expression for something good.

"You're funny. Thanks for everything."

"Hey, wait, that's not good enough. I need a hug."

He smiled and hugged her.

"Send him in. Have I got a story for him."

The security guard dashed out, and a few moments later the famous celebrity trasher Barry Banister waltzed in and plopped down on chair.

"You know you want to talk to me kid," he said.

"Indeed I do, Barry, but you're going to have to come back. Give me your number, and I'll text you when I am ready. I have a phone call to make that will be of great interest to you. Bring back a camera crew. You have my word as a fellow reporter that I'll give an exclusive, but I need a little time to get my facts checked."

Chapter 10

Sugar lay in bed watching Prescott sleep. Everything about him was perfect. His smooth, light skin complemented his dark hair and blue eyes, which now opened to see a girl completely smitten with him.

He laughed and said, "Don't fall in love with me. Let's make love, but not fall in love."

"Then you should get that adoring smile off your face. You look like you have fallen *hard* for me already."

"Funny you should bring that up, because I'm definitely feeling you."

He put his arm around her. She looked at the clock. *Oh crap. Five o'clock.* She had to call Tiffany. Even though she'd been banned from the hospital, she knew that her best friend must be waiting for a phone call. This was going to be difficult because surely by now she'd seen or heard about the sex tape. It was playing non-stop on TV.

Prescott noticed the look of panic on her face. "Uh-oh. What's that look for?" He was hoping for an evening of no more drama.

"I have to call Tiffany. She must be wondering what's going on.

I also forgot to do the interviews for her. Remember? I was supposed to do press interviews pretending to be her."

He wrapped his long legs around her body. "Let it wait. One more hour. Do it in an hour." He started rubbing her arm.

"Don't you lose that thought, sexiest man ever. I just have to make one call."

She crawled out of bed and grabbed his pants off the floor. She pulled out her cell phone that he had confiscated earlier. The thought of him putting it there and telling her to "just stay" made her wild with excitement. Plus, she wanted to tell her best friend Tiffany all the details. No, wait. She couldn't do that. At least not yet. The whole sex tape thing must be bad enough for her friend to swallow, let alone hearing that she was doing it with him every hour on the hour. She knew deep down Tiffany had a major crush on Prescott. She had a lot of explaining to do.

She looked at her phone that had been switched to silent. There were over 20 text messages from her best friend. Rather than read them all, she dialed the number. Her hands were shaking. She walked into the master bathroom away from Prescott. She paced back and forth on the white, heated marble floors waiting for a pick up. She caught a glimpse of herself in the mirror and didn't like seeing her naked reflection. She put on his robe. The smell of his cologne was intoxicating and calling her back to bed. Ring, ring, ring.

Tiffany answered and skipped the hellos. "Why haven't you called me?"

Sugar didn't mince words. "Did you see the video tape?"

"Oh please! Who didn't see the kissing cousins video tape? Really, Sugar. Really?"

"Now you know why I haven't called. If that's my best friend's reaction, what do you think the rest of the world is saying? I'm in semi-permanent hiding."

"Are you with him now? What's going on between you two?"

Sugar examined herself in the mirror and couldn't face what she saw. She'd never lied to Tiffany about anything. She turned away. Besides, how long could this "romance" last? It would be over soon enough with his record of running through women, then the two friends could go on with their lives without him.

"It's a long story. But here's the short of it. After the press conference, we got into a big fight. He tried to throw me out of his penthouse but I made a scene. Then he started to panic that the press would follow me, and I'd say something I shouldn't. The paparazzi are outside the hotel waiting for either of us to appear. So, he left instead, but he wants me out by early morning when less people will notice." Well, at least part of it was true.

"You two are freaks," Tiffany said while shaking her head. "Did you do any phone interviews? Wasn't that the deal? Selling tickets, promoting the show. You know the press is fickle. You're in one day and out the next."

Sugar took in a deep breath. "I'm sorry, Tiffany. I know I should have, but I didn't - I mean, I'm trying to figure out how to put my own life back together. You know that everyone in the office is probably laughing their asses off at me. I have to face a lot of people. Even my dad."

"Yeah, even your dad," Tiffany repeated with a particularly mean tone in her voice.

"Are you mad at me, because you sure sound mad."

"Why would I be mad? What about Hollywood and Broadway?"

"Baby girl, I am going to get on that first thing. I promise you."

"So, is Prescott out of our lives now that he slept with his cousin? Are you related to him? Is he still going to help us?"

"No, we're not related. I don't know if he's going to help. Maybe."

"Are you telling me the truth? Just tell me the truth because there is nothing I can't handle. What's going on between you two? Be honest."

"Honey, I'm telling you like it is. I'm going to get moving on Broadway and Hollywood first thing in the morning. I'll ask for his help if I see him. Now I want you to get some sleep."

"You know I could handle the press without you. Calls are coming in left and right. There was one call from your dad I found particularly interesting that we need to have a serious discussion about. I have a reporter waiting, and before I throw anyone under a bus, we need to..."

Prescott entered the room clothed in nothing but a smile. Sugar held her finger to her lips gesturing him to be quiet. He started kissing her neck. Sugar breathed in his cologne and couldn't hear a word Tiffany said.

"Interesting call, you say? Reporter waiting? I can't wait to hear all about it, sweetie. Let's talk after I've had a chance to listen to all my messages and rest up. Night-night."

"What's going on? It's only 5 p.m. And you never called me sweetie before. You only call me honey. I call you sweetie. Are you sure there isn't something you want to tell me?"

"Nothing." Once again lost in his sexual energy.

"Don't do anything stupid like drink and have sex with someone else."

Sugar's eyes widened. "Who says I've been drinking?"

"Seriously, have you been on a drinking binge? Are you drunk? Are you making up stories?"

"I've never been more sober or clear headed. Why do you ask?"

Tiffany had heard enough. "I am tired, really tired. I have to go."

"Love you."

No response.

She turned to look at Prescott. "She just hung up on me."

"Come hang out with me," he said, stripping off her bath robe. They didn't make it back to his comfortable bed.

Chapter 11

Monica sat in her girlfriend Gina's Fifth Avenue corner apartment - compliments of a sugar daddy. The two models planned to go out partying but it was only 9 p.m. Things didn't really start heating up at the clubs until at least 11.

The hot-looking redhead took a sip of her cosmo and stared at her friend's new $20,000 burgundy colored vase with blue checks. She wasn't sure if it all matched. Monica had excellent taste and loved expensive things, just not overpriced junk.

Gina couldn't stop bragging about the thing. "It's just to die for. Die for."

The two met in Milan when they were both 18 and doing runway shows, but the Jersey girl never made it in magazines because her nose photographed too big. She had it fixed, but everything didn't blend quite the way it should.. Her Italian good looks needed that original schnozz. The nose fix made her already nasally sounding voice even more annoying.

"To die for," she said again, referring to the ugly vase.

"It's killing me all right," Monica said. The two girls often took jabs at one another but were best friends at heart.

"Seriously, you're going to do a reality TV show? Eww. Jeffrey has a friend he can introduce you to." Gina had retired on a married guy's Wall Street salary and thought Monica should do the same.

"Are you kidding me? Jeffery's a short, fat jerk with almost no hair. Eww."

"Well, it's better than going out with someone who is screwing their cousin. Eww."

Monica looked confused. "Who's going out with anyone screwing their cousin?"

"You are - or were," she laughed. She sound like a nasally machine gun. NANANANAA.

Monica threw a pillow at her. "What are you talking about?"

"I'm talking about you of course. Seriously, what have you been doing all day? Duh, don't you watch the news?" She laughed again, NANANANAA.

Monica raised her dyed-red eyebrows. "Seriously, I was in meeting after meeting, signing paper work, then went back to my place only to see an eviction notice and then came here. Some of us have responsibilities."

"Oh. Well, wait 'til you hear this. Prescott Borden gave a press interview. He throws you out the door and proclaims his love for that writer girl you beat up."

"They attacked me first."

"Of course they did." She rolled her eyes.

Monica snapped her fingers. "Hey, that reminds me. I got to do a press interview in the morning. I'm going to drive over him with a bus. Did you see the fight tape? He's in big time trouble. I'm pressing charges."

"That's nothing. It might even be old news because this is **way** better. It turns out that girl, what's her name? The writer. Um...wait. I remember, it's Tiffany. So check it out. Even though he said 'she's the love of my life,' it turned out not to be true. Some fat girl named Sugar is."

"Are you crazy? Fat? Prescott Borden and fat? That's ludicrous. I don't believe it. That guy wanted me to lose ten pounds," said the 115-pound, 5-foot-10 girl.

"I saw her myself on their sex tape. Going at it, wham bam and thank you. She's a heifer, at least 140 pounds."

"Are you sure it was Prescott?"

"It happened in the same hall where you beat up that girl. I remember those big mahogany doors from when we visited. I saw the sex video tape on the entertainment channel, so it's totally legit."

"Stop saying that I beat that bitch up."

"Of course you didn't." She rolled her eyes.

"Stop rolling your eyes. Finish the story."

"You didn't tell me he was a fast finisher. Three strokes in, and it was over."

"That's for sure not Prescott."

"It was him. Maybe he was turned on so much because she's a relative. He's been doing his cousin. I think they said she was from Kentucky. Yeah that's it: His cousin from Kentucky." She laughed. NANANANAAA.

Monica looked puzzled. "Maybe this is news from a while back. The rags are always taking old news and recycling it. Remember, they did it to me when that hair dresser burned my hair. The press pulled out of the closet anyone who ever accused me of causing an altercation, including one of my cousins that I beat up in third grade. It's just a tabloid ploy."

"They're getting married. The press interviewed Sugar's dad on TV about the sex tape. He said it's no big deal because his daughter is marrying Prescott Borden. He was over the moon. Wow, that makes him Prescott's uncle and father-in-law too. That writer girl confirmed the story and congratulated Prescott and Sugar on national TV. She said a bunch of other stuff too. She looked terrible. Wow, did you pound the crap out of her."

"They attacked me first. Damn it, finish the story."

"She said the two of them are 'one and the same.' I guess it's because they're related." She nudged her girlfriend. "Can you believe it? Prescott Borden is marrying his cousin Sugar from Cincinnati." NANANANAAA.

"I thought you said she was from Kentucky. This is all bull crap."

"Just turn on the TV. It's on all the entertainment channels."

Chapter 12

Prescott and Sugar each discovered they had something else in common besides being so sexually in synch. They both loved sugar in the morning and sugar in the evening. Coffee with two lumps for breakfast and sweets at night while watching 80's movies. He ordered up truffle popcorn and sherbet ice cream. Coincidentally, every night at home in Charleston, she microwaved a bag of popcorn and sprinkled in her famous homemade toffee. She wished she had some to give him now. He'd love it.

The room service guy who brought up the treats lingered at the door quite a long time, hoping to get a peek inside and see Prescott's cousin first hand. He was disappointed. There was no freak show tonight. Sugar stayed hidden in the master bedroom and even covered her face with blankets.

"Thanks," Prescott said to the bell hop. He went to close the door but instead added, "I am sure my sister and I will enjoy it." To hell with what anyone thought. He'd worry about that later.

Tonight, the couple behaved like mischievous kids on a camping trip, swapping stories and laughing. He was getting a big kick out of her tales of growing up, like hearing about the time Tiffany fell overboard off the Good Ship Lollipop, a boat that took passengers on tours around Charleston harbor. Her 7-year-old friend had been posing for a picture while sitting on the deck rail and fell over backwards. Eight-year-old Sugar naturally jumped in to save her even though she couldn't swim. Thankfully, both girls were wearing life jackets. But what he liked the most wasn't the stories, but the way her eyes lit up with childlike charm when telling the tale. He imagined being around her would bring a lot of joy to someone's life, and that's why Tiffany loved her so much.

An odd sounding phone started ringing. "Batman, dadadadadada..."

Sugar started laughing. "Is Gotham calling, or did someone get a new ringtone? I thought we agreed to shut off all phones."

"This particular phone never gets shut off. That's one of my partners in China. Darling, I have to take this call."

Sugar liked his ringtone. For someone so important and powerful, he had a great sense of humor. Her ringtone was the song "Dancing Queen."

He got out of bed and put on his bath robe. He pulled the cell phone out of his mahogany dressing table.

"Charlie, how are you?" he asked. He walked over to his balcony window, opened the sliding glass door, and went outside. Boston looked good in the springtime. All the lights, sounds, and activity. Winters were wicked cold, and you could see the pain on people's faces. So, spring seemed 10 times better than in most cities.

If Prescott was going to be on his cell phone, she might as well check hers. She turned it on to find hundreds of "congratulations" texts. Congratulations for what? There were also friends making jokes about cousins and one super lengthy text from Tiffany.

"I really thought you were drunk and on a binge. At least I hoped that was the case. What else could explain your sex tape with Prescott? How did it go from extreme hate to sex on his hall floor?

I talked to your dad earlier in the day. Surprise! He called me to see how I was doing. He told me all about you and Prescott planning on getting married. I was shocked. At first, I thought it was a publicity stunt but then realized you would not have told him if it was a joke. So then I figured you said those things high on whiskey. I've heard you tell tall tales when you were buzzed, so once again I gave you the benefit of the doubt. I asked you if you were drunk. You made it clear you were quite sober and that nothing was going on between you and Prescott. Then you thought I hung up, but I heard you talking to him. This, after I begged you to be honest with me. He was there all that time. It's no wonder you didn't talk my ear off like you normally do. Too anxious to get back in bed?

When were you going to tell me about the two of you? Or don't I matter anymore? You put him, some ***hole player, before my play? Your lifelong best friend? For six months you made me feel like shit over Marble House. You guilted me out EVERY DAY over ticket sales and maybe losing the newspaper. I stressed out and worked my ass off for you and for us.

I guess you found a new ticket to ride. You were supposed to do interviews and start brokering deals. Remember Broadway and Hollywood? Couldn't you have at least made time for both of us? Instead you have been having sex with him and now you're engaged? HA. As if that's ever going to work out. Just don't come crying back to me when it doesn't.

All of this got me thinking about our friendship. All these years you've bossed me around. All the 'oh I was drunk and didn't mean to say those terrible things' Keeping me chained to the newspaper because you said it would never work without me there. Then holding me hostage because you put your money into the play.

I was beat to hell by a crazy person but all you and Prescott could do was FORCE me to attend the play's opening. Sell tickets. You made me risk my health, then left me high and dry.

Now the both of you are on to some new crazy thing. Good luck! Because I am done with you. You're freaking crazy and always have been. It just took me 20 some years to figure it out.

BTW congratulation on your dad finally being proud of you. He even told me so on the phone. Looks like he has lots of time for you now that you're a millionaire's screw of the week. Turn on the TV. He's been all over the news bragging about the two of you getting married. I guess getting attention and publicity runs in the family. Who cares at what cost?

I gave my own statement to the press concerning your upcoming nuptials. I know you haven't seen it or else you would have called me with some new fabricated story. Read my statement or watch it on TV. I don't have anything else to say to you other than, 'Congratulations. You two are one and the same.'"

Tears started falling down Sugar's face. What was happening to her life, and how was she going to explain this new turn of events to Prescott?

* * * * *

He continued listening to his partner and couldn't wait to hang up. The conversation really wasn't over but he said, "Well thank you. There have just been a lot of mix-ups in the press and misunderstandings. Thanks for giving me a chance to explain. I'll send you an email on that other matter. Bye."

He looked up to the stars so far away. If there's a God, what are you doing to me? He needed a drink.

He opened up the sliding window and said, "Sugar, you want to come out here? And bring a bottle of scotch."

* * * * *

Tiffany woke up covered head to toe in sweat. She looked at the clock. Midnight. She was having a panic attack. She grabbed her cell phone on the side table to see if Sugar had responded but then remembered she'd blocked her. She didn't give her any way of explaining or making excuses for her bad behavior. Like bossing her around all the time. But this latest episode just pushed her too far, and she was no longer going to be an enabler and let people walk all over her.

She made up her mind. "I am starting my life over effective this minute." She lay back down and fell into a deep, coma-like sleep.

* * * * *

Starry, starry night, the starriest ever, Sugar thought as she lay on a lounge chair next to Prescott looking up at the night sky. Boston's traffic noise had stopped and it was just the two of them on the balcony with a city all to themselves. She'd never drunk scotch before. Or if she had, nothing this smooth. It's amazing what a 100-year-old bottle tasted like. Prescott hardly ever drank and was feeling quite high.

"So, let's go over this one more time," he said.

"I just need sleep." She'd agreed to his plan earlier and didn't want to hear it again. She couldn't get Tiffany off her mind. They were each other's sister, mother, and cousin. Best friends forever. She desperately wanted to make things right between them. Tiff's texted words had gotten through to her heart. She realized she'd made some horrible mistakes.

He started slurring his words an hour ago. "We need to act like we were engaged for at least… for, er, ah, a month, or hell, maybe two." Prescott was clearly bombed. "Between the Monica breakup, the penthouse trashing, the Tiffany fiasco and the sex video with my cousin…well needless to say, my life looks somewhat…how do you say it - unstable?"

"Unstable," Sugar repeated. "That's how you say it. Unstable."

"I couldn't tell my partners our marriage is a sham too. Not after your best friend and your dad said so on national TV. And after sex on the hotel floor."

"Engagement! We're engaged, not married"

"A person can only have so many public misunderstandings in a 48-hour news cycle. International news." Hiccup. "My China guy at least believes we're not related. People will get that we're not cousins if we stay together just a weeny little bit longer and pretend to be engaged. Thirty days. YADDA YADDA YADDA. Now let's have sex."

"You forgot the most important parts. You're going to get me a Hollywood deal for Tiffany in return, right? And get my newspaper out of trouble. And no sex."

He laughed. "Hollywood is practically done already. I'll give you my cut from the deal to fund the newspaper. Hell, it's not even that much money. I'll write you a check in morning. HAH. And you can forget the no sex part. That's part of my compensation."

She rolled her eyes. "Drunkenness becomes you Prescott. You changed from wanting to make love to me to telling me you're going to get back to dating once this engagement charade is over. You already told me that I'm fat three times, after telling me how beautiful I am earlier. By the way, I weigh 142 and I am five foot five. That's not fat."

"Oh darling, I am sorry. But that's fat. But you still have pretty eyes, the hottest I've ever seen. They look really familiar to me. I've seen them before, maybe in a magazine. So you got that going for you."

"Right. And you told me this was just sex. So get off it. We're over. There is no future for us but me getting played. I am not throwing my life away for a month of the greatest sex ever. I just want to get my newspaper and best friend back."

"See, there you go. Greatest ever. That's me. Yup. Darling, just stop lying to yourself. You're going to have sex with me. We're going to be living together." Hiccup. "I'll just make you do it. You won't have a choice."

"You can't make me do anything. I'm going to bed." She got up to leave.

He stumbled along. "I'm coming with you. Get it? Cummin' with you?" He laughed drunkenly.

She pushed him back. "No, I am going to the guest room. You're staying put. You're drunk."

"Speakin' of which, why aren't you?"

"I'm not in the lightweight group of fighters. It takes more than a shared bottle to knock me down. You're a featherweight."

"SHHHHHH. Don't let anyone hear you. (Of course, there was no one to hear.) Come on. Just come sleep with me. No sex. Just let's go to sleep. Like you know, girls. Girly girls. You all want to be held. Just holding, nothin' else."

She looked him up and down. "You're too drunk to do anything. Get over yourself." Still, something inside her really wanted to be held.

"I promise. Please. Just holding."

She felt so terrible. Like she lost her best friend. Which she had. Holding someone might help ease the pain since the scotch didn't.

"OK, fine, whatever. But holding, nothing more."

They both walked over to his king-size, brass bed and laid on top of the covers. She put her head on his shoulder, wondering why it couldn't be like this. Why couldn't they really get married and just be together? Why did he need so many women, so much power and fame? Why wouldn't Tiffany just let her explain? Why couldn't she lose weight? Why was he such a freaking JERK!

He rolled over and got on top of her. "I am not, not, not in the lightweight group of fighters either. Just a different category. I can do anything. Anything I want with you."

"Prescott stop it. I can't." She tried to squirm away, but he was almost like dead weight. He was already sound asleep.

Chapter 13

Tiffany had the best night's sleep ever. As far as she was concerned, it was because Sugar Lynn Limehouse was finally out of her life. No longer a puppet but free to walk without strings attached. No longer working for the man. Or rather, the woman who never really appreciated her.

The meeting with her doctors went well, and she was going to be released tomorrow. She knew they'd kept her an extra day because Dr. DeAngelo was enjoying spending time with her. He even attended a matinee performance of *Marble House* and loved it.

She kept thinking, "I can't wait to tell Sugar all about him." But then flashbacks of the sex video tape kept playing in her mind, and she remembered all the lies. In her head she realized they were no longer friends, but it would take her a heart a little while longer to figure out that her childhood pal was gone for good. She had been hurt one too many times, going all the way back to when their mothers died.

She tried to think of happier things, but there was always a catch. The show was running seven days a week for the next six weeks, completely sold out, but there was no way of getting her cut of the profits until after the play closed. She resigned from her job at the Charleston Gazette, something she should have done years ago. But the paper's accountant told her in confidence that she wouldn't be seeing her final paycheck any time soon. The publication needed the money from the play to cover payroll.

She started worrying about how she'd get her stuff out of the apartment she shared with Sugar, move someplace else, and pay for everything. Money didn't fall from heaven. Then out of nowhere, two men walked in dressed in black power suits and carrying brief cases.

Tiffany's heart started to beat faster. "Who are you, the FBI?" She figured their appearance had something to do with Monica's charges against her.

"No ma'am, we're attorneys."

"I'm not giving any depositions 'til my lawyer is here," she said, even though she couldn't afford one.

"We're not here to depose you. We're here to help you."

* * * * *

Gina woke up and looked at the clock: 10:12 a.m.

"GET UP!" she said and started shaking Monica, who was fast asleep next to her. She had one of the best mailing addresses in New York City but only one bedroom. The guest diva refused to sleep on the pull out couch, which had a steel bar pounding into her back.

"What the hell?" Monica screamed. She was wearing eye patches with an elastic string around her head and couldn't see a thing. She tried to figure out where she was and kept turning her head from side to side.

Her friend pulled the eye contraption off and said, "Look at what time it is! You're late for your press conference."

"Who cares? Let's go back to sleep." She laid back down and tossed the blue checked comforter over her head.

Gina, the Italian-looking girl from Jersey, pulled the covers off. "Your manager cares. I care. You're not staying in my condo for the rest of time. You can't lose that reality TV job. You owe me money."

Monica had fine taste but couldn't save a dime. Gina liked expensive things but had no taste. She had a financier sugar daddy covering everything except the debts her friend was running up. It was cutting into her budget big time. She expected payment in full, ASAP.

The red head sat up with the covers bunched up around her neck. The air conditioning was turned too low.

"Gina, don't you remember?"

"Remember what?"

"The Penguin, my manager, was at the nightclub. What's wrong with you? We drank with him half the night. We worked this out."

"I couldn't hear a thing. Plus, I kept having to go to the bathroom to throw up so I could drink more."

"Why do you always do that? That doesn't even make sense. If you're drunk, you're drunk. Puking doesn't make you sober. Save your pukes for when you eat."

"I can't do that. I'd just rather starve."

"How can you purge when you're drunk but not after eating food? That doesn't make sense."

"It's easy to make yourself puke when you're drinking. You don't even notice it. Too much work when you're wide awake. It's much easier to starve. And it proves I don't have an eating disorder."

"What? Let me get this straight. You don't have an eating disorder because you starve yourself, and it's normal to throw up when you're drunk - so you can drink more. That's the most ridiculous thing I ever heard. Why can't you be like normal models and eat whatever you want, then purge? I'm not listening to this anymore. I need coffee, bacon, eggs and a toilet. Someone has to teach you right from wrong."

Monica pushed the covers off herself. She looked like a little kid in an oversized long T-shirt with white socks on. In some ways, she still was a kid. They were both were 21 years old, but managed to pack in 40 years of living into their short-lived modeling careers.

"Wait, why didn't the Penguin want you to the go to the press conference today?"

"Because I am dropping charges against Prescott and Tiffany."

"Now THAT doesn't make sense."

"It does if I'm planning on running into Prescott again." She laughed. "He won't file anything against me. He'll just be glad it's over. He's open game without a restraining order. And check this out. They are going to pay off that girl."

"His cousin?"

"No, the one that I beat up…after she hit me first. Hush money."

"Who's they?"

"I don't know - the powers that be. The lawyers are handling it all."

"Just make sure it's not you paying it off from your own check-book. You owe me lots of money."

"The show's producers, that's who's probably paying. Even though I'm supposed to be crazy on the show, they don't want any lawsuits or anything else pending. It turns off advertisers, so they're going to pay that bitch to go away. In the future, I can do whatever I want - except get into physical fights with people. If I do, I'm out!"

"But, why do you want to see Prescott? Eww. He's marrying his cousin."

"Exactly. Hello publicity department. So check this out. The show is going to start out with me getting my stuff out of my apartment for a fresh start in Newport, Rhode Island. I am going to be opening up an art gallery there. That's why the show is named 'Hanging with Miss D.' Get it? Hanging, like a painting. Can you believe it? You know I love fine art. Here is the plot line...I'm turning my life around. Done with modeling. Going for a simpler life."

"More like modeling's done with you."

The words didn't bother Monica because she knew it was true. She was only good for catalogue work now. There was no way she was going from the cover of "Vogue" to the JC Penney circular. Reality TV could put her back on top again.

"It doesn't matter. I'm like a whole new person, only the same. The Zen me. But, I still do all the same stuff I do now. I get to buy expensive things, party like a rock star, and kick box, just at a new location. Oh, and stir up trouble. They want lots of trouble. I just can't punch anyone." She sat up, crossed her legs Indian style and continued.

"Can you believe it? They're putting me up in a mansion where I can throw huge parties. And here is the best thing of all. Guess who stays in Newport all summer? Prescott Borden. It's a small town, so we'll see each other for sure. You just watch, something crazy will happen. He really loves me, he just doesn't know it yet." In reality the opposite was true: Monica was in love with Prescott, only she didn't know it.

"What about his cousin/wife?"

"Seriously? He won't marry that fat girl. I couldn't believe my eyes when I saw her. El pork-o. No way is she his cousin. She's got something to do with that play *Marble House*. I think she owns the rights to that show. Prescott must have a cut too. He's such a money whore. They must have some power deal going on. I don't know what the hell is cooking, but it smells like cat shit."

"What are you talking about? I don't have a cat."

Monica threw a pillow at her friend.

NANANANAAA. Gina laughed. "Gotcha."

Chapter 14

Prescott rolled onto his side in bed, let out a deep sigh and started laughing.

"What's so funny?" Sugar asked. She felt somewhat ashamed because she swore there would be no more sex, but they'd already "bonded" twice this morning. She still felt terrible about Tiffany's text and told herself over and over she'd make it up to her, but Prescott had been right. There was no way they could say no to each other.

"You slay me," he said, then started chuckling again. "Can't speak after that great sex." He stretched out his arms across the bed and tried to piece it all together. Meaning Sugar and him.

He couldn't really pin it down. He'd had so many different women in his 30-some years he'd lost count. What made the chemistry so much more intense between the two of them? Why did she have to have those big green eyes that turned him on so much?

He looked at the clock. "Oh crap, I have to get in the shower now," he said as he jumped up.

"Oh, that's romantic. Not a kiss or a hug, just sex like you said? Can't you at least humor me a little?" Sugar pouted.

"Nope. Not happening. No." He checked out his toned body in the mirror and smacked his sculpted abs.

"What do you mean no?"

"Because if I kiss you again, I am not getting out that bed for the rest of the day. I've got business to take care of, and then we're going for a ride."

"What kind of business, and who is we?"

"I'm seeing if I can still save my penthouse sale despite having to face a room full of men who think I'm marrying my cousin. Then WE, as in 'you and me,' are going for a ride." He lightly knuckled her head. "I am taking you down to my home in Newport, Rhode Island. It's about an hour and a half drive from here."

"Oh." She wondered if he was dumping her there. The thought obviously showed on her face.

"Darling, now don't go giving me that look. I don't even want to know what that look means." He took in a deep breath. "Sugar, you know the deal, darling. It's four weeks."

Her voice got quieter. "I just thought we'd be spending it together. That's all."

"Most the time, we will be together. I'm moving there too in the next week or two. My hotel penthouse purchase is never going to happen thanks to having sex with my 'cousin' in public view, but I at least have to try."

"Hey! That's what you get for lying to that manager guy. Telling him we were cousins. Liar, liar. Don't blame me."

"Liar, liar, we're not getting married. You never should have lied to your dad about us having wedding plans," he said and touched her nose with his finger. "No worries, your nose isn't growing yet, but it might be soon. We need to go out on dates and pretend to be madly in love. We have to be seen together by people - which will stop the cousin rumors and boost the engagement talk. Then we'll have a happy-ever-after breakup. Everyone will be happy, including my partners, who won't think I've completely lost my mind."

"Don't count on it, because you'll be miserable once I'm gone. It's going to kill you. You're addicted to sugar. You put it in your coffee in the morning, and you have some before you go to bed at night."

"Darling, I like it so much I am going to give you a lifetime free sex pass. I've never done that with anyone before. So be happy. Go get married, have kids, and if you need an hour of loving, call me. But that's it. I like my freedom. I'm not changing, and you need to know it upfront. We have a 30-day business deal, and you get a bonus check. An hour of me for a lifetime."

Sugar did a double take. "You have got to be kidding me. Do you ever give your oversized ego any downtime? Do you really think I'd actually call you to have sex after I was married with kids? Hah."

"Damn straight you will. Everyone does. You'd just be the first one I actually said yes to. In the meantime, I'm giving you lots of spending money and time with Hubert, my personal clothing shopper. He should be here in an hour. He's the one that bought you that pretty purple dress you wore on opening night."

"Oh yeah, that one you ripped to shreds. Clearly you were a fan of it. At least my pink pants suit is intact. What do I need new clothes for anyway? Not that I'm complaining. I can learn to love shopping on someone else's credit card. I'm still trying to figure you out."

"Look, do you want to get your newspaper back on the right

track? Paying off its debts isn't going to do it. You have to make some changes too. Starting with your fashion choices."

"What's wrong with the way I dress?"

"Darling, nothing if you're running a brothel in New Orleans."

Surprisingly, Sugar didn't turn sour. She loved the idea of spending time with his personal shopper. Hubert did a great job picking out a dress for her opening night. She needed some girl bonding time, so to speak. Gay guys absolutely adored her, and the feeling was mutual. A famous Charleston female impersonator once said, "She's a gay man trapped in a woman's body."

Which is precisely why Prescott wanted her attire changed. It had little to do with the newspaper and more with *his* personal taste. He didn't want to be seen with someone who looked like she was in a nightly drag queen show. His "fiancée" was at least going to dress the part. He couldn't correct her weight issues or make her 21 years old, but he could at least have her looking like a 1960's pin up girl. Confuse the press into thinking voluptuous was the new fashion trend: That was his theory.

Since the publisher didn't blow up on him for suggesting that she dressed like a madam, he decided to push his luck further.

"I'm setting you up with a consultant who's going to help turn your business around."

Ouch. She jumped out of bed. "Hold on there, honey! Don't you dare go messing with my area of expertise. No one knows Charleston news like I do. Let me get to the point. I just need your damn check book. I've never had a chance to run that newspaper without piles of debt consuming most of my time. I'll take a free shopping trip any day, but there ain't no way someone's messing with the Charleston

Gazette - period!" She softened her tone. "Especially if you want me showing up for sex after I'm married. Now darling, don't go ruining any chance you have with me in the future. Back down." She lightly pushed him.

He kissed her forehead. "Get rid of the word ain't. You're a newspaper publisher." He started heading to the shower but stopped. He turned around and said, "Wait a minute. Did you just call me darling? Publishers shouldn't plagiarize words. That's my word, not yours. Don't use it again. He went inside the master bath then yelled, "Mark my words. You will be knocking at my door 10 years from now. No question about it. By the way, tonight we are going out for dinner with a consultant friend of mine. You need more than just my money to make your business a success." He locked the door so she couldn't confront him and laughed while he lathered up.

Chapter 15

Tiffany sat up in her hospital bed listening on the phone. Finally she had a chance to speak.

"I just don't know if I can do it. I can't stand them. Either of them. But I don't think it's right to throw anyone under the bus," she said.

The male voice on the other end was straightforward and to the point. The same men who had stopped by her hospital the day before were now on a conference call with her.

"All you have to do is make a public apology. 'I am sorry for what happened to Monica. I support her version of the events and just want to concentrate on my career. I have no further comment.' Nothing else. She's dropping all charges against you and Prescott. You're not throwing anyone under the bus, just buying yourself a better vehicle. Like a new Mercedes," the attorney said.

She did need a car. "I don't know. I'm going to have to think about it some more."

"The offer is only good 'til midnight. All medical bills paid plus $300,000. If you litigate this thing, you wouldn't get any more money and it will be years of court battles. And more bad publicity for you.

Is that what you want your life to be like? You can call in a team of lawyers and they'll all tell you that it's worth more, but it's only more for them."

She let out a sigh. She knew he was right about her attorneys taking it all. She covered many legal cases throughout her years as a newspaper reporter, and that was always the final outcome. The only people who came out on top were the lawyers.

She nodded her head, but her heart wasn't in agreement. At least not yet. "Thanks for calling. If you hear back from me, you'll know the answer is yes. Otherwise, you'll hear from my lawyer."

Right - the same lawyer she had no money to hire and that she'd have to agree to give a thirty percent cut and a five-year relationship trying to settle the case. How much more time did she want to be associated with Monica, Prescott, and his "cousin" Sugar?

Tiffany stared at all the flowers in her room now starting to fade. All those beautiful flowers Prescott had bought for her only to change his mind. There were no calls from Broadway or Hollywood. There was no Ken hanging on Barbie's arm like he did the night of the show. She remembered part of the limo ride and him touching her head gently and being so tender. All just for show and lots of tell. Then he ran off with her best friend and had sex with her in the same hallway where she was attacked and beaten up. None of it made any sense. Maybe there was some game plan she was not understanding, but if so, why did Sugar tell her dad she was getting married? Maybe Tiffany didn't give her enough chance to explain, but there is just no explanation possible or plausible. And why wasn't her childhood friend pounding on her hospital room door begging for forgiveness?

Regardless, the clock was ticking on the offer and her life too.

When would she ever get another chance to start over again? Yes, the play was a smashing success but there was nowhere to go after it closed in Boston. That was looking like the final act. The only thing she had to look forward to was returning to her hole-in-the-wall apartment in Charleston she shared with Sugar and no job. Maybe it was time for a change of venue. A fresh start in New York City with more than just a dollar in her pocket.

And maybe it was time for an attitude adjustment too. No more being bulldozed by people like Sugar and Prescott. She'd be standing up for all the Tiffanys in the world who lost at love and life because they were just too damn nice.

It all sounded great in her head but so horrible in her gut.

* * * * *

Hubert showed up on Sugar's doorstep on time and as promised. They had met briefly when he dropped off the exquisite dresses for the opening night of *Marble House*. Anyone observing would have thought they were lifetime best friends. For someone who was a personal shopper, he looked more like an 80's punk rocker, with short spiky brown hair and leather jacket.

When they saw each other, they both started screaming and jumping up and down like middle school girls on a sleep over. Hue looked her up and down but decided not to comment on the gaudy pink pants suit that she was wearing again.

"Oh no you dit'nt. I can spot that Prescott Borden afterglow on anyone. When do I get my turn? With him, not you of course," he said, cracking himself up.

She held her hands to her cheeks. "Does it really show?" Her delighted voice said it all.

"Yeahhhh - like in millions of home across America. OMG and to think this is the spot where it happened," he said, while reaching down to touch the hall floor where the sex tape was filmed. He stood up and whispered, "I'm standing on sacred ground."

They both let out a squeal of giggles. It was a relief to finally laugh about it and show off for someone who appreciated the humor in it all.

Sugar bragged, "If you think this is sacred, come on inside. I'll give you a 'where we've done it' tour. As in everywhere."

He pondered for a moment. "Who knew being cousins could be such a turn on?"

"You don't know the half of it."

"Please tell me you really are related. Don't go boring me with any straight-girl sex talk. If sex ain't got a weird twist, then you must acquit." He snapped his fingers while waving his hand back and forth.

"Oh honey, we're not related, but there is nothing straight about our sex. Totally twisted and sick," she said with straight-girl pride. "We have sex 24/7, and I don't even know his mother's name! Or if he even has a mother. Maybe he's a sex alien."

"Then give me every detail on the way down the elevator. Prescott says I only get four hours with you. Sugar, no offense, but I'm dropping you off at the salon for hair coloring, cut, makeup, and lashes. You're a mess. I got a lot of work ahead of me. Most of the clothing styles I like won't even look good on a size 10." He held his fingers to his temples. "Gotta keep thinking pin-up girl and muster up the spirit of Jayne Mansfield. I'm shopping with her today – and she was a chubby girl too." He clapped his hands together like he said something intelligent. "Well, don't just stand there Sugar Puff. Time for credit card fun in the sun."

"I'm not fat. I weigh, as of today, 140 pounds," she yelled at him as they walked towards the elevator.

"Sweetcakes, you'd still be heavy even if you lost twenty pounds. Welcome to the fashion industry." They got in the elevator, and he pressed the down button.

She wanted to give Hubert the details of her adventures with Prescott, but he was too busy talking about his alter ego "Kitty Glitter" and his nights on the drag queen stage. The girl from Charleston wondered what she was getting herself into with this new cast of characters taking charge of her life. Was her moral compass pointing straight to hell? Tiffany had always been there to give her a thumbs up or down on right and wrong. Their Catholic school upbringing taught them to make sure more good boxes were checked than bad. She felt shameful acting like a naughty school girl, only it was making her feel oh-so-good being with Prescott, even though he kept saying "It's just sex." What was so wrong with that? She wanted more, but it was nice to give up control for a change of pace and let life happen, like shopping with Kitty Glitter who wanted to take her to gay karaoke at a bowling alley for drinks tomorrow night. And what about this mysterious consultant Prescott arranged for her to meet? Her life was spinning out of control like the tilt-a-whirl ride at the fair, and she for once was enjoying the ride.

The elevator doors opened on the lobby floor, and he was singing the words to "Dancing Queen" (her all time fav) and smacking his bum right in front of anyone who happened to be standing in the high-class hotel. He did a few disco style moves for the onlookers. He kept trying to push a make-believe microphone in her face so she'd sing the line, "Young and sweet, only 17." She was laughing as they spun around the rotating exit door and then started singing along.

Only to be greeted by paparazzi waiting on the other side. Four guys with cameras, microphones and insults. Asking questions about her upcoming wedding plans to her cousin, the attack on Tiffany, and if she'd met Monica or planned on being in the model's new reality TV show. The camera crew stayed just a few feet from their faces as they followed the unusual couple down the street.

Sugar and Hubert kept on singing the Abba song as if absolutely nothing out of the ordinary was going on.

* * * * *

Monica and Gina looked online at Newport mansions for rent.

"Get out," Gina said as they clicked through pictures of private estates on the ocean. "They're not going to rent one of these for you. Who the hell are you, Queen Victoria minus the royalty and virgin part?"

Monica rolled her eyes. "Queen Elizabeth was the virgin queen, dummy."

"Well excuse me. Now that you're a reality star, you're an expert in Canadian history too? NANANANAAA. Gotcha."

"I hate all these," she said, referring to the mansions for rent online. "I mean, if I am starting a new life as an art dealer, why are they going to put me in a frat-looking house with knock-off paintings and flowery print wallpaper? I'll look like I have no style or class."

"What are you talking about? All of these look fabulous. Plus they got to put you in a place you can destroy. If you can't have parties with people wrecking stuff and getting naked in the hot tub, then there's no point in having a show? Hey…I have an idea." The nasally sounding girl got all excited. "The last show of the first season can be the house being trashed. Then you being forced to move out. A real cliffhanger."

Monica curbed her friend's enthusiasm with one word. "Whatever. Hey, speaking of cliffhangers, check this out." She pointed to a home on the website. "Here's a house on Bellevue Avenue overlooking looking Newport's cliff walk.

"Whatever. Who'd want to live on a street called Bellevue anyway? That's where all the whackos go. Bellevue Hospital."

"Who cares? Look at this place. It's el perfecto." She pointed at the screen.

"Let me see it." Gina took a closer look. "Ha ha, it rents for $50,000 a month. Keep dreaming. You're not on the freaking 'Housewives of Beverly Hills'."

"No, I have my own show, not thrown in with a bunch of plastic surgery victims. Loser!" Monica smiled broadly. "Look at the address! OH OH OH. Guess who will be my next door neighbor? Prescott!" She started jumping up and down laughing. "I don't care what it costs. I'll give back some of my salary. It will be well worth the added expense."

The Jersey girl raised her eyebrows as best as she could. Even at her young age, Botox was the answer to tiny sun lines. "Hold off there. You first owe me $65,000," the 21 year old said to the other 21 year old. "I worked hard for that money."

"Let me look at your face." She gave it a quick glance. "Yeah, you worked hard for that money. I can see how sore your jaw looks. Jeffrey must be working you overtime."

"NANANANAAA - got me!"

* * * * *

Sugar spent three hours at the salon getting what looked like plastic surgery from a team of professionals. She looked unrecognizable even to herself. Who'd have ever guessed she'd make an amazing brunette with a hint of red? Changing from her blond hair brought out those exotic features that previously blended into her face. Her chiseled chin and high cheek bones were no longer lost in platinum, super-sized hair. Her green eyes were like emeralds on ice, deep and luminous.

She had just finished getting the last touch of paint on her full, pouty lips. A wine color with a speck of pink gloss to soften the shade. The team went to work on another client. She wasn't actually at a salon but a photography studio where girls were done up for print advertising. She sat alone staring at herself in the mirror as if seeing her reflection for the first time.

"Excuse me, I'm trying find my friend Sugar," Hubert said, pretending he didn't know it was her. "Are you kidding me? OH GOOD HEAVENS, I'm a genius! I love myself!" He started kissing his own arms.

Sugar stood up and bowed to him. "I can't believe how beautiful I look. I'm speechless and honored to meet a man of your talent."

He had instructed the stylists and makeup artists on exactly what he wanted. He even showed them a color swatch for her new hair shade. He went through his bags and handed her a burgundy dress and a pair of Jimmy Choo shoes. "Put these on. Prescott wants me to bring you to an undisclosed location."

His Sugar creation entered the dressing room and walked out looking like a true screen legend. The pin-up girl of any man's dreams. He jumped up and down. "Prescott will surely fall in love with me now once he sees the new you. Come on! Let's go." He practically pushed her out the door.

They exchanged few words on the taxi ride across town. He was busy texting and kept slapping her hand if she tried to interrupt him or speak.

"Where are we going?" she asked

"Sugar Buns, don't speak or move. I don't want your hair or lip gloss to get messed up." He dug his claws lightly into her hand as a gesture to stay still.

Sugar was surprised to see they had pulled up at a jewelry store. Her eyes lit up. "Are you kidding me? Are we buying jewelry to go with the outfit?" She put her hand over her mouth, overcome with excitement.

He smacked her hands off her face. "Don't touch the merchandise," he said.

They walked inside, and there was Prescott looking like Agent 007, only better. His dark, wavy hair was slicked back and he was wearing a navy Zegna designer jacket and starched white shirt. He looked at Sugar and mouthed the word "wow," then pretended to take out a knife and stab himself in the heart at the sight of her. He walked over and whispered in her ear, "You slay me."

She didn't have to ask him what he thought; she knew what he thought. They both looked at each other like teenagers on a first date. For some reason, no one else seemed to exist when their chemistry was kicked up in high gear, but this time it was a supernova explosion.

Hubert squeezed himself between the two. "Excuse me, excuse me. I am the one who deserves to be hugged."

Prescott pretended to punch him in the gut. "That's my guy."

"How dare you?" Hubert cried, acting offended. "I'm not your guy, I'm your girl."

The playboy shook his head. "How can I look at you when I need to ask this lady for her autograph?" He turned to Sugar. "Excuse me, most beautiful woman in the world. Can I have the honor of your autograph? Or would you prefer to shop for an engagement ring?"

Hubert almost fainted. "I can't believe I get to witness this moment. All the years we've been together. We lasted longer than any of your other relationships. What can I say? I am verklempt." The man really did look like he was going to cry.

Outside the store, a few media hounds gathered. One of the clerks at the store notified the press that Prescott was in the building and looking at rings before Sugar arrived. The couple walked around, and he asked to be shown a few engagement rings. Sugar remained silent through it all, smiling and nodding her head. Prescott couldn't seem to get a rise out of her even when she tried on a $50,000 rock.

He thanked the clerks and promised to be back soon. As they walked out, the media presence had doubled in size and started circling in. Prescott put on his best "come on baby" smile, which he normally used when picking up a woman for the first time. In this case, he needed to charm the press.

"Now, I know a lot of you think we're cousins, but that's not the case. We're even willing to submit to DNA testing, but I can assure you we're not related. You must have a thousand questions, but let me give it to you straight from a guy that's completely smitten with this woman. It would seem that I've had my share of dates recently. Some did not end well as you have observed from the different video tapes. (They all laughed, just as he intended.) We've been keeping our relationship quiet, but it's in the open now. We'd ask you to please respect our privacy, and if there is anything new to report, we'll let you know."

Questions started flying, but he grabbed Sugar's hand as he flagged down a taxi and made no further comment. Hubert went to get in, but Prescott shook his head no.

"Come to Newport tomorrow and bring more clothes for Sugar. Plan on spending the day and having some fun. Talk to you later."

As they drove off, Prescott felt really high about the whole situation. He had the press laughing and the prettiest girl in Boston sitting next to him. He kept glancing at her.

"Why so quiet? I never heard you not talk before." He was starting to enjoy her colorful commentary and constant chatter, even though it drove him crazy about half the time. They'd been in the cab for 10 minutes and not a peep came out of her sexy lips.

"I don't know. I guess I was thinking about Tiffany and what she will think after seeing us shopping for rings." She stared out the window.

"Speaking of which, I have good news on that front! I'm close to wrapping up a deal with Hollywood, but we'll all talk about it later. Let me get it finalized and then you can tell her. That will make everything all right. You have to trust me on this."

Something in Sugar's heart told her there was nothing that could make her relationship with Tiffany right again.

She made no response so he changed the subject. "There's a car waiting for you back at the hotel. It's going to take you to my cottage in Newport. My live-in housekeeper Lydia is expecting you. You'll see her husband around too. He does all the handiwork."

"OK, but I need to go back upstairs at the hotel and get my clothes and luggage."

"Your things are already packed and in the car." He watched her staring listlessly out the cab window. "Now don't look so sad. I'll be down later tonight. I have things I need to get done here in Boston first."

Again she said nothing. The loss of Tiffany and playing make-believe with Prescott when she wanted so much more were starting to take a toll on her. *What's my life going to look like a month from now? No best friend and Prescott gone?* Looking at those rings made her depressed. She wanted to believe that dreams can come true. But in all the fairy tales she read, none ended with the line: "And they live happily after in separate houses and had sex every now and then. The End."

Chapter 16

The limo ride out of Boston was a nightmare. The rain was coming down in buckets. *Why do people forget how to drive in rain or snow?* Traffic was at a standstill. Sugar watched as drops fell on her passenger side window. Drip, drip, drip, drip, drip, drip. The rhythm mesmerized her. There was no room for anything else in her thoughts. Her world had been turned upside down in two days. There was nothing else she could do to restore her relationship with Tiffany. She fell asleep in the back seat of the Town Car, exhausted.

"We're getting close," she heard the driver say.

She sat up groggy and confused, like being on a business trip and trying to piece together the new surroundings. That moment of panic as the brain tries to catch up with reality.

"Welcome to Newport, Rhode Island," he said.

She tried to calm her racing heart and mind. She took in a deep breath and gathered her wits.

They went through a small, quaint downtown filled with luxury shops. Just a block away were beautiful residential homes. She looked around, her head turning left and right checking out all the Victorian mansions on Newport's main drag, Bellevue Avenue. She'd never seen anything like it before: unbelievable in scope and size. During the Gilded Age, the New York blue bloods built their summer cottages on the Island trying to escape the Manhattan heat. At 2 p.m. every day, the ocean breezes would cool off the Victorian ladies dressed in the latest designer fashions. They'd travel with an entourage of maids and personal dressers, party hopping from one neighbor's mansion to the next. A summer day in Newport meant seven clothing changes in order to keep up with the Astors.

Sugar had been to the Hamptons and seen some large beach homes. But, the mansions overlooking the ocean on Newport's Bellevue Avenue from impressive cliff rocks were of another even more opulent era.

She remembered reading a book describing the life of Doris Duke, who had a huge home in Newport. The socialite allegedly killed her interior decorator/lover by gunning him down using the gas pedal of her limousine. She somehow managed to hit him at top speed in her own driveway. An investigation was started by local authorities. So, the "remorseful" Doris offered assistance (a big check) to anyone who'd buy a broken down mansion or home and refurbish it. Newport's heyday was long over, and many of the houses now left in town were occupied by rats. She also helped the Newport Historical Society purchase some noteworthy homes for educational purposes. As a result of her "good deeds," the sheriff excused the "unfortunate accident" and coincidentally he was able to take an early retirement the following month. Sugar liked reading Doris' story and admired her cleverness. She hoped she could tour her home and connect with Duke's spirit.

But long before Doris' day as a premier philanthropist/social-ite, Newport was the most watched city in the world. The glamour and decadence that it housed defined what one day would transfer to Hollywood. The 90 per cent tax laws made it impossible for the "old money crowd" to continue with their lavish lifestyles. No longer were there gossip columnists hanging around Newport to get the inside scoop, so the movie industry took its place. Hollywood's days in the sun eventually died too, along with its screen legends. The new age of the instant celebrity took over. Here, Sugar sat in the back seat of a Town Car looking every bit the part of a socialite and movie star, all thanks to having sex on a hotel floor with her cousin. Times surely had changed, thanks to social media.

The driver made a left turn into a private entrance. They stopped at a daunting set of 12-foot gates attached to two stone pillars, which appeared locked. The manicured, tree-lined driveway beyond opened up to massive marble steps that in turn led up to a towering castle. The only thing missing was a moat. Good Lord, this can't be his summer cottage, Sugar thought. That's the word he used: cottage. Maybe they were at the wrong place, or there was a smaller house hidden behind the palace.

"Welcome home," the driver said.

"Is there another house here?" Sugar asked.

"Nope - you've arrived."

"Just wait a minute. I need to get some air," she said and got out of the car.

Sugar couldn't help herself. She walked up to the gates and peeked through, like a kid first in line at Disney World. She twirled around as if in a scene from a musical. Please tell me this is not a dream. I am staying here? She pulled out her cell phone and started taking pictures and texting them to her dad.

The message she sent with them read: "Don't put these on the Internet! If you want me to marry this guy, you can't put out any more information about us. You're scaring him away. Check out his summer COTTAGE. Go Daddy!"

She knew it was a childish and stupid thing to do, but she was certain he'd only show his buddies at the bar. There was no way he was going to blow this for his little girl. For the first time, he was phoning her on a regular basis and calling her "my little baby girl." Sometimes even twice a day. She needed him running the newspaper in her absence, and these awesome photos provided more reason for him to sit tight. For once, he was showing up at the office instead of the bar on the lower level of their building. Her daddy was present and playing to win - with Prescott as the prize. He was doing everything humanly possible to make that happen, including letting Sugar take some time off from the paper. Little did he know there were no plans of anything other than 30 days of shacking up. But at least she'd be doing it in style.

She took 20 more pictures from different angles to show off the mansion.

She was startled when she heard a voice say, "I can see you."

She looked around and saw the camera. "Oh hi," she said, feeling like a fool, but then she remembered herself and added, "I'm Sugar. Sugar Lynn Limehouse, Prescott's – aah - fiancé." Take that!

She waited for the next question, but the pearly gates opened before she could react. Sugar got back in the car. The driver turned around and looked at her.

"You're one lucky lady, landing him," he said, as he drove her up to her mansion in the sky, overlooking the Atlantic Ocean and Newport's famous Cliff Walk. It was a place where visitors came to gawk at the lifestyles of the Swells, and she was feeling quite swell herself.

* * * * *

Tiffany was still at the hospital. She was scheduled to be checked out today, but her doctor kept her there. She came down with a fever starting mid-morning, accompanied by chills.

She'd taken the offer from Monica's people. After seeing Hubert and Sugar walking down the street singing "Dancing Queen," then Prescott and her former best friend shopping for an engagement ring, she'd had enough. In reality, Tiff decided to cash in before seeing Prescott's impromptu press conference concerning the engagement, but at least now she felt justified in doing it.

She was indignant. It was so ridiculous watching the media following around phony famous people. I mean, who was Prescott other than a tycoon who dated famous women? And who the hell is Sugar? At least Tiffany was beat up by the most famous model in the world.

The whole cousin thing, sex in the hotel hall after proclaiming his love for the playwright, and the violent model attack, made the entire story too bizarre for the press to pass up. To top it off, Monica had been offered a reality TV show. Tiff figured her people decided to settle because of advertisers. She saw it happen first-hand at her former job. One of the guys at the newspaper had been arrested for the assault of two women. Advertisers wanted nothing to do with him, even though he hadn't been proven guilty. The show's producers needed

Tiffany to back the model's story, or signing up advertisers would be difficult given the premise of the show: the cover girl changing her ways and starting over as an art dealer.

A knock was heard at her hospital door. Tiffany's heart started to beat faster because she was tired of surprises and had a No Visitors sign posted on the door.

"Checking in on my favorite patient," Dr. DeAngelo said.

"Dr. D, what are you still doing here?" Tiffany smiled. He wasn't wearing his glasses or hospital white jacket. He looked relaxed, tall, dark, and handsome.

"Had to finish up a few things. I'm going on vacation. Leaving in the morning. I wanted a chance to say good bye to you."

"Lucky you. Where you going?"

"Golfing with some buddies in Hilton Head, then going to Newport, Rhode Island, for a few days."

"Wish I could say the same." She paused for a few moments. All her life, she sat on the sidelines watching others win at the game of love. If she was going to start her life over, it might as well be now.

"Look, this is going to sound crazy, but what's normal in my life these days? I might as well try something new. I don't know if you have a girlfriend, but I noticed you don't wear a wedding ring. I would like to see you again outside of here." Her fever went up a notch, and her face reddened.

"How nice of you. But that's crossing the patient doctor line, and we don't do that around here. Don't get me wrong because you seem like a very nice girl."

Tiffany was ready to faint from the embarrassment of it all.

"Well, I was just kidding anyway."

"Would you mind taking a little walk down the hall? There's something I need you to see. I know you don't feel well, but would you go along with me?"

What could she say after being shot down? She didn't want him to know she felt like a heel.

"Aah, sure," she said. She got up despite feeling under the weather.

They walked down the hospital hall. She kept her head down since she was now quite famous at the place. Some staff even asked for her autograph. This whole mess had become unbelievably embarrassing, including get turned down by him. Where was he taking her now?

They got to an exit.

"Stay right here," he said. He walked out and came back inside.

"This is my last day here, and I am going to be working at the Brigham and Women's Hospital once I'm back from vacation. You're no longer my patient. How would you feel about meeting in Newport in a week? Great food and scenery there."

"That would be lovely. Can I give my cell phone number?"

"I already have it from your chart. I put it on speed dial in case you said yes. I was planning on asking you out long before you asked me, but I needed to follow protocol."

"Well played." She smiled and felt her fever break.

* * * * *

Monica stood on top of the bar pouring champagne for everyone from a magnum-sized bottle. People chanted her name, and she laughed at the sight of 200 people showing up at 5 p.m. just to party with her. All from just one tweet. "Come party with me today at Roxy's NYC. 5 p.m. First flute of champagne on me."

Gina was worried she'd never see her money out of the over-pampered diva, so she called a few nightclub owners and arranged a three-stop appearance tour of the Big Apple. She squeezed them for $35,000 and could have gotten more, but it was on too short notice.

The already tipsy Monica sat down with the bottle and undid her top, revealing a spectacular pink bra with diamond studs. The crowd went wild – except Gina who was in the bathroom throwing up so she could drink more. The night was young, and there were still two more clubs to hit.

* * * * *

Sugar laughed. "You're kidding me, right?" She and her new acquaintance sat in leather chairs in the handsome library with wood-paneled walls, glancing at the antique books but mostly at each other.

"Seriously, Prescott played hockey for years and even made it to the semi-pros," Jon Perry said. He was the consultant who Prescott had mentioned to Sugar earlier in the day.

She giggled a little bit thinking about him wanting to be a pro hockey player but also from too much champagne. She was entertained to meet one of his best buddies from college and see him through someone else's eyes.

Jon had been out of the country and so had not seen the latest in celebrity gossip. He'd just flown in from Heathrow. He found Sugar delightful, amusing, and absolutely captivating after a grueling trip and a lifetime of thinking "love stinks." He figured Sugar and Prescott were business associates because she was definitely not the playboy's type. He looked forward to getting to know her better and was feeling rather high on scotch - and her sexy vibe.

They were now on their fifth drink.

"Sugar pie, why aren't you married?" he asked.

"Why does everyone pun on my name?" She didn't expect an answer but replied to his question. "Because I'm too much woman to love. Besides, no one ever asks." She giggled, completely forgetting that she and Prescott had shopped for rings earlier. But that was only make believe. She needed to separate herself from feeling close to her pretend fiancé.

He started laughing. "I'm asking. Will you marry me?"

"Let me look over your bio again." She pretended to be holding a piece of paper and picked up reading glasses from the desk. "Successful businessman. Divorced. Tell me again how many kids you have?"

"Enough to keep you busy. Two boys. One from a first marriage and another from a one night stand. Do you want to go for kid number three?"

"Maybe. But let me get this straight first. You're raising two boys on your own, including one from a one-night stand. Does that mean if I don't like the way the baby looks I can give him or her back to you?" She giggled.

"Aha. So, you are agreeing we're going to make a baby? When can we get started?"

A voice cleared his throat behind her. It was Prescott, who'd overheard most of the conversation.

"What's going on here?" he asked in a flat tone.

Jon jumped up, embarrassed from sitting a little too close to Sugar. Not that he was doing anything wrong, of course.

"Prescott, good to see you." He gave him a guy kind of hug.

Prescott walked over to Sugar and kissed her on the cheek as awkwardness filled the room.

"Honey, would you go into the kitchen and help Lydia make up some snacks for us?"

Lydia had been living in the house since Prescott acquired it a few years ago. Her husband, Bernard, had been the groundskeeper at the estate for 20 years. They both looked after C-side like they would a beloved family member. It was named after the original owner, Calvin Chapel, who thought Seaside was too dull for its name and that C-side gave the home more character.

Sugar nodded as she left to find Lydia. This was embarrassing. Too many drinks and too many chuckles had caught her off guard. It was just so nice to finally meet a guy with real potential. Prescott told her himself it was "just sex" between them. So why was a little flirting with his friend so bad? There were no prospects in her life until Jon Perry walked through the mansion's doors ready to swoop her off to his London flat or wherever he lived. *Where did he live?* She forgot to ask.

* * * * *

Gina and Monica rode across town in a long, black stretch limo while each of them tried to put on makeup as they headed for their next stop.

"How much did you say we're getting paid for this?" Monica asked as she stared into her compact mirror and made duck faces at herself while checking out her lip gloss.

"Five thousand," Gina lied, intending to pocket the $30,000 difference.

"Are you freaking kidding me? What are you trying to do, undercut my rates and every star's in the country? I'll be the laughingstock of reality TV. That fat girl Kim K gets a hundred grand."

The Italian model put on her best mafia sounding voice. "Fuggeddabout it. It was an hour's notice. Take it while you can. You need some spending cash for our trip to Rhode Island." Then she went back to her usual nasal sounding whine. "Hello, I'm not the Bank of Monaco."

The red head rolled her eyes. "We're going to Newport, not France."

"Monaco as in you. I am making a play on your name Monica. And for your information, Monaco is a nation all by itself and not a part of France."

"I hate it when you try to be smart because that's the stupidest thing I ever heard." She cracked her gum.

"Take your money and get the gum out of your mouth, Stephen Hawking. We're here." She handed her an envelope but mixed them up and gave her the wrong one. So instead of pocketing a $30,000 commission, wise girl Gina wound up only getting five thou.

Monica started fanning out the loot as her friend's eyes widened realizing her mistake. But it was too late.

"Ginnnnnnaaaaa! Look - those idiots paid me more... HA HA HA. Finders keepers." She imitated her friend's laugh. "NANANANAAA."

* * * * *

Sugar walked back into the library carrying a tray of assorted cheese and crackers. The only person sitting there was Prescott, drinking a glass of brandy in the same oversized brown leather chair that Jon had recently been relaxing in.

"You seem to be making yourself at home in MY home," he said.

She sat the tray down on top of an antique desk with a roll top. He got up and moved the tray to a window seat in the library as if she'd committed a cardinal sin.

"What's wrong?" she asked.

"Jon had to leave. Something came up."

"Like what, Prescott? What was so urgent that he had to get out of here? From what I understood, he was staying the night," she said, with a slight annoyance in her voice.

"Why do you ask? Did you plan on tiptoeing around and meeting him later on?"

She could see that he was not kidding around. "Seriously Prescott? Don't be ridiculous. That's silly. I mean, we flirted. OK, I admit it. I am guilty as charged. Am I interested in him? You betcha! There is nothing to date back in Charleston besides Southern good ol' boys who go out with the same kind of women as you do. In a nutshell: skinny young models, with noodle bodies and brains to match. Or then there's the other option of dating…NO ONE. Have you ever been to Charleston? I can assure you there is no dating scene."

"So, you can make a fool out of me because you can't find a date? I've got headline news for you. You're engaged."

She shook her head. "And I've got news for you: We're not really engaged. It's only make believe – and over in 30 days."

He stood up and grabbed hold of her hand a tad tighter than he meant to. "Make believe or not, we have a business deal and it did not include making dates with one of my good friends."

She pulled her hand away from him. "You must be kidding me. First of all, I didn't make a date. He was teasing me about one day getting married. As if that would happen anytime soon. And who are you to talk? You just broke up with Monica because you were ready to sleep with Tiffany, 'the love of your life,' but instead ended up having sex with me. And you're going to tell me about not dating one of your good friends? Hell, if you had your way you'd be sleeping with all of us."

"I'm telling you to act your part. That's the deal!"

"I am sorry I momentarily forgot about our 'deal' since I was having a fun, intelligent conversation with someone who is interesting and interested in me. Believe it or not, some men actually like me. I have no problem getting dates, but finding guys worth two cents is a different story. Your friend Jon is perfect for someone like me. A consultant who travels the world, has two kids and no wife. An ordinary guy doing extraordinary things and raising children on his own. Surprise! He's not sitting around watching Entertainment News and following the details of your sex life. He didn't even know we were engaged, and I doubt he'd even believe it anyway. I am sure he took one look at me and thought, 'NO WAY is this Prescott Borden's property.'"

"Some brilliant consultant. He was quite mistaken in his assessment."

"What the hell does that mean? Are you kidding me? This isn't a remake of *Pretty Woman*. Wait....wait...wait...That's your point, isn't it? I am just like that movie, including the escort part, only I don't get the guy at that end. So, basically, I'm just paid help at your disposal."

He said nothing.

"You know what? Screw this. I am just done. I've had enough feeling like a game to you and not a human being who is trying desperately not to fall in love with you. Besides, you couldn't keep someone like me anyway. I require more than a mansion by the sea with a 30-day return policy. I'm out of here."

She went to leave but realized she had nowhere to go. She had no money, no car and no hope of being with him.

"I need a ride somewhere," she said.

"Now you're talking nonsense, like when I first met you. Number one: You need your newspaper turned around, and I am the one who can help with you that. Number two: You owe it to your friend Tiffany. The play is dead in the water without me. You need it not just for her but for your own financial security. I am close to a deal that will make both of you very happy. Finally: You don't want to leave me. You really don't. You just want me to stop you, but I won't."

"That says it all, doesn't it?" she said. She felt so mad at him but even more at herself because he was right.

He pulled a box out of his jacket and handed it to her. "Open it," he said.

She looked at him. Her hands started to shake as she reached out for the jewelry box bearing the label from the store where they had been earlier. Her heart started pounding along with her head. She felt overwhelmed with a headache but part of her still wanted to believe he was really asking her to marry him.

"Is this the ring I fell in love with at the jewelry store?" she said, knowing full well it was.

"Yeah, the same one. Just take it and wear it for as long as you want. I don't care if you keep the ring. Sugar, you already agreed the answer is yes. So, let's just make this temporary arrangement happen and see where it goes."

She couldn't help herself and opened the box. There it was: the promise of everything she grew up believing could happen to her. "And they lived happily ever after." She put on the ring: a beautiful three-carat, round-shaped diamond ring set in platinum gold with smaller diamonds around the band. She stared at her hand and swore to herself, "My dreams will come true."

She teared up. "How did you know this was the ring? I didn't even speak the entire time we were at the jewelry store."

"I know women and what they like." He took in a deep breath. "No…correction…I know you," he said.

She felt overwhelmed with emotion and needed to break away from his intense stare. She hugged him to catch her breath.

He held her and whispered into her ear. "You really had me nervous there. Sugar, we do have something. I don't know what it is, but I can't lose you now."

He pulled her in even closer to him. Once again, that kinetic energy started up all over again, and they made love in the library. They woke up just in time to see the sunrise. They headed up to the master suite to avoid getting busted by the hired help. They lived there more than he did and might find their underwear and clothes thrown about to be in bad taste.

Chapter 17

Monica shook her friend Gina out of a deep sleep.

"Stop it," the former catwalk model hissed. She sat up and looked at the clock. Seven a.m. "What are we doing up so early?" She punched Monica on the shoulder out of annoyance.

Monica smacked her friend lightly on the head in return. "Remember? That girl Tiffany is going on the Today show. A live feed. She's going to apologize to me."

"NANANANAAA," Gina laughed.

"What's so damn funny?"

"How much did that cost you? Wait, why am I laughing? You still owe me a ton of money girlfriend."

The leggy redhead got of the bed, walked over to the kitchenette, and grabbed her Gucci purse. She handed over yesterday's proceeds, minus the thousand she tipped a cute waiter who also happened to be an up-and-coming model. She'd collect a favor later for that payoff. He was 100 percent in love with the dazzling cover girl and would have done anything for her for free. But she was drunk and feeling generous and wanted to throw some money around just to show off.

"I'll pay you the rest of the money today once we get to Newport. I have to film a scene, and then I get my first paycheck."

Gina said nothing. She was too busy counting up the dough and figuring out how much more she was owed. She was still mad at herself for handing over the wrong envelope and giving up her 95 percent commission.

Monica waved her hand in front of her friend's face. "HELLO! I'm getting my first payment from my reality show. We're taking a road trip.

The nasally Jersey girl snapped. "There is 10 grand missing from here."

"I need something to live off of. The producers are taking money from my weekly paycheck to pay off that bitch Tiffany. Wonder what she'll do with MY money? You were right - some of it does come out of my pocket."

"Told you so! I knew it. You better pay me back soon or else Jeffery says you have to sleep with both of us as part of the payment plan."

"What the f? I wouldn't ever sleep with Jeffery and with you only if I was too drunk to remember."

"Then I won't remind you of that time…"

"Just be quiet and turn on the TV. I'm finally getting that apology I deserve and some justice."

* * * * *

Tiffany was officially discharged from Mass General Hospital. She jumped into a taxi and headed to the Four Seasons to pick up her things. The interview wasn't as bad as she thought it would be. The agreement was that the camera crew would come to her, and she spoke from her hospital bed to appear somewhat sympathetic. True, she stood up for Monica but did manage to get in a good plug for *Marble House*. She'd announced to the world that the fight was all Prescott's fault. She claimed to feel bad for the supermodel because the attack was instigated by him. She hoped Sugar saw the piece live and choked on her ham croissant, something her former friend ate for breakfast every day.

She convinced herself she didn't feel bad for "tattling" but couldn't admit to herself that it was pure lying. Throughout her life, Tiffany always played by the rules, but where was it going? She was exhausted from feeling walked over and taken advantage of by people like Sugar and Prescott. She convinced herself that telling stories out of school was something reporters do every day when chasing down a lead. They make stuff up while trying to get the facts of a story. She once even pretended to be blind in order to expose a slumlord who took advantage of the handicapped. Still, she never printed a story unless it was 100% truthful. This was a different situation though. Here she was on TV incriminating herself and a stranger who actually saved her from a black belt tornado.

She looked up her bank balance on a cell phone app. There it was: a $300,000 wire transfer had hit her account. The highest she'd ever seen her life savings was $8000. And before this bonanza, her balance was less than zero.

The cab ride was a short five minutes, even through crazy Boston traffic. She tipped the driver a twenty because for once in her life she felt rich.

"Keep the change," she said, surprised that the driver, a bandanna-wearing hippie, didn't seem all that impressed.

She almost asked, "Do you know who I am?" but then realized she was no one but yesterday's news. Another celebrity drive-by shooting, so to speak. The temporary fame had gone to her honey blond head just a little.

The cab door opened, and a smiling Four Seasons doorman offered his hand.

"Welcome back, Miss Tiffany James," he said.

Now that was more like it. He knew her first *and* last names.

He continued on with his deep Boston accent. "I must tell you that I have never gone to the theater before. But I decided to see your play, and it was magnificent. I'm going to start seeing more shows from now on. Thank you so much for introducing me to the world of theater."

"And thank you so much," she said while grasping his outstretched hand. The short conversation embodied what she'd worked so hard for, and she loved hearing it. She wanted to inspire others to appreciate the arts and be entertained by her work. In a way, the doorman's words made everything seem better, including the physical pain she suffered from Monica's attack and her considered decision to trash Prescott. After all, isn't that what the world's most eligible bachelor had done to her? Fooled her into thinking they could have a possible relationship. That he was going to help with her dreams of being on Broadway and maybe even a Hollywood movie. Instead, he slept with her best friend. If he had not been such a bastard when it came to women, she'd never be in this situation to begin with. Her face was still swollen up, while her ego was deflated from his 180-degree turn-around from her to Sugar. To hell with him and everyone else who got in the way. From now on, she was looking out for number one. She was checking out of the Four Seasons and taking a vacation in tony Newport, Rhode Island. Not just because of her coming date there with the hottest doctor in Boston, but to get a fresh start on life. Her beau wasn't going to be there for another week, but she'd never taken a full two-week vacation ever, only mini-breaks. Darn it – now it was her turn to just kick back and enjoy success. Snap - she just figured out who she'd get to pay for all of it, too. She put on her best smile and pulled on her short black skirt. She marched through the hotel lobby with a little wiggle in her walk and a new found confidence. Life was never going to be the same, in more ways than she could imagine.

* * * * *

Monica and Gina rode in a black Town Car headed to Newport from New York City. They sat in the back seat drinking Cape Codder cocktails: cranberry juice mixed with vodka. The breakfast of champions. They'd been toasting back and forth for an hour and were good and hammered. The driver rolled his eyes as he realized that they were only in New Haven. He could tell this was going to be a long trip.

"To effing no one," Monica said, while lifting her glass up in the air.

"No, to Prescott and his porker cousin. Let's track her down and make fun of her." NANANANAAA, she laughed while lifting up her glass to say cheers.

Monica rolled her eyes. "Prescott's not in Newport yet. He only stays there in the summer. We've got plenty of time to plot and figure out better ways to abuse her."

"Like what?"

"Like paying a guy to pretend he's interested in her. Already in the works. HAHAHAH – will that be hysterical. She'll think she hit the lottery. Prescott and some hot male model from the city chasing her around. HAHAHAH. It's all so ridiculous to begin with. As if a guy like Prescott was ever interested in someone like her. So, let's make it even crazier. She is sooo dumb. He's just using her for some money deal. Mark my words. There are rotten eggs all over the place on this affair, and we're about to let loose some real stink bombs. Ginaaa – WTF."

She waved her hand in the air. "Don't look at me – it was the freaking driver."

He smiled and waved at the girls in the rear view mirror. They rolled down the windows and didn't say anything for the rest of the trip, much to his relief.

Chapter 18

Prescott and Sugar sat at the very back of a greasy spoon diner. The place was filled with misfits. It was impossible to distinguish the bums from the blue bloods. Newport was filled with both. A lot of the old money townfolk were still wearing their great-grandfather's sweaters with moth holes that got bigger every year. One in particular, 79 year old Spencer Hollings, had black tape wrapped around his topsider shoes keeping them bound together. He was the beneficiary of seven different trust funds but drove a Honda with 300,000 miles on it. He was busy trying to sell the diner owner a basket of mushrooms that popped up on his lawn.

"Spencer, we don't buy mushrooms off the streets, and besides, we don't have a dish that requires fresh 'shrooms." The heavy set brunette in a pink uniform said the same thing to him every year, and his reply was identical too.

"You can run a mushroom omelet special," he said.

Prescott yelled out to the old geezer, "Get over here you cheap S.O.B., and I'll buy you breakfast."

No way was Spencer turning down free food, even though he

had already eaten. He'd take the meal on the cheap to go. The two gentlemen shook hands. Prescott offered him a chair, but Spencer shook his head no.

"Two cinnamon buns to go," he hollered at the manager/waitress. "And put it on his bill."

"You owe me now, you bastard, for not sitting down." He leaned in and whispered, "Say, what's cooking with this windmill contract I'm hearing so much about?"

The crotchety old fellow looked around the room, bent over and said, "If I were a betting man, it'd be hard to pass on Davidson Industries getting that deal. You weasel."

Prescott nodded. "I appreciate that. By the way, if I were a betting man, it would be hard to pass on a start-up in California, P.L.C. Technology. They just signed a government contract worth more than your entire family."

Spencer, the master of "a penny saved is a penny earned" to the tune of $200 million, did a double take when he noticed Sugar. Who was this fine lady with Prescott Borden? The beauty's newly colored auburn hair was pinned up, and her dark mascara showed off amazing green eyes. Now that's a deal he'd be wary of investing in. He had been warned about her type all his life. The kind of gal you want to spend money on just because you're feeling sweet on her. That's why all his family members married ugly women. But now that he was turning 80, maybe it was time to rethink that strategy. Plus he wanted to try out some of that Viagra he'd invested a fortune in.

"Is there a reason you're not introducing me to this lovely creature?" Spencer said and held out his hand to Sugar.

She giggled, and he kissed her hand. He couldn't help but notice the huge, shiny rock sparkling on her fourth finger. Now, buying something like that brand new was really overdoing it, just a bit. Besides, he had plenty of better looking family diamonds that cost him nothing. He had an unmistakable grin on his face, like a Boy Scout who found a girly magazine. He was captivated.

Prescott stood up. "Now, back down there old boy. This is my fi… fi… fiancé, Sugar." It almost pained him saying the word since he'd sworn off marriage from the time he figured out women were magnets and he was steel. About age 13, when his cute dimples and curly hair seemed to charm everyone. Sometimes, girls would pull on his hair just to see how long it really was. Even his teachers appreciated his Elvis-like persona. But Spencer wasn't impressed.

The blue-blood ignored the remark and turned to her and said, "When you change your mind, I live two doors from him. And I've got more money than he does." He laughed and walked away.

Prescott yelled at him. "Then why don't you fix up that eyesore of a mansion you call home? Tourists mistake it for a frat house." Half the diner laughed because it was so true.

Prescott sat back down. "What the hell is up with men and you?" he asked

"Everyone loves a little Sugar with their coffee," she said, while stirring some into hers.

"Seriously, what's the deal? I've dated far better looking…let me correct that. I mean far younger…wait…what I mean to say is…what the hell is up with you? Why do men fall all over you?"

"Honey, you don't really wanna know," she grinned.

"Darling, enlighten me, because I just don't get it."

"Oh please! Coming from the man who just had the best sex ever? You get it."

"What are you talking about? The best sex ever. OK, fine. It's good, but that's not the point. Why do they get all twisted around after just meeting you? I don't get it."

"Wake up. You picked up the vibe in the hotel elevator once you stopped being all full of yourself. I put out kinetic energy, and others feel it," she said, while making wavy gestures with her hands as if trying to hypnotize him.

"All I'm feeling is that you're driving me crazy."

"Exactly," she said and stopped with the hypnotist act.

"When I say crazy, I don't mean it necessarily in a good way. Don't misunderstand me, you're dynamite, but you think you're 20 times more explosive than you are."

"What? No, I don't. I am nuclear power! That's just a fact. Every day, I take 10 selfies of myself half-dressed. Just so I know how damn good I look in a lacy bra - of which I own hundreds in every color. I even practice my pouty stares," she said and actually made a pouty face. "At night, I like to dance by myself to sexy music while wearing lingerie. It's how I work out. People can feel my sex appeal when I walk into a room. It's electric. My aura enters before I do, and that's why everyone's captivated - including you. You just can't help but stare at me. Like you did when you first met me."

"My oh my, my, my. Darling, your head is way too big. Who could have missed that pink pantsuit of yours? That's called scary staring, not good staring." He took a big guzzle of his coffee and leaned back.

"Who cares what it is? You noticed, and so does everyone else. My

Grandma once told me, 'Honey child, once you got it, you never lose it. It's just your audience gets older as time goes by.' She was married four times. I can't help it that I got good genes."

He seemed unimpressed, but she continued.

"Believe or not, most men want accessible and curvy. Pin-up girls never go out of style, just out of circulation. Only dumb bastards fall for the newest Hollywood version of women. All bones, hair extensions, and big, oversized, supersonic white teeth. Most men aren't fooled that easily. They want good, old-fashioned American sex appeal, and baby, I got it. In fact, you can pick out any guy you want, anywhere we go, and if I want him to talk to me, I can make it happen, just like that." She snapped her fingers.

He rolled his eyes. She sounded more cocky than him. And no one could be more attractive to the opposite sex than Prescott Borden as far as he was concerned. No one. Not even Sugar with all her crazy energy. Crazy, just plain crazy, and some guys fall for it. Something about her did remind him of a pinup girl, but who?

He thought to himself: "If guys actually had sex with her, whoa, they'd really be dazzled." Then it dawned on him. "She's my wannabe counterpart. The female me."

Maybe he had seriously underestimated Sugar Lynn Limehouse. Men fall all over her - including him. No, he wasn't going there. That girl needed serious fixing, and it just so happened he knew exactly what needed to be done.

The waitress dropped off a plate with a ham croissant and another of egg whites and fruit. She poured some coffee and left the two of them alone. Prescott switched plates.

"We're playing by my rules now. Darling, you're not eating ham sandwiches for breakfast anymore. You think you have men chasing you now. Wait 'til you lose twenty pounds. Hell, even I might not be able to keep you."

"Who are you kidding? You can't keep me now. They're already lining up out the door to steal me away from you." She grabbed the croissant and took a bite.

"Sugar, I am serious. For once in your life, don't think you're right about everything. Trust me on this one. I'll make you better. You'll thank me one day." He took back the sandwich, wrapped it up in a napkin and stepped on it.

"What in the hell are you doing? You're not messing with my food. I like to eat. I am not changing another thing for you. You called the hair and clothes right. You win. But that's the end. Besides, I am in awesome shape for me."

"Speaking of which, I have a personal trainer I want to introduce you to." He looked at his watch. "He'll be here in 15 minutes."

"I don't need exercise. I dance half naked by myself in front of a mirror all the time, and my body looks great."

"What the hell? I haven't seen you do that. When did you plan on putting on a show for me?"

"Never, because you wouldn't appreciate it."

"I will once you're 20 pounds thinner. In fact, you should lose 40 pounds and that would put you at about a 10. Perfect!"

Sugar's blood started to boil. "Correction: That would make me a hundred pounds and I'd look like an older version of your underage anorexic dates. PASS!"

He backed down and tried a new approach. "I'll make you a deal.

You lose 20 pounds in 30 days, which you can easily do on Atkins, then I'll keep you around another 30."

"Are you kidding me? Trust me on this. In 30 days, the only thing I'm doing is calling your friend Jon. He likes me just the way I am. Sugar and spice and everything nice," she smirked.

She could see the taunting remark did not set well with him and immediately regretted bringing up his friend's name. As much as she loved Jon's attention, she really adored Prescott. There had never been another man she loved fighting and making up with more than him. Everything about him turned her on and made birds fly around her head. She wanted to marry the elusive bachelor. She wanted him to adore her as much as she did him. They seemed to bring out the best and worst in each other, and she loved it that way. For the first time in her life, she felt free to say whatever came to mind. She said things to him she'd never share with anyone else, not even Tiffany. Besides, Tiff would cut her down to size if she heard all the bragging Sugar was doing about herself.

And so what if Prescott wanted her to lose weight? What was so bad about losing a few pounds? She started a diet every day but never made it past lunch time without cheating. She wanted to lose weight too.

She did an about face. "Mr. Borden, you have deal, 60 days. But I'm warning you. I'm going to look so good you're never going to let me go. You see this ring?" She held up her hand. "With thee I do wed. Just you wait and see. We'll be Mr. and Mrs. Newportant before you know it. Don't you forget it."

Prescott started to laugh. "Make up your mind woman. Do you love me or hate me?"

She smiled. "A little bit of both."

"Good, because you should only marry someone you love, not hate. But I like having you around. LIKE being the key word. I like you more than I dislike you," he said.

"Not really. You're just kidding yourself. You love me. L- O- V- E love me. You just haven't figured it out yet. You even get jealous of old men like Spencer."

He took hold of her hands, and they pulled in close. He kissed her on the lips like a real couple, giddy with being in love. Anyone looking over would see the two love birds at the red and white checkered table enjoying each other's company while they bantered.

"So, when do I get this lap dance you're bragging about?" he asked and flashed his perfect teeth smile.

She ran her fingers through his dark curly hair and looked into his sea blue eyes.

"As soon as I lose 20 pounds."

"Now that's my girl talking."

"You know it."

Things were going well. A conversation without a fight that didn't end in sex. Almost bordering on a normal, well balanced relationship. It was time to break the bad news while things were going well.

"So, listen darling. I am going back up to Boston today. I have some business to do, and I have to start packing up some of my treasures from the penthouse. It's killing me saying goodbye to the place."

"I'll help you," she said.

"No, you stay here. I want you to meet with the trainer and do a little more shopping with Hubert. Remember? He's coming here today. He's got your cell number. You need to buy some clothes a few sizes smaller as an incentive."

"No, I don't want to do that in case I fail. I'll have to take them back and switch sizes and that will make me feel bad."

"Nope, it doesn't work that way. If you fail, the clothes go back. There are no bonus checks for people who fail in my world," he said.

Oh no! She was looking like a warship ready to launch a cruise missile right at him. Who was he to treat her like one of his employees?

"I beg your pardon? I don't work for you!"

He held up his hand. "Now, don't go getting all huffy over the comment. We still are business partners - just with benefits. Speaking of which, partner, I have good news concerning Tiffany's play. So, you just sit tight and be a good girl for the next few days, and I'll do my job. You'll be happy you did."

"A few days? You're leaving me here?"

"Darling, I have a career and a life back in Boston. I'll be back on the weekend."

She realized there was no sense in arguing. She had her own work to do on the newspaper that she'd been completely ignoring. Then a thought entered her mind. Something so disturbing she almost felt like crying.

"Prescott, promise me you won't cheat on me while you're gone. I mean, you can be faithful to me for 60 days, right? In fact, I am making that part of the deal. You set all the terms and now I have one…no, two. As long as we're together, you won't cheat or flirt."

"Listen to you, Little Miss Flirt," he said.

"I won't do that anymore. We'll both hold each other to the same standard. NO cheating and, um, um, minimum flirting. (Something she was very fond of doing!) Do we have a deal?"

He nodded while rolling his eyes.

"I am serious." She held up a butter knife in a half-threatening cute, kind of way.

"Deal." He kissed her on the forehead.

"Oh, look who just walked in. Your personal trainer. I'll introduce you, but then I have to get back to the hotel and get some business done. He'll drive you home."

Did he just say "home," she wondered.

He waved Steve over. But, seeing his workout body strutting across the room made him think twice about leaving Sugar.

Prescott stood up. "Hey, good to see you." The two men shook hands as they sized each other up in a guy kind of way. "I don't mean to be the bearer of bad news, but, umm, something's come up and we need to cancel for today. I'll cover the cost for her missed appointment."

Sugar looked confused. "What are you talking about?"

"I forgot we have another appointment." He gave her a little nudge. "Time to go." He turned to the trainer with the super-fit body. "We'll be in touch."

What was it about this girl that was making him feel so insecure?

He didn't like it, not one little bit. He suddenly was glad to be leaving for a few days. He had more important things to do then worry about women, especially one in particular who was making him crazy.

Chapter 19

Prescott and Sugar headed back to the castle after spending the morning clowning around at the dive diner. He instructed her to wait outside while he went in to "get something." Five minutes later, he drove up on his Harley wearing a bomber jacket and tossed her a helmet. She squealed with excitement and jumped on board, even though she'd never been on a motorcycle before.

Sugar held on tightly to Prescott's waist as they drove around the tiny island together. Where was he taking her? She didn't care. She felt like a bad girl out with her rebel boyfriend after a prison break. Freedom was hers for the taking. For some reason, she never thought of him as someone who owned a Harley. This was a tough guy's type of transportation, unlike his sports cars that to her seemed more like rich boy's toys. She hoped he owned a pickup truck too. Not that she didn't appreciate the high-end penthouse, the mansion and the manna-from-heaven shopping sprees, but for the moment this felt more real. She liked him raw and without walls filled with antique paintings covering up who he was on the inside. Plus, he looked like a rock star in leather. Everything about him turned her on, including the vibration from the ride.

They headed to Ocean Drive. The temperature dropped another 10 degrees from the unobstructed sea breeze. The town of Newport was protected by the harbor from the full force of nature's whims. He pulled over to Brenton Point State Park, the perfect island spot for kite enthusiasts showing off their acrobatic skills. Dragons seemed to be swooping down from the sky with long tails in every shape and form. Their colorful dance attracted tourists and couples falling in love who snuck away for a quiet getaway but still appreciated the spectacular show.

They hopped off the bike. He pulled out a blanket from a hidden compartment and grabbed her hand. They said nothing to each other. Sugar was learning to surrender to the here and now, something she'd never done until Batman took charge of her life. Prescott was like a superhero of sorts, freeing her of the need to be in control at all cost. But her fear of abandonment, like losing her mother and never seeing her grandmother after that day, loomed overhead like a heavily weighted black kite in the sky, tangling itself in other's life lines.

* * * * *

Tiffany sat in the business office of the five-star hotel with three men in power suits. The same hotel where she'd been viciously attacked by a stranger.

She cleared her throat. "As I was explaining to the desk manager earlier, I've spoken with my lawyer and I could easily sue this place for the attack on me. Monica had been here before and stirred up trouble, yet you let her back into the hotel, even after she vandalized the penthouse suite. You not only put your business in danger but paying guests as well. You have cameras everywhere, and you'd been instructed to stop her from entering by Mr. Borden."

She looked around the room but couldn't tell if her words were having an impact. "Gentlemen look at me. Look at my face. This is your fault, and you need to do something about it," she said, gesturing to her bruises and bandaged nose. She crossed her fingers hoping they hadn't seen her on TV declaring it was all Prescott's fault.

"So, what is it that you want us to do for you?" the lawyer in the group asked.

"I want my hotel bill here cleared, and I'd like to stay at your location in Newport, Rhode Island for a week. I'll sign any waiver you want. I am not out to make a fortune from this unfortunate accident. I just want what's fair. I deserve a chance to recover from my injuries in peace. In return, I won't sue you for anything. We'll be even-steven."

The group of men looked at each other. There was consensus in the room that something should be done now rather than later when she had a lawyer.

"The problem is, we don't have a hotel there," the general manager said.

Tiffany shrugged her shoulders. "That's not my problem, it's yours. Pick up my tab at the best hotel there," she said.

The assistant manager stood up. "Now hold on. Just pick a location where we have a facility, and it's workable."

The attorney chimed in. "Chuck, now hold that thought a minute. Why don't you sit back down. If Miss James wants to go to Newport, then we'll figure out a way to accommodate her. And I know the perfect place to stay: The Viking Hotel. Let's make the arrangements and include her transportation there."

The GM tried to support his assistant. "But we have a hotel in..."

The lawyer held up his hand and smiled at his negotiating adversary. "Tiffany, please feel free to go back to your room, freshen up and enjoy a meal on us. Relax and stay the night while we take care of all your bills here and arrange the trip to Newport. I'll meet you with the appropriate paperwork in one hour."

He turned away and stared down the two managers. He didn't want to hear another word from either of them. The lawyer was thrilled to wrap this up and wondered how she could be so naïve, when in fact he'd been had. None of the hotel managers had seen the interview that aired on the Today Show where she took responsibility for the fight.

"Thank you very much gentlemen, and you have a good day." She stood up and walked out feeling that the new Tiffany was about to conquer the world.

* * * * *

Sugar giggled under the Newport sun as they lay next to each other watching the clouds and kites fly by. "Which one is your favorite?" she asked.

"The blue triangle-shaped one, all alone."

"Really? What's so special about a kid's kite? Wait, I can figure this out," she said in a smirky kind of way and held her hands to her head like Karnack the magnificent. "You had one just like it as a little boy until it got tangled up in telephone wires. You went crying home to your mother, and she said not to worry because one day you'll own a private jet instead. Thus began your desire to achieve more, all thanks to your bad kite-flying skills and a hobby shop in North Carolina that lost your business because you no longer played with plastic trains, planes and automobiles. You decided to acquire your own from then on. Ta da!" She held up her arms in the air like the victor after a winning goal in a soccer match.

"I can see a future career for you, Miss Psychic smart ass. I'm thinking about getting an airplane now just to show you how amazing you really are."

She took on a more serious tone. "You show me more when you show me less. I like this Prescott. The one who likes a single kite because you pilot your own way."

"Now you're scaring me because that's exactly why I like it."

"No worries. I still can't figure you out. Most single men of your stature like having a bunch of grownup frat boys hanging around like George Clooney. People think he's a ladies man, but to me, he seems to be more about impressing his entourage. A lot of guys secretly live for other guys, which does not make them gay, just incapable of real relationships. The best they can hope for in life is pranking each other, smoking cigars and going to strip clubs as a team. But you live for impressing yourself. What I don't understand is your need for so many women. That's beyond my psychic pay grade. You sure like a lot of women around you, only on a short-term basis."

He pointed up. "I like my space and flying free like a single kite. I think people get to a certain age in life, say about 30, where they have to make certain choices. What's of value to you? At that time, I was flying high in my career on Wall Street. I had shortened my business life span because of pursuing hockey and had a lot of catching up to do. If you don't mind me asking, how old are you, Sugar?"

She paused and rolled over on her side to look at him. "What a terrible question since I happen to be 31 with a business that needs my attention 24/7. Thanks so much for reminding me." She slugged him in the arm, then pointed to the sky. "I'm more like that kite over there with 15 others tied to it. Only I'm stuck being the lead. I have to worry about making payroll and keeping a lot of people employed who have families to support. Sometimes I wish I were a single kite like you. Maybe I missed my calling as a day trader. Or maybe I should have been married with one kid and another on the way and I wouldn't be stuck flying in zigzag patterns all the time."

He looked at her closely. "What do you want from life? I mean, really want from life."

She took in a deep breath. "Funny, I was going to ask you the same question. My answer keeps changing. On paper, I want kids with a zany mom who might home school them on a farm. But, I don't like animals or manure. So, I know it makes me full of cow crap whenever I think about it. Sometimes I just want to be so successful that I'm untouchable. I can do whatever I want, when I want, kind of like you. Then I look at that little blond girl over there, and I want to steal her away." She pointed her out. "The one with the pretty pink bows. One-stop shopping. She looks like a good girl, and half the parenting is already done. Everything made easy."

"You can always have a baby without a husband."

"Oh yeah, how often does that work out for the kid? I was raised by a single dad, so that should say it all when it comes to single parenting. Look at me. I am still scarred for life."

"You seem perfectly intact to me." He leaned in and kissed her lips. He hated thinking about Sugar ever hurting and always wanted to come to her rescue when she felt down.

She loved his kisses, but needed to know. "What about you? What do you want from life?"

"I already have everything I want. Don't get me wrong. I thought about kids too. I am not void of feelings. I just don't have any desire to marry. It must be from having been the best man at too many weddings. The happiest day of a person's life turns out to be the saddest. Every relationship starts out wonderful. Marriage works like this." He cleared his throat and spoke with an English accent. "It was the best of times that turned to the worst of times." He dropped the phony inflection. "Hah. Dickens almost had that line right. I decided to make relationships simpler and happier. Two years tops because nothing works much longer after that."

"Then maybe it wasn't real love to begin with."

"Ask yourself, is it worth selling out your own happiness in order to have kids? Is that fair? I'm not saying it's not possible, but even in the best of marriages like my parents', everything is a compromise most of the time. That's really what love is, a constant compromise. Who do you know that's married and happy?"

"I think if you have children, anything is possible. You look past certain things."

"Exactly. Is that what you want? To marry someone like Jon and look past certain things?"

"You shouldn't ask a person who is in love with you that question." The comment slipped out before she had a chance to think about it. She could see it made him extremely uncomfortable and the picnic in the park was over." She tried to regroup and change the dynamic between them, afraid she'd scared him off. She rubbed his arm. "Honey, let's go back to the estate and spend the rest of the afternoon listening to crashing waves and make some of our own. Maybe I'll show you my naked lingerie dance moves if you're a good boy. The ones you wanted to see earlier."

He looked at his watch. "I am not bailing out on you, but Hubert must be there waiting for you by now. Big shopping day ahead. I have some business that I need to take care of. Darling, I'll take you up on that offer later." He held out his hand and helped her up from the blanket.

"Well, don't forget me. OK?" She felt so stupid and small in his business world. "Or at least remember your promise. It's just you and me for the next month or so. No sex with anyone else." Why did she feel like a clingy, insecure heap of nothing. She'd never have dreamed of saying that to anyone her entire life. Sometimes he tore down every ounce of confidence she had without him realizing it. Why couldn't he just feel the same way as she?

* * * * *

The director of the reality TV show pulled Monica away from the cameras and crew that were set up in front of Newport's finest real estate office on Bellevue Avenue. The same street where Prescott lived and the exact address where she planned on renting a home. The crew was shooting a scene featuring the model going inside and talking with an agent about rentals. It was seventh take. So much for spontaneous reality TV.

"Cut," Rocco the director said, pulling Monica aside so they could have a private chat. He put his hand on her shoulder. "Listen, I'm not trying to be a nag, but you're drunk."

He'd been warned his main job was going to be babysitting not directing. But, dealing with her was worse than trying to herd cats. She couldn't even stand up straight.

Monica put her arm on his to balance herself. Wow, was he built, and cute to boot, she thought. A young Rocky Balboa.

"Drinking is good," she said. "Good for the audience. Good so they'll get used to it early on, don'tcha think?" Her words were tumbling over each other.

He smiled in an irked kind of way. "The viewers will get used to your partying once we ease them into it. We can't have the first episode with you looking like a sloppy, hot mess. We want viewers to think of you as a pretty, sweet person with special issues. Once you have a big following, then you can turn into the asshole that you are. They'll love to hate you. But until then...we need the likeability factor in order to get them to tune in." His pained grin said it all.

"Ha - some director you are. Why are we filming the first episode today after everything I've been through?" She pointed to her cheek that barely had a bruise on it left over from the tussle with Prescott. "Let's film something for the fourth episode. How about me and Gina coming out of a bar, drunk in the middle of the afternoon? Yeah - that's the ticket." She started to walk away, then stumbled back towards Rocco. "Yeah, and then Gina and I will steal some kids' bikes and return them later." She yelled at her friend who was talking it up with one of the cameramen. "Let's steal bikes, bitch." Her friend ignored her.

"Are you kidding me?" He could not be more annoyed.

"Would you rather we stole a car?" she asked seriously.

"No! Of course not. We can't steal cars." He shook his head and thought for a moment. The crew was getting anxious, and he worried about them walking off. His instructions were to film everything and anything, then let the editors figure out the rest. Rocco had only signed a one season contract with an option at the discretion of the producers. His job was not secure, and there was a bar just two store fronts away.

He snapped his fingers and pointed at her. "The more I think about it, the bike thing could work. Yeah, stealing bikes. It's sheer genius! You're good, Monica. You're real good." He gave her a pat on the head.

She smiled and whispered. "Well, if you really want to know how good, you should meet me at the Viking Hotel tonight. That's where I'm staying. I'm baaaaaad. Hahaha. And I have a suite." Her sexy voice revealed exactly what she had on her mind.

He took a deep breath. "Ah thanks, but I have a girlfriend."

She rolled her eyes. "Then don't freaking bring her. Are you kidding me? You're going to let something like a stupid girlfriend get in the way of a night of sheer decadence?"

He was surprised she even knew the word.

"If you do good work today and steal some bikes, then how could I say no?" he said quietly. I mean, what kind of an idiot says no to supermodel? Plus, he needed the job security and could sue for harassment later if things went bad.

Monica screamed loudly, "Gina, get over here."

The lanky Italian model stumbled over and put her arm around her best friend.

"What do you need?"

"Go find some kids' bikes to steal. We're going for a ride."

* * * * *

"It's just sex," Prescott kept on repeating to himself during the entire drive back to Boston in his silver Porsche convertible. "It's just sex." That's it, nothing more, so why couldn't he stop thinking about her dancing around in lingerie, taking selfies, and finding it more entertaining than sexy? She was fun, so much fun, yet deep and amazing to talk to when she just let life happen. She was bringing him something that had been missing from his life. A girlfriend. A real girlfriend and not just a new playmate! Someone who stimulated his mind and not just his sexual appetite. Why did she have to ruin it with a four-letter word like L O V E.

"It's just sex," he said out loud while visions of her laughing danced in his head. The little kiss he gave her on the lips as they watched clouds and kites fly by. He could barely concentrate on the road and drifted into the traffic in the oncoming lane. The fast-approaching truck driver hit his brakes and then the horn. Prescott startled and woke up from his Sugar coma. He made a fast right swerve back into his lane. He started to sweat but not from the near-fatal accident. He pulled over to the side of the road while the trucker stuck his middle finger out the window and flew by. Damn it. He had to get this girl out of his life before something really bad happened. Like him falling in love.

In an attempt to clear his mind, he tried to think of every bad characteristic she had and the list wound up being pretty long. But, the more he thought about her quirks, the bigger his smile grew. Like: how she never shut up but said such funny things, and her zany but stimulating mind. Every negative had a positive.

He yelled at himself. "Damn it! You don't even know this girl." His mind drifted back to his first impression of Sugar Lynn Limehouse: "Chubby she-devil who thought far too highly of herself." He questioned how this all happened. Why was he giving a stranger an expensive engagement ring, gifts and a 60-day trial engagement?

He needed a quick Sugar fix. The bachelor's only solution, crazy as it seemed, was to have sex with someone else so that he could put it all in perspective. He had to put some space between his head and heart and stop thinking about her big, almond-shaped green eyes and enticing personality. It wasn't exactly breaking the agreement. The businessman convinced himself it was a necessary part of the deal in order to shift the transaction back in his favor. No she-devil was going to get the better of him. He hopped back in the car and decided to make a stop in Brookline, Massachusetts, instead of going straight to Boston.

Chapter 20

"Oh, Prescott, I never thought it would happen," Kim said while lying in bed next to him in her Brookline condo.

Their "once upon a time" romance ended long ago. But they continued fooling around with each other intermittently for the past 10 years. She was a former actress/model, once married to a famous Patriots football player. Time had changed the dark-haired beauty. She was still stunning but now in graduate school at Harvard studying to be a psychologist, a turn that made her even more attractive to him. But Thor, her pet name for his private part, clearly wasn't in the mood.

She gave him a little nudge and in a sweet voice said, "Anyway, buddy, you need to get going. My son will be home from school soon."

Prescott didn't even want to look her in the eyes. She looked as pretty as ever, but for some reason, he couldn't get it together down below and felt utterly ashamed. For him, performance was never a problem. Maybe when the girl wasn't a 10. But Sugar wasn't a ten, and this never happened with her. Kim scored 100 on a scale of 1 to 10, and he still couldn't perform.

"What's going on with you?" the leggy woman asked. She tried to soothe him by rubbing his arm since he seemed to be feeling down in more ways than one. She had blue eyes that could be seen from across a room, but at this moment, he was avoiding eye contact with her.

He rolled to his side. "I don't know. Just overworked I guess."

"Oh, come on. That's not the problem, and you know it. Talk to me."

He let out a sigh. The words started coming out of his mouth before he had a chance to think. He was not the type to spill his guts.

"I'm not really engaged. I didn't have sex with my cousin. I lost my penthouse. What's right in my life?"

Her mouth fell open, and she half-laughed. "Wait, what did you just say? You had sex with your cousin?"

Oh great, she didn't know. "Don't you watch the news?" he asked. "I'm engaged to her. But not really. It's all just a big mix-up."

She started laughing. "How does someone get mixed up enough to have sex with one of their relatives, then marry her?"

He made no response. She started to tease him, adopting a southern accent. "I forgot you're from North Carolina. That's pretty common with mountain folks. Wait…is that banjo music I hear playing?"

"Ha ha. You make a better lover than comedian," he said in a flat tone. He got out of bed and pulled on his boxer shorts.

"You're becoming a better comedian than lover," she said, pointing to his smiley-face underwear.

Oh no. Monica had bought him all kinds of silly boxer shorts for Christmas. He kept meaning to throw them away.

"Oh crap, I forgot I put these things on," he said while slipping into tan khakis. "Darling, nothing is going my way these days." He continued to avoid looking at her.

"Look me in the eyes," she said.

He rolled his eyes. Some days Kim was spooky, almost psychic, and today was one of those days. He glanced her way but still tried to dodge her stare.

"Oh no, not you! I can see it all over your face. You're in love. Why didn't I notice it before? Prescott Borden in love with his cousin. No wonder it's headline news."

"Now, there you go again. Are you studying human psychology or improvisational comedy?"

He pulled his white rugby shirt over his head.

"I don't need either skill to figure you out. I can read your mind," she said, twirling her long dark curls.

"Well, you're wrong. I'm not in love, and you better not cross me off your list of lovers or friends. I'm always here for you." He walked over and gave her a hug.

She pulled him in close. Her perfume smelled so sweet, and he felt himself finally rising to the occasion. She was appreciative, but declined the offer.

"No, Prescott." She took in a deep breath. "This is the last we'll see of each other. I can't cure you. You're suffering from something far worse than a bad case of spring fever. What you've got is incurable. Trust me, I'm almost a doctor and I once played one on TV." She kissed his cheek. "Now, get out of here and send me a wedding invite that I'll politely decline."

He had no reply even though she was wrong. Dead wrong. He gave her a salute like a soldier following orders and walked out of her first-floor apartment.

His silver 911 was parked in front of the building. It was a sunny, breezy day outside. Warm and friendly. The kind of day that makes you want to ride around with the top down. He opened the door, started the car and put the electric convertible top up. He just wanted to hide out. He kept thinking about where he could go next. The visit to his "doctor" left him even more depressed. He wasted his time driving to her place in an attempt to get Sugar off his mind. Hah! Some psychologist Doctor Kim will be if all her patients left feeling this bad. And what exactly did she mean that he was suffering from something incurable?

He started wondering if Sugar Lynn Limehouse was a curse from the gods. In the ultimate irony, he fell in love with a plus-sized girl who everyone thought was his cousin. This after years of holding himself to the highest standards of dating. Was this really going to be his fate? No way. There wasn't a woman who could pin him down no matter what she weighed. He needed to devise a plan to cut ties with Sugar while still pretending to be happily engaged. But he had to walk a fine line. He couldn't get her upset and cause another public commotion drawing further attention to himself. Maybe a business trip to China without her was the solution.

How could he keep Sugar content without being around? He still needed her in order to save face with those questioning his new personal life and future ability to make sound financial decisions. The sham engagement was the perfect solution, especially after her dad went on TV congratulating the two on their upcoming nuptials. It was time to devise a plan before she ruined everything good in his life - like being able to perform sexually at top-gun level.

He adjusted his rear view mirror but not without taking a look at his profile. Perfecto! There was no way he was falling in love with anyone. He revved up the sports car and sped off, relieved his mojo was back.

* * * * *

"Cut," Rocco, the director of the new reality TV show "Hanging with Miss Dees," yelled.

"That's a wrap," he said. The crew all clapped, and Monica took a bow. She and Gina successfully stole the bikes. Or at least the models thought they did. The assistant director paid off a couple of kids who were riding around with their families. He promised they'd film them all on another day with the star of the show apologizing for "stealing" their bikes.

The scene with the two models attempting to set the "stolen" merchandise on fire could not have been funnier. Because nothing they tried worked, like sparklers stuck in the wheel spokes. They couldn't have looked more ridiculous. Reality entertainment looks best when the "stars" are at their worst. In the final scene for the day, Gina pulled her top off as they cycled through the town holding sparklers in one hand while steering the bikes with the other. They'd just blur out the ta-tas when it aired.

The good townfolk of Newport cleared the sidewalks and smiled and waved as the two-person parade passed by. Funny how when the cameras rolled, unacceptable behavior becomes normal. Everyone wanted their mug filmed. True, some made faces and a few yelled obscenities or covered their children's eyes. But most just smiled.

The hot looking girls rode down Newport's famous Bowen's Wharf and dumped the bikes into the harbor as crew members on $10 million yachts clapped and invited them to come on board. Which they promised to do later.

Monica decided to throw Rocco overboard for a night of partying on board a hundred foot boat. After all, he had a girlfriend and was too broke to even afford a box of sparklers.

That's a wrap!

Chapter 21

Tiffany walked into her hotel room. She felt completely free for the first time in a while. Maybe it was because there was no IV sticking out of her arm. Finally a chance to really rest. She fell down on her bed and closed her eyes. She sat up after catching the scent of fresh flowers. For a moment, it was like being back at the hospital. She opened up her eyes and noticed 24 long-stem roses arranged in a beautiful vase. She pulled out the card.

"Would like to meet for a drink in the Bristol lounge at 5."

She was taken aback. This was indeed intriguing and puzzling. The flowers were in such perfect shape she had no idea they were sent by Prescott a few days earlier, before the Monica disaster. She set her alarm for 4:30 and fell into a coma-like sleep.

* * * * *

Sugar Lynn's day was going better. Shopping with Hubert turned out to be great fun. He had to rush back to Boston for his alter ego Kitty Glitter's performance at the gay karaoke bar. He invited Sugar to go along, but she asked for a raincheck and promised she'd go soon.

She looked around her spectacular bedroom at C-Side. Maybe having lots of expensive things was the answer to love. She sat staring at her engagement ring and the piles of new clothes on the bed. Here she was in Newport's most sought after real estate, inside the world's most eligible bachelor's master bedroom suite overlooking the crashing waves of the Atlantic. Maybe he was right, relationships were only good for two years. She might as well make the most of her 60 days.

She walked out on the balcony to experience the feel of the ocean breeze and to try to absorb the reality of her new, unreal life. The wind was cool and crisp and there was a light, foggy mist covering the City by the Sea. For hundreds of years, the C-side mansion stood strong and resisted the elements even though many generations of previous owners had been laid to rest. She wondered if Prescott's relatives had ever lived there. She didn't know anything about his past. She guessed him to be from old money. There were many antique paintings hung on the walls, and some of their weathered faces resembled him. The estate was full of historic treasures, each one waiting to tell a story. She wanted a guided tour of this larger-than-life home with Prescott, from its exterior white marble walls to the servant's quarters hidden above. When she ventured up there earlier and tried to peek, she came racing back down. The creaky wooden floors seemed to announce her visit to any spirits lurking in the shadows. She'd try again later when Prescott returned.

She wanted to know about his Great-Great-Great Aunt Henrietta coming over on the Mayflower. At least that's what she imagined his tales of family folklore would be about — that and so much more. Maybe even a few scoundrels who tried to kill an imagined Uncle

Albert for the family loot. Surely a man with Prescott's personality had many family skeletons stashed all over the place. Perhaps she would do some exploring on her own and unravel the truth about the man of her dreams who for all practical purposes was still a complete stranger. She had no idea the true mystery of the man was far more intriguing than she imagined. In fact, their pasts had collided before, even though she was unaware of it.

She caught a chill. Newport's island location was always at least 10 degrees cooler than the mainland. Not nearly as warm as it had been in Boston. Her phone rang, and she was relieved to come back inside. For a second, she had a wistful thought: "It's Tiffany." That had always been her first reaction to a ringing phone until less than a week ago. They were in constant communication for years. She sighed. No - it was her father.

"Hi, Daddy," she said.

"Are you okay?" he asked.

"Yes, of course, couldn't be better. Just got back from a shopping spree and staring out over the Atlantic Ocean from his bedroom balcony. La-de-da for me. Why do you ask?"

"Is your fiancé around?"

"No, he's in Boston for a few days while I'm holding down the fort or rather mega-mansion." She couldn't help but brag.

"I'm a little worried about you. I'm glad you're happy, but after I saw the interview with Tiffany, it got me to thinking. What if he tries to hit you?"

"What are you talking about?"

"Tiffany went on TV and said that Prescott had instigated the fight, that he was the first to hit Monica. She apologized for her part too."

"What? What? What?"

"Yeah, it's on all the entertainment shows."

"Dad, thanks, but I have got to go. Don't worry about me for one minute. I can assure you that's not true. Please, whatever you do, do not respond to her allegations. Let me talk to Prescott. This is really important to me. Do you promise me?"

"Sugar, you know Tiffany would never lie."

"Dad, she just did. I was there at the hospital. She told me what happened personally. This is some attempt to get even with me."

"Why would she want to get even with you? You're her best friend."

"Not any more. Oh, my Lord, what in the world has she done? We have a Hollywood deal in the works. Why would she be so stupid?" She was talking more to herself than to her dad. She came back to the real world.

"Now, Dad, you have to keep your mouth shut. This is serious business and might have huge legal implications for everyone. Especially for Prescott. Dad, I really do love him and want to be his wife. Not because of all the glamour but because I LOVE HIM." She paused a moment. She hoped Prescott would give her enough time to figure out he loved her too. This Tiffany fiasco was another roadblock against that happening.

"I won't say a word then. I love you."

"I love you too."

There was a strange silence between the two. Both had said those words without thinking because "I love you" was something they never said to each other. Only on a greeting card during the holidays and then written by some anonymous writer from Hallmark.

They hung up at the same time. Tears fell down her cheeks. She felt terribly conflicted. She started thinking about all the years of being in second place to alcohol and his newspaper. How he ran it into the ground and she had to step up and be the family bread winner. There was never peace between the two but never big fights either. He didn't like conflict and would ignore her for days on end if she tried to bring up any emotional issues. Especially if it concerned her mom who died of alcoholism. That was an out-of-bounds subject. She wanted to know so much more about her. But after her death, he cut off all ties with her mom's family. She vaguely remembered her Grandma and the box of ribbon candy she always had on hand. She was a robust woman who gave her mint chocolate chip ice cream for a special treat. She didn't like it but would pretend it was yummy because it made the big lady with the funny accent happy. As an adult, she wondered what country her grandmother was from but couldn't remember those kinds of details from when she was a child. Or the sound of her Grandma's voice. Sometimes she'd stare into the mirror trying to figure out her facial features and what were her ethnic origins.

On her father's side, they were strictly Irish Catholic even though his mom had been married four times. She was a hard woman with a giant personality and a taste for beer. Quite a novelty in her day. Working class men loved her. She prayed the rosary daily and frequented the bars at night along with her husband, or rather husband at the moment. She was actually married five times because she married one man twice. Two of her exes became best friends and kept in touch with her every now and then.

Even though her grandmother Marion O'Brien was outgoing and witty, Sugar couldn't talk to her about anything because she was so loyal to her son. What he said was the law. That's how she treated all her men until they got on her nerves. Her son never did. No matter what trouble he caused, she'd make excuses for him. "Mimi" (her nickname) wasn't a girl's girl and wished Sugar had been a boy. She liked the company of men, and the little girl seemed too clingy after her mother died. Her dad and grandmother ganged up on the child, and she became the source of many problems between the two. She was neglected and emotionally cut off.

Her only friend through it all was Tiffany. Tiff's mom became her surrogate mother. She'd comb her hair and make sure she was bathed and looked nice. Sadly, the sweet woman passed away a year later from breast cancer. The two girls took care of each other while their Dads did whatever it was they did. Worked and drank and didn't say much.

All these memories came rushing back to Sugar at the same moment she was trying to process the evil her former best friend had unleashed on Prescott. What would make her do such a thing? Her heart weighed heavy as the words of her best friend's text haunted her mind. About how Sugar had treated her so badly for many years and made her life impossible. Always pushing her to do things her way and never letting her just be herself.

Maybe it was because she was never shown much love herself. Often-times, hurt people lash out and hurt others. Maybe she had done unto others what had been done to her. All the adults in her life pushed their will on the little girl. She had to accommodate her needs to the very people who were supposed to take care of her. Instead of loving Sugar, they ignored any of her emotional concerns.

But, isn't that what she did to Tiffany all these years? She fell down on her knees and started to sob. The thought of her Dad saying "I love you," the memories of her sad childhood and now her lost friendship overwhelmed her heart. She didn't really believe in God or that if he did exist that he cared about her at all. So, she prayed to her mom's spirit as she done many times as a child and asked for help.

"Momma, I know I haven't talked to you in a while but I need you. I so need you right now. Please send me a sign about what to do. Something so obvious I'll know the right answer. In some ways, my whole life has been a search for you. Looking for things that would make you proud of me. I'm sure you're not proud right now with the news of my life broadcast for all the world to see. And all the lies I'm living. I didn't mean any harm to anyone during all this. Most times, I just go forward full steam ahead without thinking. But, now I am not so sure what's right or wrong. Help me."

Chapter 22

Tiffany signed the legal documents stating she had received payment in full, releasing the hotel from any further obligations from her injuries. She was excited about leaving for Newport in the morning. She'd have some time to recover from her injuries and get the first real vacation of her lifetime. Then a weekend with the hottest doctor who had ever examined her. Ooh-la-la. She was hoping to be a little more recovered from her injuries when Dr. DeAngelo arrived so he could see how pretty she was. The same kind of pretty that Prescott Borden did back flips over. The attractive blond had no idea that black belt Monica was staying at the exact same hotel she'd be checking into. Or that the hotheaded model was on a drinking bender with her out-of-control friend Gina and wreaking havoc on the town already. Or that Sugar Lynn Limehouse was living in Prescott's seaside mansion a half-mile away. She just thought it was all going be fun in the sun with $300,000 in her back pocket and a two week, free stay.

She left the management offices grinning like a groupie who just was given a front row ticket to a sold-out show. Which was true in more ways than one. She was getting a first row seat all right! She had no idea that the latest contract she'd signed with the devil included an oversized spotlight waiting to shine directly on her. And not because *Marble House* was debuting on Broadway. A whole new screenplay with her as the leading lady was about to unfold.

She wanted to make sure Prescott was nowhere around and inquired at the front desk to see if he was checked in. The answer was a firm "no" from Jackie O. The same girl who originally started the media frenzy with the text about the model trashing the bachelor's penthouse suite. The same girl who was forbidden by management to ever say if a famous guest was checked in or not. The same girl that almost got fired thanks to the billionaire player. The same girl who today added a card with Tiff's flowers because she knew Prescott had drinks at 5 every day in the lounge.

Ha-ha. Jackie might not be able to contact the media again, but there was nothing wrong with stirring the pot for the sake of personal entertainment. The best kind of revenge.

The receptionist whispered, "Between you and me, he's checked out for a few days. He went to New York," knowing it was completely false. She saw him getting on the elevator a few minutes ago and knew he'd be returning soon for a cocktail. The trap was set.

The receptionist spoke under her breath. "I don't blame you for never wanting to see him again. He's bad news. Hey, it's happy hour at the bar. You deserve it after all you been through." She smiled.

"Thank you." Tiffany felt relieved.

Yes, indeed. The playwright needed a drink before meeting the mystery man who sent her roses and without the fear of running into Sugar's cousin. She was sickened thinking about the two of them and their escapades. Besides, everything was going her way. Another new admirer was a few steps away. She was starting to feel like a starlet with a busy roster of men hoping to spend time with her.

The people in the lounge all turned to stare at the bandaged woman. Many recognized her from the tabloids. They whispered amongst themselves about her being front page news and wondered what she was doing there. Some saw her press conference earlier in the day dissing Prescott.

She ignored the gawking. Who cared what they thought. "You're a short time alive and a long time dead" was her new motto. Maybe she'd put it on a bumper sticker of the used car she planned on purchasing in Rhode Island. Hopefully an old Boxster or BMW convertible. She liked older-looking cars and their prices too. Nothing too extravagant. She gave herself a $20,000 budget for what she figured would be the purchase of a lifetime. Something she could keep as a memento. A gift that would signify a new beginning and attitude for the small town girl who was no longer settling for a small time life and what others thought.

She sat at a wooden tall table with two chairs across from one another in anticipation of a guest joining her soon. She didn't wait for a waitress. She gave a wave to the bartender. "Gin and tonic." She didn't even say please. She stared at the mirrored wall directly in front of her. She looked awful but didn't bother to switch seats. For the first time in her life she was happy with the person she saw on the inside.

* * * * *

Gina sat in the hotel suite reading a text while Monica blow dried her hair. Most people would have needed to rest after such an exhausting day, but the non-stop party girls kept on rolling. They'd been lounging around for a little bit, drinking and watching celebrity news, including Tiffany's apology, but mostly hoping to see themselves. They weren't disappointed. Photos of their infamous bike trip were popping up everywhere, including Gina's bare-chested ride, looking like Lady Godiva except on two wheels. They cracked up. They were exhilarated seeing themselves, and it overcame their fatigue. They planned on napping, but it just wasn't happening. Too much excitement in the air. So they decided to go out and party some more.

"OMG." She yelled loud enough that Monica shut off her blow dryer.

"What the hell?" she asked.

"You have to read this. Get over here."

"Don't tell me something else went wrong. What did Prescott do, call me a liar and file a suit? I figured he was too much of a gentleman for that kind of crap."

"No, it's worse. You need to see this text."

Monica walked over, grabbed the phone and started reading aloud.

"Saw your performance on TV today. You're a whore. Don't bother coming back to New York. The locks are being changed as I type. All your crap including the clothes are staying since I bought it all anyway. It was a loan not a gift. Feel free to call my wife because she's known about you for a year. She just has enough class to say nothing and not ride through any old town drunk and naked on a kid's bike. Have fun on your reality TV show with your slutty friend. Or should I say your new sugar daddy? She owns you now. Come anywhere near me, and you'll have an order of protection and some unfriendly types covering your bare naked ass. You know EXACTLY what I mean. Jeffery."

"What does he mean? What does he mean?" Monica asked twice.

"He's talking about a guy they had beat up in prison for ratting on him and some buddies to the feds over insider trading." She put her head down in shame as big tears rolled down. Mostly because she realized he was not kidding around and Jeffery was a scary character when crossed. That informant mysteriously died too, but she decided not to mention it.

"What a dick."

"Jeffery looks like a short, harmless bean counter but he's one nasty prick. He's done all kinds of bad things to his enemies, but I never thought I'd be one. What am I going to do?" she cried.

"You're not going to do anything. Like he said, I own you now. You'll come work on my TV show, get paid, and as long as you do exactly what I say, then I'll make sure you're never fired. And if you don't, then good riddance. But you never have to worry that I'll hire someone to screw you over. Because that's what friends are for."

"What are you talking about? Friends don't screw each other over."

"Exactly. They don't do it themselves. They hire people to do it for them. But I'm not that kind of person, unless your name is Sugar Limehouse. Or that Tiffany what's-her-name? I'm not letting her steal $300,000 from me and get away with it. Her on-air apologies weren't enough. And you're going to help me. We're partners now."

"OMG, you touch my heart so." She went to hug her friend.

"No, don't. My hair is almost perfect. I don't want to mess it up. Get dressed and let's go."

She took a second look at Gina, who still looked really overwhelmed by Jeffery's text.

Monica leaned in close to her. "Hey, if you don't want to go anywhere tonight, we'll just stay in and have a girl's slumber party." She put her arm around her friend.

"I'd really like that."

The redhead picked up the phone. "Room service? We need three chilled bottles of your best champagne." She winked at Gina and said to her, "You can take that off my bill from the money I owe you."

* * * * *

Prescott sat at the head of the dining room table in his soon-to-be-former penthouse. Hard to believe he was saying goodbye. He wasn't feeling disappointed over losing his Boston home, just empty. Like something should be there that wasn't. He hoped to God his feelings had nothing to do with missing Sugar. Something needed to be done about his feelings for her. He'd only known this girl for a few days. What the hell was wrong with him?

He pulled out his laptop and started writing a Dear Jon letter to his friend the consultant with that name. The same man he asked to leave his house because his flirting with Sugar made him furious. Thankfully, Prescott didn't make a scene and handled it like a gentleman. He politely explained that something came up and he would like to reschedule on a later date. Still, it was awkward reaching out since Jon had originally planned on staying the night. And Prescott hadn't returned any of his phone calls.

Dear Jon,

I just wanted to apologize for my behavior the other day. Too many long hours.

I hope you'll still work with Sugar. She needs help and has 50 employees whose jobs may end soon. This is a 30-year-old family owned publication, with no current market value. If you could help her out on this, I'd be most appreciative. I will pay your standard fees and expenses.

Give me a call to discuss details.

Best,

Prescott

He debated if he should hit send. But this was his only hope of getting her off his mind and giving her a life that he was unwilling to provide. A chance at marriage and having a family. Let those two fall in love and she'd be happy, which would make him feel good about letting her go. He didn't want to disappoint her any longer. This way, everyone wins, including Jon. So why then did he feel like a loser? Like he'd lost something far greater than just his beloved penthouse. He convinced himself the condo was the real source of him feeling so choked up.

He knew Jon would respond and step up to the plate and work with Sugar for a number of reasons. The consultant specialized in turnarounds and worked primarily with publications, generally putting smaller businesses together to form a powerful conglomerate. His friend grew up in the newspaper business and his family currently owned a popular magazine. He had taken a struggling farming publication to the national spotlight as a "Food to Table" magazine featuring organic eating. He'd saved and created many jobs. No one had a heart bigger for this type of work than his good friend.

He knew Jon liked Sugar as much as he did. He never saw him act like that with any woman before, including his first wife who left him a single father of a little boy. They were roommates for six months as he helped him get back on his feet from that terrible ordeal. They'd been friends since their days at college. Never once did he remember Jon so captivated with anyone besides his kids.

The two newspaper publishers were meant for each other. He hit send. That was that. He needed some human company and decided to get his last drink at his long time hangout and enjoy the company of his old friend, Henry the bartender, who'd been there since Prescott was in business school.

* * * * *

Jackie O chuckled as she watched Prescott get off the elevator and head into the Bristol Lounge. She even waved to him, but he didn't acknowledge it.

The wide-eyed looks on people's faces seated at tables in the restaurant's dining area seemed far more intense than usual to the handsome bachelor who always turned heads. What's up with that? It must be from the whole cousin thing, he thought to himself. He had no clue the patrons had just observed Tiffany headed in the same direction. He walked a few steps up to the bar where there were only a few people standing around. He checked out the back of a blond woman's head. He considered himself an expert on good looking women, even from behind. Rarely was he wrong, and the woman turned out to be unattractive. With the exception of rock star Justin Strange, whose long, dark, wavy locks didn't belong on a guy that gruesome. It gave him the shakes for two days.

Henry the barkeep waved to him in an unusual way, like he was holding up a stop sign, and started shaking his head, "No." Prescott walked over, not picking up on the signals.

"Don't tell me the press turned you on me too," he laughed. "Aren't you happy to see me?"

Henry pointed at the blond woman sitting less than a foot away with her back to them. Confused, Prescott walked to the front of her small table. Who is this mystery lady?

"You have got to be kidding me. What is wrong with you? Things not going well with your cousin?" Tiffany couldn't believe those words were coming out of her mouth. She was overwhelmed with all the inner hostility she had towards him, completely forgetting she'd lied to the world about an innocent man.

"Darling, you need to slow down there."

"What are you doing sending me flowers? What's wrong with you?"

"I didn't send you flowers."

"You're so full of yourself. Of course you did." Her voice was louder than she anticipated. She paused. She could feel all eyes were upon her. You could hear a fork drop since everyone wanted to hear what happened next. A few onlookers pulled out their cell phone cameras, hoping to catch the next big wave of celebrity gossip.

Prescott sat down and smiled like everything was normal and lowered his voice. Oh great, another tabloid moment.

He whispered, "I didn't send you flowers."

Tiffany rolled her eyes and handed him the card but smiled as if to say: Everything is normal here.

"This isn't from you?" She mocked him in the quietest tone possible.

He looked at it and shook his head.

"No. I didn't send this. But, yes, I did send you flowers, but that was days ago, before we met."

She started to laugh. "What kind of freak are you? You sent me these before we even met? Did you set up the fight too?" She started to stand up.

"Shhhhhh. Sit down. Just stop. Let me just tell you something. One thing and then you can go."

She sat back down worried about drawing more attention to herself. She had enough already.

"Sugar is heartsick over you. We have a deal for *Marble House* with Hollywood. You need to stop thinking she's against you. She loves you." Prescott was always a man of his word and intended to deliver on it, even if he and Sugar were over.

"You have a Hollywood deal for me? Hah. What kind of bullshit is this? After today's press conference, you went out and got me a Hollywood commitment. What are you trying trick me into now?" Her words convicted her the second they came out. She held her hand over her mouth in shame over what she had done and knew she had been busted.

"There is no trick. The deal is ready to close and only needs your signature. Wait – what did you say? Press conference. What press conference would that be?"

Tiffany's face shone bright red, even through her white bandages. Prescott's heart started to beat faster. He scrolled through his cell phone looking for a news update as she made a fast exit with patrons' cameras rolling.

Chapter 23

Sugar woke up at 2 a.m., confused and dripping in sweat. She had a horrible dream about a car crash. She was in the accident but observing from outside the scene as well. She saw herself covered in glass and blood. Her eyes were open as if she had died. She leaned in close and tried to shake her other self. There was no movement from the body. Her green eyes looked haunted and had no spark of life. She screamed for help. Prescott jumped out of the car and appeared unscathed from the incident. He looked at both Sugars: the one in the accident and the one begging for help. He turned his back and walked away. She yelled out his name. "Prescott!"

The sound of her panic-stricken voice woke her up. Was the dream an omen of things to come?

She was scared. The kind of terror you experience after seeing a horror film. She turned on a light at the side of the bed and tried to calm her racing heart. She got up and walked into the master bathroom and turned on the lights. The white marble room was too bright, but she didn't dim down the harsh glare. She needed to see the naked truth in the mirror, but was almost too spooked to look at herself.

She turned on the cold water, splashed some on her face and looked up. She almost didn't recognize herself. Her newly colored, dark reddish hair didn't look good without makeup. Her skin was washed out and looked pale. Too pale for the living, she thought. Her semi-permanent eye lashes were the only thing making her look pretty. But they weren't real either. Just like her life.

She put on one of Prescott's robes hanging from their brass wall hooks. There were four of them altogether, each one with his initials embroidered on the front. Property of Prescott Borden, they seemed to be shouting.

She walked back into the master suite and sat back down on the king-size bed. The grandeur of the room opened up her eyes in a way she hadn't considered before. Not in the same way it had when she first entered wide-eyed with loads of shopping bags filled with designer clothes. Like Cinderella after finding out the glass slipper fit and making herself at home in her new castle in the sky even it was for only 60 days.

The room seemed empty now, even though it was filled with treasures acquired from around the world. A rug from Tibet with vibrant colors made from vegetable dye that took two years to create. An old, wooden seaman's trunk at the end of a hand-carved sleigh bed imported from Spain. Newly sewn pillows, created to match the burnt orange European drapes made in the 1800s, were scattered all over the floor along with bags of clothes and boxes of shoes.

She had fallen asleep while praying to her mother for guidance. It was eight hours later, and the clock had already struck midnight. The size seven shoes fit, but there was no fairy godmother to tell her what to do or think next after her Prince Charming ran away from hearing the words, "I love you." Nothing was making sense to her. She was just too far out of her comfort zone to collect her thoughts.

She checked her cell phone. There were no calls or texts from him. She frantically dialed his number. Maybe he could save her from the thoughts of "What am I doing? I don't belong here." The emergency call rang and rang. What was he doing that was so important that he could forget all about her?

The unanswered phone call, along with no texts from him since yesterday, seemed to be sending the same message as his unspoken words. "I'll never be there for you." Maybe he never directly said those things, but isn't that what it all amounted to? A temporary business arrangement mixed with a lot of pleasure. Then goodbye forever.

There was no emotional depth to their relationship on his part. She was a commoner, hired help for that matter, and way out of his league. The only reason she was queen for the day was because of having sex in a hallway and all the confusion created by the press. Otherwise, she'd be nothing more than a one-night stand. Like so many others before her.

She wanted to believe that her feelings for him would change his heart and mindset. That he'd come to love her as she loved him. Was having so much stuff the consolation prize for women who had little emotional support from the wealthy men they loved? Or maybe they just sold out. But, everything in the mansion was just on loan to her. Nor did she care about any of it. She didn't really want those things, she wanted Prescott Borden for her soul mate, best friend and confidant.

She felt a disturbance in her heart. She laid down on the bed and looked up at a heavy crystal chandelier with gold trim hanging over her. Not a spot of dust. Sparkling as if it were brand new. An heirloom that been hanging there for centuries. Was it really secure and not going to come crashing down on her? Of course not, because it was handled and hung with museum quality care.

Was Prescott capable of caring for her in the same way he did his priceless works of art and his manor home? She pondered the question and kept going back to his own words and how they made her feel. She simply wasn't good enough for a guy like him. Not tall, not young, not skinny, not well dressed, not smart enough to run her own publication. Even her hair was the wrong color. She didn't remotely resemble all the beautiful things that he'd accumulated, including people. Ironically, the objects he treasured while the people he dismissed. She wasn't in the same league as his other lovers. They'd just move on and find another rock star and easily forget him because they never cared in the first place.

What would become of her? She'd be packed up and sent back to Charleston with a broken heart. How could she be so stupid as to fall for him? In that moment, she determined that Sugar Lynn Limehouse with all her infectious zeal for life could never be enough for Prescott. When the 60 days were up, he'd just walk away and leave her for dead. Just like in her dream – a sure sign from her mom.

She'd have to shut down all her feelings for him in order to continue with the charade of being engaged. He was like owning the Boardwalk property in a game of Monopoly. Just a temporary investment that made game players winners. She hated that kind of thinking, but what choice did she have? She needed to use him in order to save the people who really cared about her. She needed to gain back their confidence. Like Tiffany, who deserved to have her play on Broadway or Hollywood despite trashing Prescott at the press conference. She was her best friend and always believed in her up until now. Or all her employees who needed their jobs at the newspaper. Many had been working for the Charleston Gazette for years and had families to support. Some were having doubts about Sugar, given the sex video and Tiffany quitting. They no longer felt their jobs were secure. She was getting phone calls from other publications asking for references on her top people. And what about her dad? He was so concerned for his daughter's well-being that he called to warn her about Prescott. He even said, "I love you," something she'd never hear from Prescott Borden no matter how hard she tried.

Even if she lost twenty pounds she still wouldn't be good enough. There would always be someone prettier, younger, thinner, and more perfect waiting to take her place, and he'd keep looking for that opportunity. Because qualities like being loyal, understanding, joyful and fun loving, not to mention being totally in love, weren't of any value to a guy like him. Not someone who believed relationships were only good for two years.

She got up and grabbed her laptop out of her suitcase. The same pink suitcase that held her folded up pink pants suit that he despised. She wanted to put it on as a show of defiance but decided it WAS pretty damn ugly. She sat back down on the massive bed and googled Jon Perry's name. Maybe she could cut a deal with the consultant. He'd give her some upfront cash in exchange for ownership of the paper and she could at least move out of the mansion, a place she no longer felt comfortable in. It just reminded her of all the things she was not.

She couldn't call off the engagement. She still needed Prescott to finish Tiffany's deal and to silence all rumors of the two of them being cousins. People were mocking her openly on social media with the incest rumors. And how she was a pig compared to his other girl-friends. A real bunch of haters.

She'd make sure that in 60 days her name was clear and that she was the one who broke up with him. She was going to leave on her terms and with some dignity. Not feeling like she was worthless to him, or to anybody else for that matter. She had enough of hating herself for caring too much about him.

Everything about her outgoing manner and fast talk was a front for feeling unloved and lost inside. She was still that little girl looking for an adult hand to hold on to. Someone to guide her. She thought Prescott was that special someone who'd pick up on that vibe and show her the way. She admired his charm and certainty about life. But he couldn't be trusted. He was just too damn far removed from his own heart. Hell, maybe he didn't even have one.

How does a person become so cold? That's what she intended to find out in order to be like him. Successful and untouchable. Having feel-ings hurt too much. She'd go on a scavenger hunt tomorrow looking for clues about what made him tick. Like when she'd gone up to the servants quarters earlier but got too scared and changed her mind. She was going to figure him out and what made him the man he is today and master every one of his skills. She hoped it would not be at the cost of her soul.

Every home had hidden secrets, and she'd be sure he had nowhere to hide, even if he was going to stay hidden emotionally from her.

* * * *

The two models had been up drinking. Neither had a bite to eat other than chocolate-covered strawberries. They both were bombed but still capable of intelligent speech for a change of pace. Usually by 3 a.m., they'd still be at the clubs practically passed out but still trying to party on.

They laid on top of the king size bed with chocolate stains all over the covers. The music was blaring with the TV on, and they were chugging directly from their last bottle of champagne. Gina checked her texts and started jumping up and down on the bed like a little kid.

"Sugar is a pig. Sugar is a pig," she said over and over in a na-na-nah kind of way. "I started it, and now all these people are following." She squealed in delight.

Monica stood up and tried to grab her friend's cell phone to see what she was talking about. The quick motion caused them both to tumble onto the floor. Bam! The fall was a hard one. Gina's nose started bleeding right away.

"You broke my freaking nose," she yelled

"NO, I didn't. You were the one acting the fool." Monica stood up. "Don't move."

She got up, grabbed a towel and dunked it in the ice bucket intended for the champagne.

"There now. Just lay down with this."

"No, I need a doctor. I want to see a doctor. I don't want my face effed up."

"You're face has been effed up ever since you got that ridiculous nose job."

"You better shut up," she said, while blood dripped all over her.

"If you can't have me telling you the truth, then who will? Jeffrey? Hah!"

"EFF you."

"You better not be talking to me like that bitch."

Their words were getting louder and louder.

"You want your walking papers now? Because you're my employee, and it's best not to bite the hand that feeds you." She was half tempted to whack her on the head.

There was a knock at the door. Both women froze. Monica started racing around and shutting off the TV and music.

"Get in the bathroom," she whispered.

"NO, I want to go to the hospital now."

"NO." She tried to lift her friend, who smacked her across the face in return.

Monica grabbed her hands.

"You listen to me, and you listen good. Get in that freaking bathroom or I'll kill you."

"NO!"

The knock got louder.

"Is everything OK in there," the hotel security guard asked.

"Just give me a minute." Monica yelled. She turned to Gina and whispered. "Look, if you don't hide right now, they are going to cart you off to the hospital and everyone will think I DID IT. No matter what you say. I'll lose my job, and you'll never get your money back."

"If you don't want me going to the hospital, then you're going to sign a contract with me tonight that I am your equal partner on your new show and that you will be paying me as your co-star."

"No way am I doing that! Hey, if I don't get paid, you don't get paid. It's just that simple."

The knocking increased.

"If you don't open this door, I am going to get the police and come in." The guard was being overly dramatic. He just wanted to meet the supermodel in person.

"I'll tell the police you kicked me in the face and everything's all a lie. You hurt that girl, and me too, and just paid her off." The Italian girl had learned a thing or two hanging out with Jeffery and with the Jersey shore crowd.

Monica looked at her friend's smashed up face. Her eyes were already turning black and blue and started to swell.

"Oh, screw you - fine. Now get in the bathroom."

"OK, well if you think you're going to change your mind and not sign in five minutes, I'm calling the police myself."

And that's how "Hanging with Miss Dees" turned into a reality show headlining two scuzzy models, not just one.

Chapter 24

The sun was bright in the master suite at C-Side. Orange hues from the heavy drapes filled the room, along with the smell of coffee and bacon compliments of the help. It was amazing how the smell of food could fill a small house or even a mega mansion.

Sugar rubbed her eyes. Morning had arrived at the castle, and she didn't turn into a pumpkin for not fitting in. Perhaps she'd been a little harsh with her judgements. She was, after all, startled by her dream and hurt by not hearing from Prescott. Maybe she let her imagination run wild like in the fairy tale "Cinderella" when the mice became coachmen. It was just a make believe story. And the exterminator took care of any rodents at this beast of a home.

She smiled, feeling like there was no reason to completely give up hope on Prince Charming because he resided here and not in a children's story. She checked her cell phone in anticipation of getting a message from him.

What she saw instead was a text from her dad.

"Did you see this? Call me when you wake up."

She clicked on the link to gossip columnist Barry Banister. The same one who interviewed Tiffany twice. Once to talk about the engagement to Sugar and the second telling the world: "It was Prescott's fault. He is the one who hit Monica first."

Sugar's heart started to race and her hands shook. *Oh no. What was happening now?*

"Guess who had drinks with Prescott Borden last night? Was it super-model Monica Dees, who from all accounts he was dating, when the relationship ended two days ago after he slapped her across the face? Or did he have dinner with playwright Tiffany James, who was injured in the knockdown between the infamous couple? He claimed Tiffany was the love of his life but changed his mind and decided to marry his cousin Sugar Lynn Limehouse instead. This story is so weird even I don't know what to think anymore. Yesterday, Tiffany accused Prescott of beating up Monica but then had a romantic rendezvous with the billionaire. Earlier, he was seen making out with his cousin Sugar, who is currently living in his Newport mansion. This in the same town where Monica's new TV show is filming. The plot line looks pretty intriguing because Dees and a model friend rode naked through the town holding sparklers! Don't believe me? Click on the link - the pictures say a thousand words. Stay tuned because I am not going to quit on this trashy cast of characters until the truth be told!"

* * * * *

Tiffany woke up relieved to be in Newport. The confrontation with Prescott made her run away rather than expose herself to more guilty feelings. She didn't want to take another chance of having to face him again and checked out of Boston permanently. She paid for her first night stay at the expensive Viking Hotel rather than risk another episode of feeling bad about herself. Still, she didn't sleep well. She felt like the thunderous waves outside her balcony window were about to drown her.

She kept telling herself that he was a liar and there was no Hollywood deal. And even if there was, she couldn't handle his ridiculously elaborate schemes and having "cousin" Sugar back in her life. *What that hell was that all about anyway?* When she first met the handsome bachelor, he seemed smitten with her. She thought there might be a possibility that she was destined to be his next love interest. They were supposed to be a "couple in love" in order to save her play and get the press writing about *Marble House*. Go to Los Angeles together. Make money. Maybe even really fall in love in the process.

His motive was to save his own butt from Monica, is what she reminded herself over and over. It had nothing to do with him liking her - but then why did he send her those flowers before they ever met? Or did he lie about that in their most recent meeting? Were the flowers and the meeting at the Bristol Lounge by design and just another attempt to scam her out of something else? He already stole her best friend. Was *Marble House* next on his agenda of things to use to ruin someone else's life? Most likely, he was going to steal her work and pay nothing but a tiny percentage for her years of effort. He was just bad news and not to be trusted.

The problem was, everything Prescott predicted came true. The press went wild, and Hollywood was knocking. Only now there was no one to open the door.

She'd have to do it all on her own with $300,000 in her account less $500 for the room and two large for the Town Car ride there.

Seven hundred bucks. How did the rich stay rich? By investing of course, but $300,000 wouldn't go far in New York or L.A.

If she was going to play the game and get herself noticed with potential investors, she needed to look the part. Newport was a perfect place to meet so-called "yacht owners" in need of another hobby besides wearing sailor hats, blue-and-white-striped shirts, and hitting golf balls off the deck while hired hands fished them out of the water. A hobby like producing a Broadway show, her original goal. She needed to put on her investigative reporter's hat and figure out how to play the role. But one thing for sure, she needed a new wardrobe. One that reeked of success and a car that turned heads as much as her smile. She couldn't come across like the naive small-town girl who just got lucky to have a smash hit on the Boston stage. Which for all practical purposes was the truth. If it had not been for the ill-fated hit from Monica, that play would have opened and closed without anyone ever noticing. Monica saved the day. So, in some ways, she was in debt to her. Yes, that's how she could justify her actions with Prescott. Because of the black belt, she had another kind of hit: *Marble House*. It was all thanks to the supermodel.

And to think, she had no idea her "good friend" was only a few floors up, playing nurse to a new patient with a broken nose, Gina.

* * * * *

Sugar finished reading about Prescott and Tiffany having drinks together and tried to absorb the meaning of it all. She clicked on a link from the article to photos that she thought would be Monica's naked ride through the city.

They captured Tiffany and Prescott smiling at each other. Both looked quite content holding their drinks and enjoying each other's company at the swanky bar. Another, a snap of Sugar grinning, holding bags of clothes and having a conversation with Hubert. Then one of her and Prescott at the diner holding hands across the table. Spies are everywhere, all thanks to social media, where everyone's a photojournalist. A shot of Monica and Gina riding through Newport with their tatas blocked out, even though only one was actually topless. The beauty of the "blur" is no one knows what's actually showing.

Damn it. Prescott and Tiffany really did meet up and looked happy together. *What the hell? And how in the world were there pictures of me shopping and... What? Monica really is in Newport too?* Her brain was as scrambled as the cold eggs waiting for her to eat in the kitchen.

The phone rang. It said "unknown number." She hesitated to pick it up, scared to death of what to expect next.

"Hello?"

"Hello, Sugar Lynn Limehouse. This is Jon Perry."

"Oh Jon. Oh my. Hi." She half wondered if he knew that she'd looked him up on LinkedIn last night. *Oh crap, of course he did since it shows profile hits.* She'd forgotten about that feature.

"I'm looking forward to having dinner with you and Prescott tonight. Reservations are for 7 p.m., but I might be running a few minutes late. I need you to bring the newspaper's financials with you, even though it's a social occasion. It will give me a chance to review them later."

She was completely taken aback. She cleared her throat so as to not sound like she was about to choke. "Dinner? Where? Dinner with you and me? And did you say Prescott is going?" *What was that dirty rat up to now*, she wondered.

"Yeah, we talked this morning and he gave me your number. He's going to meet us at the White Horse Tavern. I hear it's the oldest restaurant in town and the first tavern in America and haunted too. We'll be drinking with the ghosts of many lushes past." He was trying to sound witty but not too unprofessional. Trying to be an interesting type of guy. The kind of guy she'd want to know better. He too had just seen the photos of Tiffany out with Prescott and was holding onto a little hope. Besides there was no way his "player" friend was capable of a long-term relationship.

He was still angry over being kicked out of the mansion by him and ended up driving to Providence since all the rooms in town were booked. Under normal circumstances, he'd never do business again with his old friend after being treated so disrespectfully. Jon may not have Prescott's money, but he was worth ten million and didn't take crap from anyone, even if he did flirt with his "cousin." As far as he was concerned, it was game on. The meeting tonight was more than just business. *Eye on the prize*, he thought. He wanted to win her heart.

Sugar continued. "Well, dinner sounds quite lovely, but everywhere I go, and Prescott too, it causes a big media fuss. Maybe we should all just grab a bite to eat here. I don't like waking up to page 6 gossip."

"Who would want to be a six when they're a 10?" *Oh no, did that just come out of my mouth?*

Sugar giggled.

Score! She was amused, so he pushed his luck. "Maybe I can get out of my meeting early. I could be there at 6. Just the two of us?" *Ouch. Great job, moron,* he thought to himself.

The photos of Tiffany and Prescott having drinks and smiling away kept flashing through Sugar's mind. They looked like goofball kids at an elementary school playground declaring their undying love for one another while swinging on the monkey bars of life. *What a bunch of crap,* she thought.

To hell with Prescott and his games. "In fact, forget about the media frenzy, let's meet at the restaurant. Let's make a little gossip news ourselves and have fun. Are you up for a good time?" Ha - she'd show that no good, two-timing fiancée of hers. She'd throw her affection for Jon in his freaking face tonight at dinner. It was about time someone put him in his player place.

"Asshole," she said to herself. Damn, she hated swearing, but there were no 50 cent words to describe her soon-to-be ex. And jerk was not strong enough.

There was dead silence.

"Did you just call me an asshole?"

Oh crap, I said it out loud.

"No, no, no. I said, umm rascal. You're quite the rascal." Thank God a rhyme came to mind.

"See you tonight."

"For sure!"

* * * * *

"You don't have much to say today. Do you feel proud of yourself? You forced me into being your business partner, and now I get the silent treatment? Not that I care. Nails on a chalkboard sound like Mozart compared to your nasally whines." Monica spoke to Gina as they sat having breakfast on their hotel balcony. Or rather coffee with non-fat cream. The breakfast of champions for models.

"I am purposely trying not to speak and move my face too much so my nose stays in place," she said, while barely moving her lips and keeping her teeth gritted together. "I'd like to punch you in the face, but I can't take a chance and move that fast."

"Don't be a fool, I'm a black belt and capable of breaking your neck if provoked."

The phone rang. Monica went inside to answer it.

"Hello?"

"Miss Dees, this is Howard from hotel security. Remember me? We met early this morning."

"Sure, I remember." *Fat boy with horn rim glasses.* "It's not often I'm asked for an autograph at 3 a.m. after I'd fallen asleep with the TV and radio on."

"Well, I just wanted to give you heads up. It seems you might have a stalker hanging around."

"A stalker? What are you talking about?"

"Tiffany James. I believe she's the same person who said that Prescott Borden harmed you. I just wanted you to be aware she is in the building and that I'd be happy to escort you around in case there is trouble."

"She's here?"

He looked at his computer. "Yes, checked in last night and staying for two weeks. I'll be at your beck and call if there is any issue. I am ready in a flash if there's a problem!"

Monica rolled her eyes. *Hah. As if a guy wearing a size 26 uniform and actually needing one in a 28 could waddle that fast.*

"No thanks, I am perfectly capable...wait. Wait, wait just a minute." *YES!* She held her hand in the power fist like a fan of a football team that just scored the winning touchdown.

She grinned and put on a soft helpless type of voice. "That would be so kind of you. I really am concerned for my safety with her around. I need you protecting me. Will you be sure to keep an eye on her comings and goings and report to me? Are you able to follow her around and not be seen? For my security, in case she tries to hurt me again? I'll give you my private cell phone number, but we'll need to be in touch constantly." She said the word "constantly" in her best sexy voice. "I don't want to be a bother."

He cleared his throat and starting to speak in a higher than usual tone like the idea was too much for his heart to handle. "I am getting off now, so I will have lots of time today." He got a hold of himself and now spoke in a deeper than normal kind of way. "You'll be safe in my hands. I have an online degree in the art of espionage. I know that does not sound like much and may be laughable but this was at a school in Russia taught by agents who were former KGB. I am not at liberty to say much more."

Oh, for gosh sakes. She was peeing her pants and bent over trying not to crack up. How'd she ever get her next words out? She had no idea. Only she could find a stool pigeon who fancied himself a foreign-trained spy with underwear as large as Moscow.

"From Russia with love. What's your rate?" She covered up the phone mouth piece and started to laugh like someone in church who was struck by something funny but trying not to lose it. She smacked her own face in an attempt to get it together.

"What? I have no rates for a damsel in distress. It's all part of my job as the first assistant to the head of security."

She barely managed to get hold of herself. "Well, you don't want to go reporting this to your superiors. This is your chance to move up and protect a guest who is need of serious privacy. When I hire a security guard, he signs the strictest of confidentiality agreements. I am sure a man of your talents knows exactly what I am talking about and has probably signed hundreds in your lifetime. Let me get it prepared, then meet me in 15 minutes. I want it be our secret until the right moment, then we'll let the world know. You'll be getting security work from here to L.A."

"Ten-four. That's code for 'got it.' See you in a few, and don't worry, I'm on your team."

"Ten-four. No worries here."

She hung up and knew she had to make up with Gina quick since she was an expert at putting together a contract fast - like she did last night.

She yelled, "Gina, I love you, and I am so sorry. You and I just hit a bonus jackpot. Don't be mad at me. Get your ass, I mean, your beautiful stellar bum in here. This is going to be fun."

Chapter 25

The clock struck noon, and finally, Sugar's phone pinged. She was standing in the kitchen with Lydia, the full-time housekeeper, trying to dig up dirt on the master of the house and getting nowhere. But, the newspaper publisher's nose for news smelled there was an elephant hiding under an imported Persian rug somewhere in the mansion. Maybe even in the carriage house where the cleaning woman lived with her husband the groundskeeper.

Text from Prescott: *Meeting you and Jon for dinner at the White Horse Tavern. I'll do my best to get there but if not he's welcome to stay at the house. I've already extended the invitation. Be as friendly as you can to make up for my behavior the other night.*

Her hands started to shake and she could not type back fast enough.

Oh - do you have another date with Tiffany tonight or perhaps meeting up with Monica? She hit send faster than her mind had a second to think.

That was a chance meeting. No harm done. We'll talk later.

She threw her arms up in the air and shook her head, even though deep down inside she felt devastated. She realized there was no sense in trying to make him jealous tonight in an attempt to revive his cold heart. He was pawning her off on Jon. Her eyes teared up, but she tried to cover it with a smile so Lydia wouldn't notice.

"It appears we'll be having a guest tonight. One of Prescott's friends, Jon Perry. Is there a room you'd prefer he stay in?" she asked.

The housekeeper didn't answer, but instead replied, "Will Mr. Borden be returning as well?"

"I don't know." Her voice had a slight shake like a little girl who just realized she lost her favorite doll.

"Jon can sleep anywhere he sees fit. Even the third floor servant quarters. No one has been there in quite a while. Although it can get drafty up there at night. This time of day, though, it's usually quite warm - an interesting place to explore." She looked at the green-eyed girl as if suggesting she should go there.

"What are you saying? Is there something there I need to know about?"

"The Rose Room across from the master suite is suitable for a guest," she said, then exited. Sugar thought for a moment but not about the mystery of the servant quarters. Something about Lydia reminded her of someone. Then it dawned on her: Lydia spoke with a German accent. She'd never paid attention to her inflection until now but suddenly remembered it was the same as her grandmother's. She finally made the connection: Her grandmother must have been from Germany - something she'd always wondered but never got an answer about.

As a child, she had trouble understanding the lady who spoke oddly because of her thick accent. But to this day, Sugar still ate mint chocolate ice cream, even though she was not particularly fond of the flavor, but because it was her grandma's favorite. The minty taste made her feel close to the lady who showered the little girl with sweets. Her father ended that relationship abruptly after her mother's death, and the old woman passed away before Sugar became an adult. At least now she knew her nationality.

She opened up the freezer just in case there was a pint of mint chocolate chip. Her eyes started to tear up. There it was on the bottom shelf. She lifted up the green treat like she'd discovered buried treasure. She pulled out a spoon from a nearby drawer. She scooped up a spoonful and held it in the air. "Here's to Grandma, Mom," she said out loud. She ate the whole pint while praying for the courage to return to the servant quarters after yesterday's abandoned attempt. It was too scary up there. She needed supersonic mint chocolate chip power in order to follow Lydia's lead.

* * * * *

"She's at a car dealership looking at a used Porsche," Howard texted to his new "girlfriend." He'd been telling friends there were some sparks flying between him and Monica. He even showed a few buddies the exchanges despite the fact he'd signed a confidentiality contract with the payment of $1. Something Gina saw on a TV show about how to cut someone out of a will. She figured the security guard would have to honor the contract once he accepted the payment.

Monica responded to his text: "Let me know when she's coming back to the hotel."

"Roger that."

"What?"

"That's spy talk for will do."

She laughed out loud but didn't type LOL. "Talk to you later Rodger Dodger."

He put down his phone, picked up his binoculars, and continued staring out at the parking lot. He panicked. His target was out of sight. There was a heavy knock on his car window. He startled and spilled the super-size Coke resting between his legs. He looked like he'd soiled his extra-wide khaki pants.

"Can I help you with something?" Tiffany yelled through the glass. He rolled down his window. "Me and everyone else at the dealership are wondering what you're doing. I saw you earlier too. Why are you spying on me?"

"Umm – me? Well, nothing. Just on my lunch break having a bite to eat." He lifted up three empty fast food bags. She noticed on his seat a note pad, mini camera, and tape recorder.

The blond pointed her finger at him. "If I see you around me again, I am calling the cops. You got it?" She stormed off.

* * * * *

"Here's the plan," Monica said to Gina.

"We have to take the elevator at the same time she leaves her room. We'll cause a huge scene on the way down. Then, as we all get off, act as if she just hit you in the face. This way, it's out of the view of any cameras. It will be our word against hers. She stalked us and attacked you. It's all legal since she really is stalking me. What's she doing here anyway?"

"You got that right. Psycho stalker. We'll sell the story to the

National Globe and hit a mini lotto! Then I can go to Boston and get it fixed by one of those Harvard guys."

"We're geniuses." Monica went to hug her friend

"No, don't touch me. I don't want to mess up my face any more than it already is."

* * * * *

Sugar turned the black knob on the old wooden door to the servant quarters. The squeaking sound seemed louder than yesterday. Like the door was as hesitant to open up as she was of going inside. She looked up and remembered the same stairs she'd climbed yesterday but ran back down out of fear. Twelve steps straight up. Today there would be no turning back as far as she was concerned. She flashed the light switch off and on few times. Like a warning to let anyone in hiding that she was coming up.

"Hello," she yelled, knowing full well no one would be up there. Only the ghosts of days gone by. Still, just in case, she didn't want any surprises if someone was there. Why did she have to go up all alone? Clearly, Lydia was giving her a coded message. Couldn't she have gone with her?

As she walked up the steps, each one groaned like no one had tread on them in some time. At the top was a small banister rail that she grabbed ahold of trying to keep herself steady. The climb left her feeling faint and light headed. She was trying to keep herself from tumbling back down, not from the burst of exercise but more like a nervous patient going in for surgery. She needed some reassurance, but there was no one there to hold her hand.

The room was massive and once housed a large staff back in the

Gilded Age when having 25 servants in a house this size was not un-common. Now it was a place to store things that no longer had a home in the master's quarters. A rocking horse, shelves filled with magazines and newspapers. Boxes labeled with words like Christmas decorations, train sets and books, scattered everywhere. Tables with lamps, vases, a broken chandelier. Paintings leaned against the wooden walls, some upside down.

I'll be up here all day, Sugar thought. She had no idea of what direction to take or why Lydia sent her there. Unlike the pieces to a store-bought puzzle, there was no picture on the box to follow. What was she looking for and what would the final answer look like? The room was packed with boxes and "disregarded" antiques. Or maybe she had read too much into the words of the current caretaker. Maybe she was in a place that was just none of her damn business. She looked at all the boxes with photo albums on top. She figured that would be the best place to start and inched over a few steps, still trying to find her comfort zone in the spooky place.

The servant quarters started to take on an unfriendly glare as the sun changed directions and dark shadows grew in the corners. She felt unwelcome there. Every hair on her body stood on end, and she wanted to make a fast exit. Like a little kid on a camping trip who can't sleep after hearing scary tales and wants to go home. It wasn't rational, but she headed for the stairs and raced down the steps. She closed the door and wished she could lock it from inside the hall. She caught her breath and vowed to go back up - just not right now. Maybe with someone like Jon. She just had to think of an excuse as to why she was snooping. But even she didn't have an answer for that question.

Chapter 26

Six p.m. Sugar sat at the White Horse Tavern waiting for Jon, wondering if meeting him was a mistake until she knew exactly what was going on between her and Prescott. She knew one thing for certain: The world's most eligible bachelor wasn't going to show up tonight on a white horse - although that would be quite appropriate given the name of the restaurant. She doubted he'd show up at all.

Jon walked in, not looking quite like she remembered. He wasn't as attractive without the half bottle of champagne she consumed at their first meeting. Short, kind of balding, and very consultant-looking with glasses and a bow tie. He tripped on the steps leading down from restaurant to the bar but recovered nicely and tried to walk in a "Joe Smooth" kind of style.

"You caught that didn't you?" he said to Sugar, who smiled and tried to look as if she didn't notice his fall. But some things are obvious, considering everyone at the bar turned to stare.

"Yeah, it's OK. I trip over my own shadow on some days. It's always a little wider than I think and gets in my way." She hoped her words eased the awkwardness of the moment.

"Nothing wrong with a woman having wide curves. It's when they become a four-lane highway that you have to be concerned." He hit his Buddha belly and laughed.

"Yeah...you're funny." Sugar practically chugged her Cosmo trying to block out that visual. *Oh great, this might be a really long night.* "Can you excuse me for minute?" She could hear her phone vibrating in her purse. Could it be Prescott? She didn't want to look rude and take a call the second after her date sat down. She headed for the restroom while searching through her overstuffed purse, panicked she'd miss the call.

"Hello?" she said after entering the ladies room and stopping in front of the mirror for a lipstick check as if he could see her.

"Baby girl, did you see the news?"

"Oh, it's just you. Hi dad. More news? What are you talking about?" Her heart skipped a beat.

"What do you mean, 'Just me?' I'm your number one fan. I'm calling to tell you that Tiffany's been arrested."

"What?"

"Yes. She's in Newport and has been stalking Monica. At least that's what the media is reporting. It just came over the AP. I'm still at the office. Tiffany used mace on a security guard who tried to stop her from going to the model's suite at the Viking Hotel. Do you know where that is?"

"Yes, I do. Oh my gosh. I don't know what to say. I need to call Prescott. Let me call you right back."

She hung up and thought for a moment. She would give Prescott one last chance to explain everything and help bail Tiffany out of jail. He couldn't be so heartless as to continue ignoring Sugar with this new crisis crashing down around them. At that exact moment, a text came through from him.

I have an emergency trip to China for critical business. I will explain later. At the airport now. My phone is going dead. I'll be in touch in a few days. Prescott.

She took a deep breath. That was it. That was the moment she'd finally had enough. She realized he was never going to be the man she fantasized about. She was wasting her time. There was no more reason to believe he was secretly hiding loving feelings for her when everything he said and did indicated otherwise. She lowered her head in defeat. She looked in the bathroom mirror and felt ashamed. Here she was with a nice guy like Jon and judging him the same way Prescott had judged her. By appearances alone. Even though Sugar was beautiful, she wasn't model caliber and never would be, even if she lost 20 pounds. She'd still be the fat girl from Charleston who weighed a whopping 140 pounds, not that big at all, and who everyone now called a pig on Twitter. Besides, what difference did it make how she looked or what strangers thought? What truly makes a person beautiful is the way they love their friends, family, and soulmate with all their heart, mind, and soul. He never was going to love her in that way. She transformed her appearance to fit his taste, and it still wasn't enough. All he wanted was temporary arm candy only to be tossed away like a Tootsie Roll wrapper for a more appealing sweet. She was just a nice girl from Charleston with a big personality, fun to be around, and that didn't hit the mark with him. She was the only one in their relationship going through the emotional roller coaster of truly getting to know someone while falling head over heels in love. She was alone on this thrill ride going nowhere but the exit station. Love requires caring for someone else, and he cared only for himself. How could she be so foolish to waste tears on a narcissist who was incapable of real feelings? Hell, he probably left the country to avoid more bad publicity. She was sticking with people she loved and who loved her back. Even if he walked through the door and swept her off her feet, the scenario would include a guaranteed promise that he'd go back to his single life. That's what he'd been saying all along, and now was the time to take him at his word because he'd proven who he is deep down inside. No more second guessing herself and day dreaming about a man who didn't actually exist. His actions with her said everything she needed to know about Prescott Borden.

She almost burst out crying, but time was of the essence and she needed to move fast in order to bury her feelings for him permanently. She had to bail her best friend out of jail and needed Jon's help to do so. She had no money, but she'd pay back him back once all the receipts from *Marble House* were distributed. No, better yet, she'd pawn her engagement ring in order to pay him back and have enough left over to cover this week's payroll. She'd leave Prescott the claim check for the diamond ring as a parting gift.

She vowed from this moment to give Jon a chance. She never loved anyone before the infamous bachelor and now wanted to be with someone who would love her equally and unequivocally back. Just like Tiffany had for so many years and now her father too. And many of her employees who stood by her for years despite not getting raises, just promises of a better future. The publisher was going to deliver on everything she said from here on out and treat others like she wanted to be treated. Sugar Lynn Limehouse was back in her take-charge glory, only now she was a better person for having been treated with disregard like the forgotten antiques in the servant quarters at C-Side.

Who knows? Maybe there was a real chance for a "happy ever after" with Jon Perry. Sugar Perry - she didn't like the sound of it, but love can move mountains. Besides, Limehouse was her name and she would keep it no matter who she'd marry. She was finally at peace with herself.

* * * * *

Gina guzzled down an apple martini at the Clarke Cooke House terrace bar overlooking the Atlantic. The ceiling was made up of white cloth panels that danced to the ocean breezes. Newport's hottest night spot designed for the swanky rich dressed to the nines. The place hadn't heated up yet. There were still a few tables with restaurant goers and a guy hovering nearby wearing a blue blazer posing like he owned a yacht. She rolled her eyes at the wannabe, but he couldn't tell since she was wearing dark sunglasses and a blue floppy hat trying to hide her bruised up face from the drunken fall the night before.

Monica nudged her friend. "Can you believe our luck? Tiffany came up to our floor at the exact moment as Howard and then maced him. Haha, the fat bastard wet his pants. I saw him two seconds later and called the cops. What would make her randomly attack a 300 pound guy on the verge of a heart attack? That's just outright mean."

"Maybe she didn't know he's a security guard. He is kind of creepy and might have freaked her out."

"OH, please! What was she doing on our floor?"

"Maybe she was going to up to the widow's peak. It's open to guests. I went up there earlier and the views are great."

"You went up there? No wonder you missed out on all the action.

What a fascinating life you lead as a bird-watching tourist. Let's get back to the point of conversation."

"You can see the whole city, not just seagulls flying around looking for food."

"What do I care about a flock of crapping birds? Stop being ridiculous." The redhead cleared her throat. "Think about it. Why did Tiffany check in to the Viking Hotel for two weeks when everyone in the world knows I am here?"

"No one knows you're here. We just sat down." NANANANAAA, she laughed.

"Stop being a smart ass minus the smart part. This is serious. Gina, you have no idea what it's like to have psycho fans. Now we know the truth of what she was doing on Prescott's floor the night I beat her up. Do you wanna bet me a million dollars Tiffany's stalking me?"

"Hah. I'll take that bet and then raise you another $300,000. The same amount your lawyers paid for her silence. Even worse, to blame Prescott. She has no interest in ever seeing you again. It's all by chance."

"Whose side are you on? The one who is paying your drinking tab or the bitch who extorted money from me?"

"Yours, of course." Gina put her head down trying to look remorseful. She wanted another drink without the guilt trip. She decided her best bet was to butter up her skinny cash cow and see what else she could get out of her. "I'm sorry. I'm just very upset with life right now. I shouldn't be standing up for Tiffany after everything she's put us through. I was looking forward to selling my story in the tabloids and telling everyone how she broke my nose. But instead, she maced Howard and ruined any chance of me making a quick buck. That girl belongs in jail for getting away with murder. I can't keep living this shitty life waiting for you to pay me back in full. All my clothes are gone and my New York apartment. My face looks terrible all because of trying to help you out. Hey, here's an idea. Since it's all your fault, maybe you should at least pay to get my nose fixed." She perked up when the bartender walked over. "Another martini please."

Monica lowered her voice. "Stop blaming me for all your problems and broken nose. You fell down drunk. It's your own damn fault. In fact, you should go up to Boston and get it fixed from the money I've already given you. I'm broke for the time being. Plus, I need you out of the picture for a while. I need time to sell the producers on giving you a permanent role on my reality TV show. I can't afford to carry you. My name is not Jeffery."

"Are you backing out of our contract? Because I'll scream you hit me right here and now," she threatened.

"Shhhh. You're talking too loud. Put on your rocket scientist thinking cap for a change of pace. The show will be cancelled if you accuse me of beating you up. Use your brain and play the game. Right now, the higher-ups are seeing dollar signs from all the publicity, and we should do the same. We have to keep making headline news and building an audience. The network will order more episodes, which means they'll need additional characters to keep viewers tuned in. Ta-da! That's when you come in. You won't need half my salary when you're being paid as a full-time featured performer. All you have to do is stir up trouble so the fans will want to see more and more of you."

"Why should I work at being a fool when I have you to do that for me? Look at all the problems stealing bikes and riding naked through town caused me."

"Wake up to your new reality and do something crazier. You might get a spin-off show. You can't keep mooching off others for the rest of your life. You have to make a living somehow."

"Look who's talking, Miss Moocher. You owe me money and everyone else in New York. You've been working like a dog in heat, and where has that gotten you? I'm not in debt to anyone, unlike you bitch. I have more class than that."

"Yeah, real classy getting paid by a guy like Jeffery. And you're calling me names? I am being extremely nice about all of this. There are a lot of names I could be calling you right now, Miss Hostess Ho Ho.

"Don't do that. Don't even start. It'll make me mad." She made a mean face.

"OK sunshine. But think about this. You need your own reality show and paycheck just in case mine gets cancelled. Or you'll be on the street. Or rather, Wall Street and looking for another fat ass like Jeffery."

"You know, the more I think about it, you might be on to something here. I do have star quality, and I'm just as pretty as you." She fluffed up her dark curls.

"Of course you are – not! That's why I'm the most watched woman in the world and you're screwing bankers to get by."

"I could go back to modeling."

"Get real, and forget that subject. You're a has-been who's never been anyone. You're 21 and way too old for the fashion industry. Even my manager told you so. We have to be thinking about our future.

Like how to make the show bigger and better through free publicity. That's how reality stars make the big bucks."

"Hmmm…Ratings will go through the roof if you and Prescott get back together."

"Oh do tell, how to make that happen, Einstein? He won't even talk to me."

"You said he hates publicity, right? So, have the security guard call Prescott pretending to have evidence concerning Sugar being in danger. Have him say the hotel management is giving all parties involved a chance to straighten things out without police involvement. But surprise – you'll be at the meeting too. We'll get photos of the two of you together. Everyone will think you're a couple again. Tabloids will run wild with speculation. Who knows, maybe sparks will start to fly?"

"OMG! How did God give us so much talent? We really are going to have the greatest reality TV show of all time and be as rich as that guy who turned into a woman."

"Can I please buy some clothes in the meantime? We can't have him dressed better than me."

"Yes, my genius friend. Yes, you can. Let's do some shopping. I'll spot you the cash. I can't have you looking ugly on OUR show." She winked.

"NANANANAAA! You're my best friend forever!"

Chapter 27

Tiffany, Jon, and Sugar sat in the mansion's den enjoying aged Scotch and discussing the night's events. They were still buzzed about the intense drama of bailing someone out of jail. Never something easily accomplished as the wheels of justice are seriously slow. Money talks, but bureaucrats take their sweet ass time moving. It was already midnight.

Lydia came in with a tray of chocolates imported from around the world, accompanied by ripe red strawberries. Always on call like any well trained help.

Wow, I am going to miss being here, Sugar thought to herself as she looked around the masculine-themed English club room with all the beautiful things she hoped Prescott would someday tell her about. The painting of Grandpapa that seemed to be staring back at her. The alphabetized books placed perfectly, some leaned on their side like they had just been picked up and not arranged by design. Did he read the leather-bound classics, or were they just for show? The pin striped seat in the arched window that looked down on jagged rocks and over the town harbor. Did the dignitaries of days past sit there and discuss world events and smoke cigars? The room did have a tobacco flavor that seemed to permeate it, but she'd never seen Prescott smoke. He did enjoy an evening snack and unwinding there at the end of every night. Today there was only one servant to care for the master's needs. How many did it take to the run the home back in the day when the blue-bloods lived lavishly and it was not uncommon to attend seven parties a day? All these questions she'd never know the answer to. She felt sadness creep over her and not because she was fantasizing about being married to Prescott. He was only make believe - he was not the man she'd imagined him to be. But this home, after all, was a symbol of every girl's dream of living happily ever after. Even though there would be no fairy tale ending to their romance, she understood why some princesses learned to be happy enough with just the "stuff" and discounted the romance.

"Should I just plead guilty? I did mace him. But he'd been following me all day, even outside the hotel. When I saw him, he was just a few feet away and I yelled for help. He kept coming at me, and there was no exit, just stairs leading up to a balcony that looked over Newport. I went up there just to see the view. But I got scared and sprayed him, then ran down the hall for help. That's when Monica spotted me and called the police, and I was arrested," Tiffany said.

Sugar was fully alert now and tuned in to the conversation.

"Didn't you understand she was in Newport? That article by Barry Banister about you and Prescott said so." The best friend wasn't being accusatory. This was her reporter's way of finding out what happened that night.

"My meeting with Prescott in Boston was quite by accident. It was so awkward after I did that press interview blaming him for the fight with Monica. I didn't bother looking at the gossip reports about the chance encounter. It didn't dawn on me that our short exchange would draw so much media attention. I guess I'm going to have to give him back the money payoff from Monica. I'm not supposed to talk about it, so please keep this confidential."

They both nodded.

"What made you come to Newport? Is it because you wanted to see me?" Sugar was still in investigative mode and hoping it wasn't to see Prescott. She loved her friend and totally trusted her, but there was still that doubt. They each needed to rebuild the relationship.

"No, I wish that was the reason. I didn't even know you were here. I met a doctor and we planned a weekend getaway. Actually, he's not just any old doctor, but my plastic surgeon at the hospital." She held up 10 fingers to Sugar out of Jon's view, their way of saying: he's hot. "But, listen to this. He must have seen that I was arrested because I got a text from him canceling. He claimed he needed to return to Boston due to an emergency. Right. His final words to me were: 'Good luck.' Another moment ruined by Prescott."

Sugar rolled her eyes. "Don't you dare give him back a penny after all the pain he has caused you and me. I'll disown you." She took in a deep breath. She had to let go of her habit of bossing people around. "No, wait...I'm sorry honey. I will never disown you, but take a good long look at this place. He's not going to miss your money. Hell, that painting is worth more than the three of us in this room." She walked over, hugged Tiffany, and sat on the corner of her leather chair.

Jon shook his head. "Not more than me. Just saying. Anyway, I am staying out of this. I can't even imagine why you're talking like this. He's been my friend for a long time, but you two have been through an awful lot. I never heard anything so crazy. Sounds like you deserve something for your pain and suffering, but enough said." He poured himself another drink.

"Sugar, did you know he sent me flowers before we ever met? If not, he lied at our recent chance meeting. I found flowers in my room with an unsigned card saying, 'Meet for a drink at 5.' I'm going to be honest with you, I think he's been conning us all and enjoys the freaky publicity. Or maybe he's the anonymous producer on Monica's TV show. I mean, everything is a set-up including your phony engagement. I'm so glad you're not really his cousin. Even I started having my doubts, and I've known you my whole life."

"You know, I was sort of half listening when you brought up this 'set-up' thing earlier. Too much information to digest at once. But, I'm starting to come your way. This was all a big game that we'll never fully understand. We are so done with him, but for the life of me, I'll never figure out why he did these things. Hell, he's probably hanging out with Monica as we sit here."

"Ladies, let me remind you, we are in his house, drinking his hundred-year-old Scotch and being waited on by his help. Let's show a little respect and trash him after we're gone from here tomorrow. We should wait to run him down until we're all sober-minded and not in his lovely home. Ho hum. I won't ever have to worry about being thrown out of C-Side by that scoundrel again. I'm kicking myself out." He held up his drink and tossed it back.

Sugar looked at Tiffany. "After you were put in jail, he texted me that he left for China on emergency business. Dodging trouble and drama is my guess. Meanwhile, I look like a fool who had sex with

my cousin in public, forever branded a sow, and everyone thinks he
went back to you."

Jon chimed in. "Don't forget your phony engagement that looks
just like that now. Completely phony."

"Thanks for reminding me." Sugar smirked.

Tiffany came to his rescue. "Don't be upset. I have it worst of all.
If it weren't for Prescott Borden, I wouldn't look like a bandaged-up
mess after being beaten by a woman that he clearly drove bonkers. Or
waiting to go to trial for stalking and assault charges."

Jon stood up and put his hand on Tiffany's shoulder. "My dear,
you don't have to worry. I am going to get you the finest attorney.
You still look beautiful even with all the stress you are under. Who
couldn't help but notice those gorgeous honey brown eyes and your
even lovelier disposition?" They both smiled at each other a second
longer than a friendly glance should take.

Oh, geeze. What was going on here? Sugar was so out of step she
hadn't noticed the mutual attraction. Oh heck, everyone was drunk,
and it was time for bed. She was letting her imagination run away.

"Kids, it's bed time for Momma Sugar. Kisses on the cheeks, good
night, and I'll see you both in the morning."

They both gave her a peck.

Tiffany held her best friend's hand. "I am so, so, so sorry. How
did we ever let a scoundrel ruin the best thing that ever happened to
either of us? We are family, and nothing will ever change that again."

"Here, here," Jon said, as they all toasted before retiring for their
last night at C-Side.

Chapter 28

Sugar woke up to the mother of all storms. The thunderous sounds shook her out of bed. Without a second thought, she said to herself, *the servant quarters. I have to go up there,* as if struck by some mystical force from the electricity in the air.

It couldn't wait until morning. There was no way of getting around it. Just before going to sleep she booked an 8 a.m. flight. The time had come for her to go home, save the newspaper, and spend time with her dad, something the two never had done in the past. But, how could she fly out without discovering the mystery locked away in the attic? No reporter leaves the scene of a crime without checking all the facts. Her heart and her reputation had both been stolen from her. Maybe she'd find an answer as to why.

She went into the master bathroom and grabbed one of Prescott's robes since her usual night time attire was to sleep in the buff. She looked at herself in the mirror. "You have to be a big girl about this," she said aloud. It was scary enough going up there in mid-afternoon, but during a thunderstorm? No matter, she was the new, calorie-free Sugar and could no longer allow baggage from the past to weigh her down. If she didn't go up there now, she'd never know the full truth of whatever mystery was hidden there.

She headed out to the hall and searched for a light switch. The lightning flashed, and she screamed bloody hell. Standing a few feet in front of her was an apparition, who happened to look just like her best friend Tiffany.

"It's me," Tiff said, turning on the light. She was dressed in a full length, cranberry print granny nightgown.

"What in the heck are you doing up? And what are you wearing? You look like the ghost of bad taste."

"I was scared and going to sneak into your room. And you bought this for me 10 years ago."

They hugged each other.

"The question remains....What are YOU doing? Sneaking into my room like a little kid?" Tiffany thought she'd busted her best pal for being a scaredy cat too.

"No, I'm going up to the servant quarters on the third floor."

"What's up there?"

"Besides a lot of boxes, I have no idea."

"Then why are you going?"

"Because Lydia the housekeeper hinted I should go up there but didn't tell me why. All she said was Jon could sleep there or anywhere else in the house. I think she was giving me a clue."

"Oh, that makes perfect sense. Not at all! I'm going to bed. See you in the morning." She turned to leave.

"No, wait." Sugar stepped in front of her friend. "I went up there twice already. The first time I started up but quickly changed my mind because the floor creaked so much. Then the maid suggested I go there, but in an indirect kind of way. I went up again and ran back down because I got scared out of my mind."

"And Miss Scarlet killed Professor Plum with a pitchfork. You're making no sense whatsoever. I'm going back to bed. Good luck."

"What do you mean, good luck? You're going with me! This is a sign that we're supposed to go together."

"Oh no. You can play this game of Clue on your own time. I am not going to any attic that scared you twice in broad daylight. You're the bravest person I know, and if it freaked you out, then I'll be having bad dreams for a month. I am not doing it. I will, however, consider it in the morning at a sane hour, when it's light out and if accompanied by an adult. And you don't qualify."

"I'm leaving first thing in the morning. Oh, come on, I never asked you do anything for me."

"That's right, you never ask me do anything. You just tell me what to do. And I am telling you: NO WAY."

"Please, please, please. I am begging you." Sugar got down on her knees, fell at her best friend's feet, and started pulling on her nightgown.

"Oh, stop that. It's embarrassing. You look ridiculous."

"Pleazzzzzzzzzzzzze."

"Groveling does not become you. Get up. Now!"

"NO, I am not moving until you go with me. Otherwise, I'm attaching myself to your leg, and you can walk around with me glued on to you." She started whimpering like a dog and grabbed her leg.

Tiffany shook her head. She knew there was no getting around it. Sugar wasn't going to stop. She'd seen this act many times as kids growing up, and her friend really wouldn't quit until she got her way.

"I don't believe this. Fine, I'll go. But, I'm telling you right now, if we don't find anything you're going to pay me back BIG time. You already owe me like a million favors as it is."

She stood up. "If we don't find anything then I only owe you 500,000. Deal?" She extended her hand.

"Oh, stop it. I am not shaking hands on anything. You sound like you did back in third grade when you conned me out of my dream Barbie Corvette."

"Follow me," Sugar ordered.

They walked down the hall to the wooden door that held so many secrets to the home.

She continued. "Look, we have to just run up there and not think. NO thinking, just running up and going on a mad dash for clues. When I open the door, don't think about how scary the steps look going up or pay attention to all the creaking sounds or shadows on the walls that seem to be a warning of…"

"Do you want me to go up or not? Stop freaking me out, and let's go."

Sugar quickly opened the door, flipped on the light switch, and they ran up, making more noise than the thunder boomers outside.

They got to the top, and Tiffany found another light switch.

"Hah. This scared you? It's just a big room full of junk."

"Well, I couldn't find the light up here earlier."

Tiffany crossed her arms. "I thought you said it was daylight?"

"It looked more terrifying then. Just start looking!" She nudged her friend.

"OK fine, but for what?"

"I don't know. You go over there and check it out." She pointed to the dark corner of the room.

"I am not going over there. You go over there." Tiffany pushed Sugar toward the unknown shadows.

"I thought you weren't scared."

"Let's just stick together."

They both walked over to the same photo albums on top of a dusty box that Sugar spotted earlier. The amateur detectives opened up the album.

Inside were old photos of a chubby lady holding a baby and smiling at the camera. Pictures of the baby all dressed up in white on a swing set with the same smiling woman pushing from behind. Then a 5-year-old little girl holding a kitten and the lady beaming with pride.

Sugar's eyes widened. "What's going on here? That's me. In my favorite outfit. That's me," she repeated. "Tiff, remember that cat? Look, that's our backyard. What am I doing in pictures here in this place?"

Tiffany let out a deep sigh. "Oh, sweetie, don't you see it? Can't you see it?"

"See what?"

"Look closer. The woman in the pictures. That's Lydia. Lydia is your grandmother."

"No, it can't be. She's dead."

Tiffany came to eye-to-eye with Sugar. "Can't you see the photo at the bottom of the page? It's the three of you together. Lydia, you, and your mom. I can remember what she looked like now, even if your dad tried to erase all memories of both of them. Seeing the pictures jarred my memory. Your grandma is here in this house and very much alive."

Chapter 29

Morning came and went at the castle, and Sugar missed her flight. Knocks went unanswered. She posted a sign on the door. "Please allow me my space. My flight has moved to 7 p.m. I'll be out before then."

* * * * *

Tiffany and Jon chatted in a sitting room on the second floor overlooking the grand foyer, perched on a yellow tapestry couch between two tall columns. They both reclined in regal fashion as they sipped on English tea and spoke in soft whispers so not to draw attention to their conversation.

"So, let me get this straight. The housekeeper is Sugar's grandmother, who she thought was dead but has been living here. Grandma never let Sugar know she's alive but now tells her to look in the servant quarters for clues. Even though Sugar has no idea what she's looking for."

"Exactly." Tiffany took a sip of her tea.

"Did you say it's been 23 years since she saw her last? Are we sure this is not some elaborate hoax on our Prescott's part? He seems to have webs cast everywhere. Does he already know about all of this?"

"Doubtful. That gentleman, who is no gentleman, is in China hiding out from bad publicity. Gosh, if the press knew Sugar's grandma lives here, that would really confirm the cousins rumor. What a mess."

"What was Sugar's reaction to finding the photos?'"

"At first, she was in complete denial and then shock. She just piled up the stacks of albums and went downstairs. She said nothing other than 'I don't want to talk about it' and locked the door. I have tried over and over to coax her out. I'm afraid there's nothing I can do to help."

"She didn't even cry?"

"I was crying, but tried to hide it. Seeing all those pictures of her mom brought back a flood of memories. She was a terrible alcoholic. There were many wild fights in that house. I could hear them from next door. Sugar and I would play a game. We both had flashlights and would shine them back and forth since our bedrooms faced each other on the first floor. We'd message through a kind of Morse code that we created. Two flashes meant keep the sliding glass door unlocked, and she'd come over and stay the night. My mom would find her in the morning and promise not to tell. No one was ever awake at breakfast time at her house, so they never noticed Sugar was gone. She'd just go back in the morning after my mom would make her a ham and egg sandwich. Something she did every day, even if she didn't stay the night."

"What a terribly sad story."

"There were happier moments. When Sugar's mom wasn't drinking, she was witty and quite funny. Just like her daughter. We always had so much fun when her mom was sober. She'd take us to downtown Charleston and we'd walk up and down the Battery and pretend we lived in the rainbow painted mansions. There were picnics at Patriot's Point and baseball games at Joe Riley Stadium. We still are huge River Dog fans, a farm league baseball team. We have season tickets."

"What happened to her mom? Is she still with us?"

"She died of a combination of too many pain pills and drinks. An accidental death, but Sugar found her. She came over to my house and said, 'Mommy won't wake up.'"

"What did your parents do?"

"My dad was never around, just like her father wasn't. My mom went over there but told us she was asleep and then called for an ambulance. She was a nurse and knew it was too late to revive her. She didn't think it was her place to tell Sugar all the details as to what was happening, so she took us for a ride down to the newspaper to get her dad. He never seemed to be bothered by much, either good or bad. My mom became Sugar's mom, even though she had been a stand-in parent long before the overdose. She always cared for both of us like we were true sisters. Then she died a year later from breast cancer. From then on, we pretty much raised each other."

"Oh my. This sounds like a novel, a story that needs to be told."

Tiffany laughed. "You'll have to see the play I wrote, *Marble House*. It's about our childhood and is being performed on stage now in Boston. It's sold out for the next six weeks, but since I know the writer pretty well, I might be able to arrange for two tickets. That is, if you'll go with me." Her heart started to race. The old Tiffany would never have the courage to say such a thing.

"So, you're not only resilient, you're also brilliant. I'll be compliant like any fan of a writing giant."

Tiffany smiled. "Are you a poet?"

Jon continued. "No, I'm a businessman in the publishing industry. Very successful highbrow, kind of material. I'm also a single father of two boys. Are you fond of perfect children?"

"No, I like them wild and totally out of control and in need of guidance. I've had plenty of practice after raising Sugar Cane."

"Perfect, then I don't have to lie anymore. You already met my kids."

"Are you telling me the truth about your publications being highbrow? Don't tell me you're really a publisher of girly magazines."

"No, mostly for the restaurant trade, but there's lots of naked food on the covers."

"I once wrote an article about cooking as a single. How to make three meals from one."

"I saw that! It was featured in a magazine I own named 'Food to Table.' I believe the article was titled 'Cooking for one on the run.'"

"Yeah, that wasn't my best work. I needed money so badly then and would have sold it to a dog publication. 'Cooking for your pooch with hooch.' In all honesty, I'm a horrible cook."

"Good, because I hate giving my chef a night off. Care to join me for dinner after attending the play?"

"I'd be honored."

"Then I'll book tickets. I presume you'll want to fly first class since my main residence is in London. The West End is a great venue for new playwrights."

* * * * *

"Yes sir, it's extremely important you get here as soon as possible. I can't discuss details over the phone. I think you'll find the information vital to you and your fiancé's security. If you don't have time to stop by, I'll be happy to contact the authorities instead," the security guard said.

Monica punched Howard in the arm. She was mad. She thought Prescott might opt for going to the police rather than coming by the hotel.

He moved the phone from his ear and mouthed, *he's coming.* "That's just great. Then I'll see you in a bit. Meet me in room 1215. There is something here you need to see."

Prescott hung up. He never had left for China.

* * * * *

Sugar sat down in the kitchen with Lydia, who offered her a bowl of ribbon candy. The same she ate as a child.

Both women started crying, then stood up and hugged each other. The emotions were deeper than either had ever experienced. Like the way an adopted child feels after meeting her birth mother for the first time. Nothing was said as they both stood there trying to get a hold of themselves. Their sighs were so deep they struggled to get their words out. They both needed to let the moment pass and waited to speak.

"Why didn't you come to see me?" Sugar asked as she held her nana's hand.

"I wanted to, but your dad threatened me. He didn't do it to be a bad man. He just was overcome with grief and had no way of expressing himself. Keeping you away from me kept his own pain from surfacing. That and the drinking. I regret the day Gretchen met your dad. So pretty just like you. Such a loss. Do you remember me from those days?"

"Your voice sounds a little like I remember. Very German – but your pronunciation of words is much better now. I wouldn't have recognized you. You're so thin now, but I should have figured it out from the mint chocolate chip ice cream. I even ate some right here on this counter and thought about you."

"My English has improved since you were a child. I still eat what I want, but I go to the gym every day. I'm a very modern grandma but still a big woman. I'll never be skinny."

"Why didn't you contact me when I turned 18?"

"This is hard. Very hard to explain. I must be honest. My visa ran out long ago. And I never returned home. I'm not here legally. This is how your father kept me out of your life."

Sugar pulled away and sat down at the kitchen island. She looked like a lost little girl at the oversized counter. She pounded her fist on the granite.

"I'll never going to speak to him again for lying to me. He said you were dead. I was finally starting to have a relationship with him."

She walked over and shook her finger like a grandma instructing her grandchild. "No, now don't talk nonsense. I spoke with him since you've been here. He wants you to know me. This has been a very good thing for him. He needed to stop drinking and face the future. We have been talking every day, and I've been encouraging him to return to the newspaper so you don't have to work so hard."

"Why didn't he tell me the truth? You both have been deceiving me."

"We are not deceiving you. We are protecting you. We've been trying to figure out the best way to go forward. Some things require a little more thought before rushing in at full speed."

"Then why did you let me stay here knowing what a horrible man Prescott Borden is?"

"He's not horrible, just misguided. Like most people in life trying to find their way back home. He's very much in love with you."

"That's rich. Prescott Borden's in love with me? Do you see how many mirrors there are in this house?"

"They were here long before him. He bought the home with everything you see in it."

"You mean, all those paintings aren't his family"

"No, his mother is a dear friend of mine and lives down the street. She is a humble woman with a big heart. She used to work here and had my job.

"I thought Prescott was from North Carolina."

"After Louise's husband died, she moved here to be closer to Boston. Prescott was in college then, and she wanted to give him space but be nearby. After he made it big, he bought this house for her, but she never moved in. Not her style. She lives in a tiny house a few blocks away."

"Prescott Borden has a mother who's alive? Something about this is almost incomprehensible. I can't see him with a mom that tells him what to do. Or being in love with me. None of this makes any sense. I just don't see it."

Lydia glanced down at her phone that was vibrating.

"Ohh, he's quite his mother's son, and they talk daily. She's been telling me he's in love with you ever since you arrived in town. Louise wants to meet you. She's waiting for you to come by for a visit. Hold on one second."

She texted something into her phone. "I just told her you'd be over soon."

Sugar's heart sank. This was just too much emotion too fast. She didn't know if she had the courage to meet Prescott's mom. Or if she'd believe anything about him having feelings for anyone.

Lydia looked her granddaughter up and down. She went to the freezer and pulled out a quart of mint chocolate chip.

"Let's finish this up, and then you can go over there."

Chapter 30

Sugar knocked on Louise Borden's red door. The house was a tiny, white Cape Cod style home, simple but with elaborate landscaping. Colorful tulips were popping up everywhere.

Louise opened the door. She definitely was Prescott Borden's mother. Same hypnotic, blue eyes with a playful glow. She looked almost star struck, but Sugar knew that was not on account of her. Some people just know how to make others feel special.

Her dark, wavy hair, streaked with silver, was pulled back in a bun, and she was thin but not bone skinny. Walking over to the home, Sugar imagined that's what she'd be, since Prescott seemed to be obsessed with weight.

"Do come in. It's so nice to meet you. I have known your grandmother for years. She's one of my best friends and speaks of you often. She's waited for this moment for a long time, and now I get to meet you too."

Sugar smiled and stepped inside. The room was cozy with a white brick fireplace lit up with candles in the hearth. The floor was original to the home, a dark plank style that seemed to be slanted but in a way that gave the house lots of character. Blue and white nautical style furnishings, along with paintings by local artists featuring seascapes, filled the entire house like a sailor's retreat. The open floor plan made all the rooms visible to the eye, including a renovated kitchen that seemed a little out of place for a single story home built in the 1800s.

"Sit down," Louise suggested as she escorted Sugar to a blue checked couch.

The two looked at each other. Sugar turned bright red wondering if Prescott's mom had seen the video. "That damn tape will haunt me for life," she thought to herself.

"I'm sorry. I'm really nervous about meeting you," Louise said.

"I am so glad you said that because I feel the same. My hands are shaking."

"I feel as if I know you. Your grandmother has shown me pictures and is so proud of you running the newspaper. You can't imagine our shock when you and Prescott became a media sensation and suddenly there you were living in his house."

"I am so embarrassed about that. I don't even know where to begin. I hope you don't think badly of me."

"Darling, some things are better off unmentioned. Tell me about my son asking you to marry him."

"Prescott always says 'darling' just like you do. It's so darling." Sugar giggled and tried to change the subject. "I'm going back to Charleston today. I have a lot of work to catch up on."

"Under normal circumstances, I would know that. Prescott tells me everything about his life and the people close to him. We talk daily. But, ever since you came into my son's life, he doesn't phone me. That's part of the reason I know you're the one. I'm sure my boy is struggling with being in love. He's always had a heart for the ladies but has needed to settle down for a long time."

"I'm not so sure he's ever going to settle down to be honest with you, Louise."

"Oh, yes he is, and you're the one. I could have pointed you out from a lineup of 100 women and said, 'That's the girl he's going to marry.'"

"Why would you say that?"

"You have to come see his childhood bedroom. It's just around the corner. Would you like to take a look inside his mind?"

"Excuse me, I thought he was raised in North Carolina."

"When I moved here, I took his all his teenage belongings with me. I decorated his room here exactly the way it had been. I thought it would make him comfortable coming home for visits since his dad passed on and I sold the home. He still stays the night on special occasions like holidays. So, the magic works. I think it helps him stay close to the little boy inside. He's a powerful man and needs that connection. Why don't you go and take a peek?"

Sugar was hesitant. She still hadn't come to terms with discovering the photo albums and reconnecting with her grandmother. She wasn't sure she needed any more surprises in her life.

"I'm going to make us some coffee while you look around. Or do you prefer tea?"

"Sweet tea please."

"You have a southern girl's heart. Delightful."

Louise went to the kitchen as Sugar lingered a little longer. She really did want to see Prescott's life as a boy. She stood up and walked down a narrow hall. There were two open doors. The first one was clearly not Prescott's. It had a canopy bed and flowered wallpaper.

His room was loud and proud. Hockey posters everywhere with what she assumed were famous players from days gone by. Prescott had photos of himself pinned up with some of the players. He looked so cute in his sports gear. On a picture of the 1980 Olympic team, he'd pasted his picture over one of the player's faces. It made her laugh.

There were sporting trophies and ribbons all around the room. Prescott not only competed in hockey but also track and field. On a corkboard, there were pictures of him with many girls on dates. Good Lord - he must have gone to every high school prom and dance in the entire state for three straight years. All pretty cheerleader types but no supermodels. One photo of a cute blond with him down on his knee like he was asking her to marry him caught her eye. She unpinned it and looked at the back. "Michelle Russo" it said, along with four hand-drawn stars next to her name. "Her dad will kill you - watch your manners." She smiled, but as she started turning over more photos, each one had ratings with stars and words like "talks too much, too chunky, not fun, too easy." *What the heck?* He was judging women and putting them in categories as far back as age 14. There were at least 50 photographs.

What the hell did that say about him? Yeah, she was getting some real insight into his mind. He was as sleazy then as he is now. She walked around the room, but there wasn't much else to see except more of the same. Even the bedspread on his twin bed was a print of race cars. Kind of goofy and a little childish for a teenager. She was about to leave but noticed his closet door. *Might as well take a look while I'm here,* she thought. She looked inside, but there was nothing to see but old sports jerseys. She went to close it when a poster hidden on the inside caught her eye. A 60s-style pinup photo of a woman who was a dead-on Sugar Lynn Limehouse lookalike with the same large, almond-shaped green eyes. The hair color was a clear match to her new look. And they both had the same zaftig proportions. "Marry this girl" was written in bold, red marker at the bottom.

What did this all mean? Prescott was in love with an image on an old poster in his teenage closet? Is that what this relationship was all about? Him reliving a boy's fantasy?

"There you are," Louise said, which startled Sugar and she jumped.

"I am so sorry! I didn't know you were there."

"He's been in love with that girl in the poster his entire life."

"But I am not that girl."

"Yes - you are. I believe God imprints in each person's mind an image of the girl or boy they'll marry one day. That's why you see people getting divorced and marrying a look alike to their first spouse. God made one soulmate for each person."

"I'm not very religious."

"I'm not either, just spiritual and close to God. I have prayed about the woman he'd marry for years. When I saw the interview you did with Prescott, I watched it over and over and I said, 'That's her.' Imagine my surprise when you turned out to be my best friend's granddaughter. More validation."

"Louise, you are such a sweet lady, but I need to be honest with you. Please forgive me for misleading you and others. This whole engagement thing is not real. Prescott asked me to do it so that he could save face with his business associates and so that I didn't look foolish with my employees. He's in China right now and won't even call me back. I am going home tonight. There is no engagement. There never was. He told me so many times over and over that this was just temporary."

"Don't you believe him! Trust me. Let me talk to him."

"No, Louise, don't talk to him about any of this. I can't have Prescott Borden in my life anymore. It just hurts too much."

"Do you love him?"

She started to tear up. "Yes, yes I do."

"Then why are you giving up so easily?"

"Believe me, this is not easy. He's given up on me. I am not skinny enough, not pretty enough. I am just not enough for him. He won't even take my phone calls. Now I have to deal with the embarrassment of going home after being headline news. I look completely foolish. He doesn't care."

"I wouldn't be so quick to come to that conclusion. Prescott loves you. I know it. I'm his mother, and I see it all over his face when he's on TV. Something has changed for him. The way he's avoiding me is another tipoff for me. Please give it some time."

"You have given me a lot to think about Mrs. Borden. In the meantime, I need to go home. I have a newspaper to run."

"Just make sure you have a newspaper to run and that you're not simply running away."

"Thank you. I'll reflect on your words in my heart. I promise. I have to get going."

The two women hugged, but Sugar's tears made it impossible to see the same tears in Louise's eyes. Deep blue eyes that looked identical to his. She thought about the beautiful kids she and Prescott could make, with this lovely lady as their grandmother. Something so close that felt so far out of reach.

Sugar walked back to C-Side with a heavy heart. *Was she giving up and running away from someone who was as confused as she was about the relationship? Don't moms know everything?* She never really knew her mother and couldn't properly evaluate the idea. But, in every movie she ever saw, the message was clear: "Mom knows best."

Her cell phone rang. She held out hope it was Prince Charming. Indeed it was not. Still, she smiled. It was still good to see Tiffany's picture come up on her I-phone. She'd missed seeing her best friend's pretty face while they were on hiatus.

"Where are you?" Tiff asked in an urgent way.

"I'm just leaving Prescott Borden's mother's house. What do you think of that? Louise – that's her name - says that Prescott is in love with me and I'm giving up too fast. Wait til you hear this - Lydia, I mean my grandmother, is her best friend."

"So, you haven't seen the news?"

"Oh, don't tell me there is more news. My heart can't take it." This was partially true since once again it was racing out of control.

"Prescott isn't in China. He's with Monica in her hotel room. The paparazzi caught him leaving there 15 minutes ago."

Sugar stopped dead in her tracks, even though she was in the middle of crossing a busy street.

"Mothers really don't know best," she whispered.

"What? What about moms?"

A car came zooming by with the horn going full blast. The compact would have hit Sugar if the driver had not made a sharp left turn and hit a fire hydrant. Water started spraying out everywhere. The driver got out and started cussing out the jaywalker.

"Oh, my Lord. I have to go. There's been an accident. I need to wait for the police to arrive. Some guy just about hit me but knocked down a fire hydrant instead. I am getting soaking wet. It's my fault. I can't let him get in trouble for something I caused."

"You don't have to make up stories. If you're going to the hotel to look for him, I'll go too. Wait...I can't go because Monica has a restraining order against me. Just get back here, and I'll help you pack. We have a lot to talk about before you leave. I can't leave Rhode Island as part of my bond, so I'm going to get a hotel in Providence. I don't want to take a chance of bumping into her. Jon's going to drive me there in a few hours."

"I have to go. This is urgent and I am getting screamed at..."

"Sweetie, I know you're hiding from me. Stop being upset over Prescott. You should be happy. This proves he's just bad news. I don't want you to ever cry over him again. Please get back here so we can have some time together."

"I have to go - now."

Chapter 31

By the time Sugar arrived back at C-Side, Tiffany was ready to leave. She was in the long stone driveway with Jon loading her suitcase into his rental car.

"Where have you been? You look like you've gone through a car wash. Is this how you looked when you went to see Prescott's mom?" Tiffany half-teased but did wonder what was going on.

"I told you there was an accident! The driver hit a fire hydrant instead of me. All the water drenched me and ruined my cell phone. Then I went for a long walk on the beach just to think about what the hell was happening with my life and where it's going."

"Oh, sweetie, I'm sorry. I didn't take you seriously when you called. Are you OK?"

"I don't know. Sorry I snapped. Everything's gotten to me."

"Well, just stop thinking about everything. Let's get back home to Charleston where we belong." She gave her friend a hug and then whispered in her ear. "Things are heating up with me and Jon."

Sugar made no response.

"Are you interested in him? Because I'm never letting a guy get between us again."

"No, he's totally not my type. Way too conservative. You two are perfect together."

"Really? 'Cause I think so too."

Jon walked over. "Look at you two sisters. Beautiful in every way."

Sugar smiled. "Thanks. You better take good care of her because I know where you live. Wait, actually I don't know where you live."

"I spend most of my time in London and the rest in New York City unless I have business somewhere else in the country. I will be making quite a few trips to Charleston and we'll get the Gazette back to her glory days."

"We never had one."

"One what?'

"Glory day. The newspaper has always been in trouble."

"We'll change that."

Sugar took a deep breath. "Jon, I'm going to be honest. I can't afford you."

Tiffany jumped in. "But I can, thanks to Monica. I'm taking care of it."

"Ladies, I am not taking a penny from either of you, just stock options. That's how much confidence I have in this team. Together, we're going to make the Gazette the jewel of the town." He looked at his watch. "We better get going. We have an early dinner reservation. Can we drop you off at the airport? What time is your flight?"

"No, I'll be fine. Just go without me, and I'll call for a driver. I need to get a few more things done. Crap, I just remembered. I don't have any money, just his credit card. I do need a ride. Give me five minutes, that's all it will take. I'll just throw everything into a suitcase." She raced off.

Tiffany yelled, "Take your time. We can be late."

Sugar stood inside the mansion and took it all in for one last time. The two-story grand foyer took up most of the first level of the home. The massive entrance moonlighted as the grand ballroom in the Gilded Age. Parties featuring the who's who before Hollywood came into prominence. Everyone from blue bloods to Broadway stars. Even presidents. Now a small time girl from Charleston was a part of C-Side's history.

Bernard entered carrying Sugar's packed bags.

"Lydia took the liberty of getting everything together for you. She is waiting to say goodbye in the kitchen."

"Thanks, Bernard. Thank you for everything, especially for loving my grandma."

"She's easy to love," he said.

"Yes, she is." Sugar headed to the heart of the home, the tucked away kitchen where meals were prepared out of sight from visitors. There was Lydia making chocolate covered strawberries.

"Grandma, thank you for packing everything for me, but you don't ever have to wait on me again. I am going to take care of you from here on. I'm going to help you get your visa issues straightened out."

"I'm sorry things didn't work out for you and Prescott. I thought you were going to be here for good. I don't know what's wrong with him. Hanging around women like Monica has really brought his character down."

"Nothing's wrong with him. He's perfectly happy with having lots of women problems. He's quite accomplished in that way. To each his own."

"When will I see you again?" She walked over and started gently touching her granddaughter's hair.

"That depends on when you're coming to see me. I can't come back here again." She put her head down.

"In that case, I'll be there next week. We have a lot of catching up to do."

Sugar smiled, and Lydia handed her a package of wrapped chocolate strawberries.

"These are a gift for you father. Don't you go eating them. I'm going to put you on a strict diet so you don't end up overweight like me."

"I would be honored if I ended up just like you."

They hugged each other.

Chapter 32

Sugar sat in the back seat of the small Japanese car listening to the blossoming chatter of newfound love. Obviously, Jon and Tiffany were beyond just having a crush on each other. They were practically making wedding plans.

She wanted to yell "slow down" but figured they'd think she meant the speed of the car not the fire truck careening straight for the altar. Who moves this fast? Enough already. She'd had it with love. Strictly for cartoon characters with birds flying around their heads. Life is a big, damn serious deal, and she wasn't going to waste her time with thinking about flowers that die quickly, disposable wedding gowns, and Prince Charmings with glass slippers that break. She was tired of walking on broken glass. Everyone should get real about fairy tales. She vowed never to read one to her children - if she ever did have kids. From the sound of things, Jon's two boys seemed like hellions on Big Wheels, and she'd dodged a bullet by not hooking up with him. Blah to love and children too. Very over rated.

Why are they so damn giggly and not paying attention to driving? She shook her head. A police car siren was music to her ears compared to the lovebirds' conversation - until the men in blue pulled them over. Everyone was ordered out of the car.

"You must be kidding me!" Sugar yelled.

"Ma'am, get out of the car - now."

"This is such bullshit." She complied with the instruction but then was immediately arrested for disorderly conduct.

"You can't arrest me for no reason. All I did was swear. I'm going to miss my flight, which would piss anyone off. There is a thing called free speech. I am a newspaper publisher. I am Sugar Lynn Limehouse, and I'm already headline news. You will not get away with this," she said to the baby-faced police officer who was clearly not listening and probably in someone's back pocket. She yelled to Tiffany, "This is some kind of Monica pay back."

Sugar was put in handcuffs and escorted to the back seat of the police car. She banged her head on the door by not ducking down enough. She tried to balance herself with hands cuffed behind her but wasn't too successful.

"That sounded like it hurt," a voice said. Sitting next to her was the devil himself: Prescott Borden.

"What's going on here? Who the hell are you, Mr. Damn Newportant getting an innocent person arrested?" she demanded.

"I knew you wouldn't listen to me unless you had no place to go, so it's jail or you'll hear me out. First, I want to introduce you to my friend, Howard." He was sitting shot gun in the front. "Howard's the security guard maced by Tiffany."

"Charmed to meet someone who had my best friend arrested after stalking her," she said in a sarcastic tone. She turned to Prescott. "Is this another one of your setups? What kind of game are you playing here? I am a real person, and so is Tiffany. You are single-handedly destroying our lives. What is wrong with you?"

Howard jumped into the conversation. "I'm sorry about all that. I was set up by Monica because I was convinced your friend was stalking her. So, I was trailing Tiffany. I'm also the one who called Prescott and told him you were in danger. That's why he came to the hotel. Monica put me up to it. After I met Prescott and saw the look on his face when Monica walked in, I knew I did something really bad. So I 'fessed up, but the press already got wind he was with the super model. She's just a super bad person."

She yelled at Prescott. "I thought you were in China. You lied and said you were there."

"Sugar, just listen. I was trying to hide from you. I can't get you off of my mind. I thought if I just stayed away from you long enough, I'd come to my senses. Everything about you dances around in my head, and I can't stop the music. Your smile, your enthusiasm, your sense of humor, even the way you talk too much. Your smoking hot green eyes. Nothing can replace you. I even visited with an ex-girlfriend who's a psychologist, and she told me that what I have is 'incurable.'"

"How much did she charge you for that diagnosis? Or did you pay with sex?"

"Don't be ridiculous. I mean, I tried to have sex with her but I couldn't - because of you. I only want to be with you."

"You tried to have sex with another woman? After you promised me you wouldn't have sex with anyone else until our relationship was over? How could I have been so stupid as to make that deal? No one goes into a relationship knowing it's over in 30 days. A guaranteed breakup is all you promised me."

"I want to start over. I want this ring that I bought for you to have real meaning." He tried to grab her hand but realized her hands were cuffed behind her.

"Real meaning? What about the poster girl. Aren't I just a kid's fantasy?"

"I'm not following you."

"I went to your house. I met your mom. I saw your bedroom and the poster on the back of the closet door."

"What about it?"

"I look just like her. You wrote on it 'marry this girl' like all the ridiculous things you wrote on the photos of all the girls you dated back then, including ratings stars and notes about them being easy. How many dates did you have in high school? Will the state of North Carolina ever allow you back?"

"You do realize you're talking about me as teenager."

"I am talking about a lifetime of cheating."

"I've loved women. Lots of women. You can't hold that against me. In fact, I take that back. I have enjoyed the company of the opposite sex, but there is only one that I love and that's you."

"Are you sure it's not because I look like the poster on your wall? The one you used to fulfill your teenage boy fantasies? I hate to think what you did while staring at that."

"I am quite certain I didn't have to do those things because I always had a girl that was happy to do it for me."

"Oh, that's a real romantic thought."

"Well, how's this for romantic." He got down on one knee. "Sugar Lynn Limehouse, will you marry me tomorrow on a sunset cruise in Newport harbor? Without you, I'm not Newportant at all. I'm just a middle-aged guy without the love of his life. Will you be my Mrs. Newportant? You told me once that's who you wanted to be."

"Say yes!" Howard yelled.

Prescott pounded on the glass window used to separate the police from the criminals "Can you give us a moment please." Howard got quiet but stayed in the car.

Sugar lowered her voice. "Why does everything in this relationship have to center around you and your needs? Maybe tomorrow is not a good day for me or the next. Maybe not even in a month."

"Darling, you tell me then. You tell me what's good."

Sugar looked away. Here she was in the backseat of a police car with the threat of going to jail or getting married. She turned to him and in a matter of fact way said, "Nothing tomorrow or the next or for years to come. My calendar is full."

"Don't you think you're being a little harsh?"

"No. I am telling you like it is. The only time I have open is tonight. In fact, I'm asking you to marry me and not the other way around. Prescott Borden, will you marry me tonight? Because my calendar is filled with days and nights of being your wife."

Howard yelled again, "Say yes!"

"**YES!**"

"You may now kiss the bride-to-be," Howard said.

Sugar took in a deep breath. "Can someone maybe uncuff me first?"

Prescott took hold of her face and kissed her like she'd never been kissed before. Every one of his kisses felt like the first one ever.

She pulled away. "How am I going to explain this to Tiffany? She really hates you, more than I ever did. What will she say?"

"She already knows. Howard and I went over there after leaving the hotel. He apologized to her and is getting the charges dropped. We waited for you to get back and then decided to do something a bit more dramatic. In fact, this was Tiffany's idea. She was afraid you wouldn't sit still long enough to hear me out, so my new friend here called up one of his buddies at the police station."

"Does my grandmother know too?"

"Can you believe that? You were living in my attic and closet for years, and I didn't even know it."

"Does she know I'm coming home tonight?"

"That's what I wanted to hear. You're coming home with me. To our home, not just mine. Yes, she knows. Everyone knows. I haven't talked to my mom, but Lydia's there now. Everyone is waiting for your answer. Jon's the best man. Tiffany the first lady in waiting, or whatever you girls call it. The yacht is booked, but I can try to push it up for a ceremony tonight."

"I suppose I could wait one more day so my dad and grandma can give me away together. Then Tiffany and I can shop for a maid of honor's dress and a proper wedding gown. Omigosh, I think I am going to faint."

"Then we have a date?"

"Yes, Prescott Borden, I'll marry you tomorrow."

Howard teared up. "This is has been the greatest moment of my life."

"Hey, Howie," Prescott said. "You want to come?"

"I'd love to be your security."

"No, you'll be our guest."

* * * * *

Monica sat sulking in her room with a bottle of vodka. No champagne tonight. Prescott had no feelings for her other than disgust.

She could see it the moment he walked in. Howard added to the humiliation by squealing on her. Gina had left for Boston so at least she didn't witness the beat down, but she hadn't called yet. Monica debated if she'd share the details with her. She looked at her phone and noticed a text she'd missed earlier.

"Hi M. I'm going to get right to the point. This whole reality TV thing is just not for me. I called your agent, the Penguin, to see if he had any ideas for me. Guess what? I'm going to be on the cover of Playboy, something I always wanted to do. He liked my naked ride through town and so did a lot of other people. Including this super-hot doctor I met with today. Dan DeAngelo. Look him up on Google. Definitely going to make something happen there. Jeffery had a change of heart and put some cash in my account. We still are finished, but he didn't want me to go without my clothes and a chance at a new start. Not too bad for a guy who had someone whacked. I forgot to tell you about that.

Now, I want to tell you something heart to heart. I think you need to let go of your obsession with Sugar and Prescott. You should have the charges dropped against that girl. She's done nothing to you. It's time to move on with things. I'd say you're a better person, but the truth is…you are capable of being better. I know deep down inside you're good. You just need to get more connected to the good side of you.

Don't you dare forget me when you're a big reality TV star. Until then, let's just give each a little space to work out our lives. I need to become a better person too.

I'll always love you.

Gina. NANANANAAAA. I know you say you hate my laugh, but deep down inside you love it. Find that girl, and you'll be happy. The inner you and not the outer one."

Monica fell back down on the bed and stared at the ceiling. She didn't cry. Not her style. But she knew Gina was right. Still, it felt like being broken up with twice in one day. She really did have secret hopes that maybe Prescott would come back to her. It never dawned on her she'd lose her best and only friend too. She stood up and grabbed the bottle of vodka on the side dresser. She went into the bathroom and stared at herself. She had plenty of sleeping pills on the counter. She lifted up the bottle, then poured it all into the toilet, along with her prescription drugs. There had to be a better way. She had promised herself to find an AA meeting many times in the past. She had the phone number of another model who went to those meetings and turned her life around. She grabbed her cell and started looking through the directory. Mostly numbers of men she'd gone out with, all of whom didn't speak to her anymore. The Monica everyone knew no one wanted to be around, including Gina. Every relationship ended badly. Her good looks felt like a curse. An easy excuse not to really connect with others because her beauty should be enough to get by in life. In reality, it was getting her nowhere: no love, no friends and no modeling career. Loretta Farrell. That was the name of the girl. She said to call her any time. Well, one a.m. was any time.

"Hello?" a sleepy voice said.

"Loretta, this is Monica Dees."

"Wow, I've been waiting a long time for your call. You ready to do this?"

Monica wept for the first time in years until 4 a.m. while Loretta talked to her as she drove from New York City to Newport. Just to be there for her first meeting and introduce her to a new cast of characters. People trying to live clean and sober lives and helping the next person.

Chapter 33

The hundred-foot yacht *Great Gatsby* left the dock in Newport harbor as people standing by waved to the passengers on board. Everyone recognized Sugar and Prescott, and Tiffany too. They were all part of the American culture now and had become household names overnight in this age of the instant celebrity. Cell phone cameras were flashing, and people shouted their names.

They all waved and posed for pictures. There was no sense in hiding from the paparazzi and the curious public. Eventually, they'd go away once their 15 minutes of being Newportant faded away to the next tabloid fodder.

Hubert grabbed Sugar's hand. "Look at you, bride-to-be. Aren't I a genius? This is all because of me and my handiwork. I'll even give you a B-plus on your wedding dress. I saw it hanging up down below. I've taught you well."

"Hey, give me a little credit. I've watched enough of those wedding dress shows to know the gown that makes you cry is the dress you say yes to."

"I'm so jealous. Hey, who's the big guy? Quite the chunk. Is he gay?"

"No. That's Howard our new friend. He's straight, or should we say round."

"Oh, thank the stars. I thought he might be my date. I don't do XXL sizes. Not going there. Just saying. But the older gentlemen looks nice."

"That's my dad. You're not going there. He's Irish. He'll punch you in the face and throw you overboard. Just sayin'."

"I guess I'll fill my dance card with Mrs. Borden. Now if you'll excuse me." He twirled off.

The minister gathered everyone together. The sky was pink like a sailor's delight. The yacht was as spectacular as the first-class deck on the Titanic but with more than enough life jackets in case they hit an iceberg. There was even a small ski boat on board.

The minister cleared his throat. "I know we haven't had time to rehearse, so I'll be brief. Who is going to giving the bride away?"

Lydia and Sugar's dad, stood by her side. The man of the cloth continued. "You will be walking her up the aisle. You'll get a chance to kiss her, then I'll present her to the groom."

Prescott smiled. He looked as dashing as ever in his tux. His best man, Jon, was by his side. Tiffany wore a yellow chiffon Marilyn Monroe-style outfit that tied up around her neck. Mr. Perry couldn't take his eyes off her.

Prescott gave him a nudge. "Hey, pay attention Jon. This is serious business. You can marry your girl tomorrow. Today's my day." He smiled broadly.

The minister opened his Bible. "Ready to get started?"

Sugar and Tiffany headed below decks along with Howard, who was to be the official photographer. They'd called around, but everyone was booked. He had plenty of cameras he'd purchased for all the spy jobs that never came to pass. He found he had quite the knack for photography and had some lovely shots of Tiffany with a telephoto lens that he shared with her. Creepy, but the pictures were stunning.

Louise Borden walked over to her son.

"I'm so proud of you for making Sugar an honest woman after the video. That's never happening again. You got that?" She squeezed his arm in a tight, motherly kind of way.

"Yes, ma'am."

"George, the father of the bride, seems quite nice. We had a lovely chat. He's single, you know," she said, with a sparkle in her eye.

"Mother, don't even tell me that. The world thinks I am marrying my cousin, and now my step-sister too?"

"I'd never remarry, but it's nice to have a travel buddy."

"As long as you stay in separate rooms, or I'll be forced to have him make an honest woman out of *you*."

"I am a woman of God. I would not even think of it. Don't you ever be thinking you'll get away with going back to your misguided youth. You're officially an adult today. It only took my boy 35 years to grow up. If you ever get caught so much as looking at another woman, I'll have the Lord and his team of angels after you. By the way, when can I expect my first grandchild?"

"I'll work on that tonight. Now, let me having a little breathing room please." He winked at her.

A pianist started to play Pachelbel.

Tiffany walked down the aisle first. She'd changed into a green gown with spaghetti straps that Hubert clapped his hands over. He was so excited by the magnificent outfit, he decided he would borrow it since they were the same ladies size six.

Sugar emerged from below decks along with her father and grandmother. Her dress was a white mermaid cut with a sparkle belt. Her hair was swept up on one side with a decorative comb.

Prescott pretended to stab himself in the heart. The same thing he did the night he saw her walk into the jewelry store where they shopped for an engagement ring. That was the moment he realized he really did want to marry Sugar Lynn Limehouse. She sent butterflies to his stomach, something he heard girls talk about but never guys.

George Limehouse had more tears in his eyes than anyone else. This was indeed the proudest moment of his life. Not because his daughter was marrying a tycoon, but because he could see she was finally happy. Like the carefree girl he remembered as a child before her mom had passed on.

Prescott whispered to Sugar, "You slay me."

The "I do's" went off without a hitch. Monica didn't jump out from a corner with ninja knives when the minister asked if anyone opposed the marriage.

The cruise around the harbor lasted a little longer than expected because there was so much LOVE in the air and everyone wanted to jump ship. Hubert lusted after the dress and couldn't wait to try it on. Tiffany and Jon had yet to consummate their love and wanted at least the opportunity to sneak in a few stolen kisses. They planned to wait a little longer and linger in their lustful thoughts. Staring into each other's eyes was enticing enough for the time being. George and

Louise were enjoying their chat and wanted to continue where no one was in hearing distance. Lydia and Bernard thought about swimming back to the castle and cuddling up for the night. Howard was busy looking through all the photos and realized he'd found his true calling. Every picture caught the romance of the moment.

Unfortunately poor Prescott had business to attend to, after the promise he made to his mother about getting started with making babies. It was time to grow up and be a man of his word.

THE END

Printed in the United States
By Bookmasters